# Putting It
# Back Together

# Putting It
# Back Together

Rhonda M. Lawson

## URBAN BOOKS

http://www.urbanbooks.net

URBAN SOUL is published by

Urban Books
1199 Straight Path
West Babylon, NY 11704

ISBN-13: 978-1-59983-082-7
ISBN-10: 1-59983-082-5

First Printing: April 2009

10 9 8 7 6 5 4 3 2 1

Printed in the United States of America

*To the men and women who work every day to bring
the city of New Orleans back to its former glory.
You are loved and appreciated.*

# Acknowledgments

Every book I've ever written has been a labor of love for me, albeit for different reasons. This one, in particular, was the most fun for me because it gave me the chance to walk down memory lane, allowing me to feature many of the things that make my hometown of New Orleans the crown jewel that it is. However, it was also the most difficult because although the characters are fictional, the places, history, and dialects were real. I needed to make this story as true to life as possible so people could understand why we New Orleanians love our city and why, no matter where we go or how long we stay away, the Big Easy will always hold a special place in our hearts.

I began writing this book in my barracks room at Camp Red Cloud, Korea, but I was fortunate enough to be in the Big Easy as I worked on the edits. I was able to visit many of the same places highlighted in this book. As I rode through the historic neighborhoods, I was reminded of things I almost forgot. I was able to talk with people who reminded me, not just by words but with actions, how special this city truly is. It reminded me why in many ways, I'll always be a modern southern belle.

So to the wonderful people of the city of New Orleans, thank you for inspiring this book! To the residents of the Lower Ninth Ward, keep your fighting spirit. I thank you for making me who I am today. The house on Caffin Avenue that I, my sister, my mother, my aunt and uncles all grew up in was washed away, leaving only three concrete steps on a patch of grass, but you will always be my original home. The news may not reflect it, but I know you're coming back slowly, but surely. If you can survive Hurricane Betsy, what can Katrina and Rita do?

To my best friend, Dhana Hunter, thank you for your friendship, support, and laughs. I won't tell everyone how long we've been friends, but I pray it's for a lot more. We don't get to talk as often as I'd like, but I plan to change that. You with me??? I wish you and your family nothing but happiness, and tell Damion to keep beautifying our city with his artwork.

To my sister, Renee Livious, I will always acknowledge you because you are the epitome of what a sister should be. I want to thank you for not only how you've always supported my writing career, but how you've taken care of both me and Beautiful. Keep looking ahead. You're on the right track, and if you keep God first in your life, there is no limit to what you can do!

As many of you know, I've been out of the country for the past two years. However, when I hit the scene again with *A Dead Rose*, many people gave me love as if I hadn't been anywhere. To the Divine Literary Tour, S. James Guitard, Victoria Christopher Murray, and Jihad, thanks for welcoming me back to the fold!

To Michele Lewis of the Afro-American Bookstop, thank you for your support and congratulations on reopening your wonderful store! I wish you all the success in the world as you continue to provide an avenue for new and established authors.

D. C. Bookman and Tia, thank you as well for all you've done for me and the host of other authors who have been fortunate enough to work with you.

I also need to send a special shout to Gladys Knight and Ron Winans Chicken and Waffles in Largo, Maryland, for your love and support. Special thanks also go to Borders Bookstore in Largo, and Barnes & Noble in Harvey, Louisiana. You guys really know how to make an author feel special!

To my sorors of Zeta Phi Beta Sorority, Inc., you remain a special and virtuous group of women. Thank you for all your love during the 2008 Boule. I can hardly wait for Detroit in 2010! Special thanks to my chapter, Pi Eta Zeta in Seoul, Korea, for all you've done for me, from supporting my books to reenergizing my fervor for my beloved sorority. To my longtime friends and sorors Lillian Ebanks, Cheryl Robertson, Shamone Stephenson, and Nicole Hampton, here's to fifty more years of love and friendship!

To my friends of the African American Literary and Media group, including Denise Spiller, Tyson Hall, and Hotep, thank you for all of the encouragement you sent while I was in Korea. You just don't know the smile you bring to my face when I see your numbers pop up.

To all of the up-and-coming writers I've met along the way, keep your eyes on the prize. This is not an easy road, nor is it always paved with hundred-dollar bills, but keep the love of your craft. It will pay off in the long run, but as long as you're inspiring and entertaining your readers, you have succeeded.

To the people who continue to push and encourage me and have boosted my writing career, Urban Soul Books, Misherald Brown, Kimberly T. Matthews, Fred Williams, my readers, and the host of others who've sent notes of encouragement, thank you. Your phone calls, notes, and e-mails kept me going when I felt overwhelmed and ready to give up.

To my family, thank you for your patience and generosity when money ran short, when book signings became plentiful, and when I just neglected to keep in touch because I was either studying or writing the next best seller. I love you guys, and pray that we remain close.

Lastly, I have to thank God because without Him, none of this would be possible. He is the source of my strength and the reason for where I am today. He is the center of my joy and I give Him the praise.

There you have it. As always, I pray that this story will both entertain and inspire you. Visit my Web site at www.rmlawson.com to look for upcoming events or to just drop a note to say hello. You can also visit me at www.myspace.com/rhondamlawson.

Thanks and God bless!

# Chapter 1

# Sweet October?

It was a perfect Thursday afternoon. The cool October wind blew softly, but just hard enough to cause the waters of Lake Pontchartrain to slap the concrete steps just below Alexis's feet. The sky was so blue, no artist could replicate it, and the sun shone just enough to warm her bare arms without burning them. It wasn't cold. It wasn't hot. It was comfortable.

Most people were at work this time of day, so she could hear the seagulls squeal as they flew above her head. A few feet away, two children screamed in laughter as they struggled to keep their kites in the air as their parents watched from a few feet away. A few minutes later, a couple walked past her hand in hand, oblivious to Alexis and the rest of the world. Of course, the music blasting from the occasional passing car broke the peace, but nothing held enough power to break her tranquility.

The lake had always been her favorite place to go when Alexis needed to escape reality for a few hours. Back in her college days at the University of New Orleans, she would come here to do homework or clear her mind. There was something about that water that kept her coming back.

For a while, she couldn't understand her attraction to the lake. It was here that one of her childhood friends had died while fishing with his cousin. Apparently he'd gone too far down the steps and slipped, hitting his head. His ten-year-old, unconscious body landed under the steps, and he had drowned before his cousin could return with help.

Then there was Katrina. It was Lake Pontchartrain that broke through the London Avenue Canal levee and washed away much of Gentilly, the area she'd called home all her life. So many lives and homes lost. She still shivered at the thought of all those people stranded at the Superdome and the Ernest N. Morial Convention Center awaiting help that took days to arrive. It could easily have been one of her own family out there, but she thanked God every day that it wasn't.

But New Orleans was coming back. Although the memories would never be erased, the Superdome and the convention center had been scrubbed and repaired. Many of the homes in her neighborhood had been rebuilt, and the area continued to show signs of revitalization. She and her mother had moved back into their home after only three months of renovations. The children again played in the streets. Businesses were returning. Many of her favorite restaurants still had yet to return, but Alexis no longer had to drive five miles into neighboring Metairie in search of food.

Unfortunately, with progress comes sacrifice. She'd lost her fiancé, Tony, who'd refused to leave Houston. However, her mother, Mary, remarried after too many

years of being a single mother, giving Alexis a stepfather
and a stepbrother. Alexis had to struggle to keep her
private medical practice afloat in a city full of people
trying to rebuild their lives. But through it all, life would
go on.

It wasn't all bad. The lake did hold good memories
for Alexis. This was the site of the traditional Senior
Skip-out Day, in which all of the seniors at John F. Kennedy High School ditched school and had a picnic.
Kennedy was practically down the street from the lake.
It still had yet to reopen, which was a shame. For an
inner-city school, there were so many smart and tal-
ented kids who went there. Many of them went on
to graduate from top colleges both in and out of the
state. Some remained in New Orleans after college and
opened their own businesses or medical and law practices. Just yesterday, as she drove down I-10, she saw a
billboard with a former classmate's face on it, advertising his very successful car dealership. Alexis could do
nothing but smile with pride.

The lake was also the hangout every Sunday. People
from all over New Orleans, even as far as the West Bank,
would converge on the lake to have their own beach
party. It was like a fashion show and car show all in one.
Alexis never went home without at least ten phone
numbers back in those days. Some she called, and
others she stuck into a jar for later use.

But none of those guys compared to Reggie, her first
love, whom she'd met at a college party. She'd actually
ditched her date just to meet him. It was at that very spot
on the lake just a few months later that he convinced her
that he loved her. She didn't want to believe him then,
but later realized that she loved him just as much.

Alexis shook her head as Reggie's name danced
across her mind. How in the hell did she ever mess
that up? Why hadn't she tried to contact him after

graduation? Had it not been for her pride and her quest to keep the world wrapped around her finger, she'd probably be married to him today. She shrugged her shoulders. No need in bringing back those memories. Reggie had long since married and was enjoying a successful career with the New Orleans Saints, who'd made it to one game shy of the Super Bowl last year. They'd started off slow this year, losing three straight regular season games, but Reggie still played well. She'd even heard about him receiving a few awards for his work with the kids and his rebuilding efforts around the city. There was no way he was thinking about her.

Alexis glanced at her watch as she brushed her long microbraids from her espresso-colored face. Ten more minutes and she'd have to head back to the office. She had a two o'clock appointment with Tavarious Johnson, a six-year-old boy with a bad respiratory infection. She'd been treating him for the past six months, and was having the hardest time trying to convince his mother that the FEMA trailer they lived in was most likely the cause of his problems.

So many of her patients were former victims of Hurricane Katrina, it scared her. Many of them came from poor families who couldn't even afford to pay for her services, let alone have insurance. Alexis didn't have the heart to turn them away, even though she only received a percentage of what she was really owed. This forced her to have to live with her mother and stepfather for longer than she wanted, but oh well. At least she could help her parents get back on their feet and still afford a few amenities of her own.

Alexis reluctantly rose from her seat and took one last breath of the New Orleans air. She smiled as she caught a whiff of the steaming crawfish at Joe's Seafood Restaurant. *I know what I'm eating for dinner tonight,* she thought to herself. She stretched deeply with her arms spread out to her sides, then turned and walked toward her car.

"Hey, Latonya," Alexis greeted as she walked through the door of her clinic. "Tavarious here yet?"

Her receptionist looked up from the appointment book and smiled. "Well, look who finally decided to come back to work."

"It pays to be the boss," Alexis replied, lifting her eyebrows in triumph. She looked around her tastefully decorated office. She'd been in the Touro Medical Center only for the past three years after completing her residency at Touro Infirmary. Since she'd gained a lot of confidence with her patients, starting her private practice wasn't hard. She'd started off with seven regular patients. Today, although she'd had to close for a few months to evacuate, her patient number had tripled since so many private practices moved out of the city.

This would be wonderful if more of her patients had insurance. If at least ten more of them had insurance, she might be able to hire a paid intern. Until then, she'd have to make do with her one nurse and her young receptionist, who was actually her smart-mouthed cousin who needed some direction.

"I hear you," Latonya said. "But while you were gone, three people called for appointments, you're going to have a walk-in at three-thirty, and yes, Tavarious is in the examining room. Ms. Kay is taking his vitals."

Alexis sighed and donned her lab coat, which hung behind the reception desk. "The work never ends."

"It pays to be the boss," the receptionist mimicked as Alexis headed toward the examining room.

"Don't get smart!" Alexis shot back.

*That's what I get for hiring family,* Alexis thought to

herself as she walked into the examining room. She
had to admit that Latonya was thorough and actually
enjoyed working in the medical office, but her mouth
was going to get her into trouble sooner rather than
later. She just couldn't draw the line between personal and professional conduct. And that inability to
draw the line convinced Alexis more and more that
she needed to hire someone else and let Latonya try
to make it on her own. Yet her heart wouldn't let her
do that to family. She was intent on giving her cousin
a chance and being an example to her just as her
older cousin Brenda was once an example to Alexis.

She forced her thoughts to the back of her mind as
she walked into the examining room. Tavarious sat on
the operating table looking pitiful while his mother
leaned against the wall with her arms folded. Alexis
sighed, knowing her tranquil day was about to take a
bad turn.

"You still got that cough, T?" she asked, fingering
through his medical records to review his last few visits.

Tavarious tried to reply, but went into a coughing fit.

"Po' baby been coughin' like that fah da pass week,"
said his mother, Paulette.

Alexis shook her head and rubbed Tavarious's cheek.
"You been taking the medicine I gave you?"

"G'on and tell her," Paulette said.

"It's nasty," he whined in the way only a six-year-old
could.

"I understand. I don't like taking medicine, either,"
Alexis said patiently. Her four years as a pediatrician
had prepared her well for the protests of a stubborn
child. "But you have to take it if you want to get better."

"Okay," Tavarious relented, his shoulders rising and
falling with his defeated sigh.

Alexis examined the boy's tongue and throat and
listened to his heart. She then sent him to get a lolli-

pop from Latonya so she could talk with Paulette. She blew out heavily, already knowing how this conversation would turn out.

"How you comin' rebuildin' your house?" she asked, placing Tavarious's record on her desk.

"Slowly but surely," Paulette replied, folding her arms.

"When you think you're going to be done?"

"When I get some money."

Alexis sat down, trying not to roll her eyes at Paulette's attitude. The woman just didn't know that Alexis could get an attitude right back, but only hid it because it was the professional thing to do. She tapped her pencil's eraser on the desk, struggling to choose her words carefully.

"Ms. Johnson, I understand what you're saying, but you have got to get out of that trailer," Alexis said slowly. "You're living in that cooped-up space with little air circulation, and the hot weather is causing toxic fumes that T just can't handle at his size and age."

"Dr. White, I understand dat, but what you expect me ta do?" Paulette asked, raising her hands in resignation. "My house ain't nowhere near ready for us to move into. My mama ain't movin' back to New Orleans, and my cousin is on crack. I'm doin' the best I can as fast as I can, but right now the trailer is all I got."

Alexis sighed and rocked back and forth in her chair. "The longer you stay there, the worse he's gonna get. I can keep giving him medication, but it's going to cost you way too much money, and eventually his body is going to get used to it and stop responding."

"Well, tell the state to hurry up and give me my fuckin' Louisiana Road Home money so I can hurry the hell up!" Paulette shouted. "In the meantime, I'm usin' da air conditioner and I keep da windows open."

"Please, don't get loud with me, Ms. Johnson. I feel what you're sayin'."

"Don't try to talk like you're from the streets," Paulette snapped. "You think just because you some fancy docta you got da ansa to everything. Well, it ain't dat easy. I'll get us out da trailer as soon as we can. You think it don't hurt to see him like this? You know how many kids at his school are goin' through da same thing? On top of that, the fuckin' holidays are comin' up and my son has to go another year havin' one fuckin' dry-ass present under da tree! You know what that's like, *Docta* White?"

Alexis almost had to smile. If only Paulette knew where she *really* came from. She never lived in the projects, but it wasn't as if the Seventh Ward was the best neighborhood in New Orleans. Being the only child of a single parent, she'd had her share of sorry Christmas mornings, and if it weren't for Brenda and her family, Alexis and her mother, Mary, would damn near have starved for Thanksgiving. But then again, even if she had been born with a silver spoon in her mouth, it wasn't Ms. Johnson's business. She needed to take responsibility for her own damned life and do what was best for her son. But of course, Alexis couldn't say that—it would be unprofessional. She leaned forward, trying hard to erase the irritation that was building inside her. "Don't let the smooth taste fool you, Ms. Johnson. Like I said, I feel you. I won't push the issue. You know what to do. I would suggest getting with some of the local churches and seeing if they might be able to help."

Paulette cocked back her head and sucked her teeth. "Thanks for da help, *Docta* White. I'll leave your payment with your secretary."

With that, she left the examining room and slammed the door behind her.

"You do that," Alexis said quietly to the closed door, as she leaned back in her chair.

She wondered how many of her patients thought she was rich. Could that be why so many of them weren't rushing to pay? Did they figure that she could afford to do without a few payments? That a couple of sixty-dollar medical bills wouldn't make a difference? If only they knew she was living with her parents. If only they knew that while she had a BMW, it was not only used, but had needed a tune-up for the past three months. She wasn't sure how much longer she could drive it. Yeah, her bills might be paid, but when was the last time she could treat herself to a nice dinner without depending on a date with her on-again, off-again boyfriend? And what if they knew the real reason she decided to work with children?

Ms. Kay poked her head into the small room. "You ready for your next patient, Doctor?"

Alexis rolled her eyes and decided to shake off the confrontation. How she longed to return to the lake and feel the salt air brush her skin. The squawking from the seagulls would be a welcome change from the madness she was sure she'd face for the rest of the afternoon. It had been a good day, and she was determined to keep it that way. "Sure, why not?"

# Chapter 2

# Family Matters

"Wassup, lil' bro?" Alexis greeted her stepbrother, Roman, as she waltzed through the front door.

Roman, a nineteen-year-old college sophomore at nearby Dillard University, lay on the couch reading what appeared to be a textbook. Once he heard his sister's voice, he looked toward her direction and gave her a sideways smile, then walked right in front of her, his one-hundred-fifty-pound, six-foot, five-inch body towering over hers.

"I done told you 'bout that 'lil' bro' shit," he said. "You might be older than me, but I'm still a grown-ass man."

Alexis laughed and pushed him away. "A grown-ass man that's gonna get his head conked if he doesn't get out of my face."

Roman chuckled. "Like I'm just gonna *let* you kick my ass."

"Boy, you don't have to *let* me do anything," Alexis

replied, flexing her right biceps. "I don't exercise five days a week for nothing."

Roman backed away, knowing his sister had a point. He sat back on the sofa and picked up his book. "Strong ass."

Alexis laughed again and playfully pushed her brother's head forward. Although she and Roman routinely had their battles, she enjoyed having a younger brother. She'd grown up as an only child, so when Roman moved in with them shortly after starting college, she saw it as a perfect opportunity to experience what her friends with larger families had all the time.

"Where are my mama and your daddy?" she asked as she walked into her room. She threw her purse and messenger bag on her bed, then walked to the kitchen to find a snack. She settled on a few baby carrots. No need in reversing her workout with junk food.

"They were gone when I got here," Roman replied with a shrug. "I'm 'bout to be out myself."

"Where you going?"

"Ole girl is picking me up in a few. We're gonna go see that new flick about Jesse James."

"Oh, I heard that was good," Alexis said, taking a seat in the love seat next to the sofa. "Let me know how it is so I can scare up a date to take me to see it."

"That shouldn't be too hard," Roman said. "You know them fellas are always on your ass. You stop actin' so stuck-up and you might get a real man."

"Ooo, no, you didn't!" Alexis exclaimed. "I know you ain't talkin'. I bet you any money you're goin' out with Sheila so early because Tameka is comin' over later."

Roman smiled and popped his collar. "Shoot, Sheila knows the deal. And she knows ain't no way I'm droppin' Tameka, so she's just tryin' to get whatever time she can get."

Alexis raised her eyebrows and considered his words. She remembered being just like him when she was his age. It was no secret that a lot of men wanted her time, but back in college, each of them would have had it. She couldn't believe she could see so much of herself in someone who wasn't even related to her by blood. "You better be careful."

"You ain't gotta tell me," her brother bragged. "My stuff is straight."

"Okay."

"But on the real," Roman said, quickly changing gears. "When are you gonna stop giving these fellas hell and get a man?"

Alexis looked at him as if he'd lost his mind. "When my practice takes off, when I find the right one, and," she said, picking up a pillow and flinging it at him, "when you get your young ass the hell up out of my business!"

Roman ducked just as the pillow sailed over his head. It plopped on the floor behind the sofa. "Okay, but don't come to me for lessons when you forget how to do it, 'cause I ain't gonna have no words for ya."

Before Alexis could reply, there was a knock at the door. Roman jumped up to answer it. Before he could get the door open all the way, a cocoa-colored beauty with microbraids similar to Alexis's rushed in and attacked him tongue first.

Alexis rolled her eyes. *God, please tell me I was never that bad back in the day,* she thought. "Hello, Sheila."

When she received no reply, Roman suddenly pulled away from the girl and looked at her disgustedly. "I know you heard my sister talkin' to you."

"Hi, Alexis," Sheila said quickly, wiping away her smeared burgundy lipstick. Alexis rolled her eyes because not only did the shade do nothing for the girl, but she couldn't understand how she let Roman speak to her the way he did.

"That's better," Roman scolded. "You need to respect your elders. *Especially* if they're related to me!"

"You right, Roman," she said, biting her lower lip. "My bad."

He pecked her on the forehead. "Go on and get in the car. I'll be there in a minute."

Sheila nodded silently and backed out of the door. Roman stole a glance at his sister and winked before calling after her, "And don't forget I gotta be back here right after the movie. Tameka is coming over, and you know how she is."

Alexis heard a disgusted grunt come from outside the house, followed by a snicker from her brother. *Poor Sheila*, she thought to herself. *I wonder if she knows how stupid my brother makes her look.*

Once she had the house to herself, Alexis smiled and picked up the cordless phone. "Roman doesn't know as much as he thinks he knows about me," she said aloud as she dialed the numbers.

"Hey, Jamar? Yeah, I'm home now. Pick me up at eight."

Once she hung up, she headed straight for the bathroom and took a shower. Jamar was nobody special, but he was always good for some company. She hadn't dated much since moving back to New Orleans. There just weren't many men to choose from. Many were underemployed and looking for a side hustle. Others were unemployed and weren't looking for anything that even *looked* like a job application. There were a few professional men around the area, but most of them were married or trying to capitalize on their status by sleeping with every woman who looked at them cross-eyed. Then there were the tourists who were only in town for a few days and looking for a fling, thinking the poor women stuck in New Orleans would go for the first piece of bull they heard. Alexis wasn't the one.

Being a doctor, she was choosy about with whom she was seen. New Orleans was a small city, and she worked hard to ensure that she would always be taken seriously in her profession. The wrong associations could mess that up for her. She always had the fear of running into one of her patients' parents and being seen with a thug or, worse, someone's husband.

She tried not to think of herself as materialistic, but being an up-and-coming doctor who worked out five days a week, she knew she deserved better than what she'd been offered lately. Her days of "Sexy Lexy" died along with the baby she aborted when she was twenty. She'd gotten pregnant by a married man who only used her for her body. In fairness, she had used him as well, but that experience, the one that caused her to lose Reggie, made her do a lot of growing up.

Her telephone rang as she slid on a pair of designer jeans. Thinking it was Jamar, she quickly snatched up the receiver and said, "You here already?"

"No, but I will be soon."

Alexis looked at the phone, puzzled. It definitely wasn't Jamar. "Brenda?"

"You forgot my voice? I know it hasn't been that long."

"Long enough! I don't think I've talked to you since the beginning of the summer."

"I know, my bad. The life of a nurse is never easy, but you should know that."

"Correction—I'm a *doctor*!"

"Well, excuse me, Ms. *Doctor*."

The cousins shared a laugh. Alexis and Brenda had been like sisters since childhood. Since they'd both grown up as only children, they naturally gravitated toward each other, establishing an unbreakable bond. Even the infamous affair, which happened to be with Brenda's best friend Andrea's husband, Christopher, couldn't tear them apart for long. Since that time, they'd grown even closer, now knowing they could talk to each other about anything. It wasn't an easy road, however.

They both had to overcome trust issues, embarrassment, and anger, but their love brought them through it.

"So what do you mean 'you'll be here soon'?"

"You won't believe this."

"Then tell me!"

"Darnell got orders to go to Algiers!"

"You're lying!"

Algiers was a city on the West Bank of New Orleans. A navy base was located there, which was where Alexis assumed Brenda's husband would be stationed. Fortunately, Algiers wasn't as adversely affected by the flood, so many people had relocated there once the waters receded.

"I'm lying, I'm dying," Brenda replied. "Not only that, but he's thinking about retiring in New Orleans."

Alexis scrunched her eyebrows. "Why would he want to do that? Ain't nothing here since Katrina hit."

"Well, we're playing it by ear, but he is definitely retiring in two years. We'll see what happens after that."

"Well, that's two years away. In the meantime, my sister-cuz is coming back!" Alexis exclaimed, jumping up and down. "When will you be here?"

"He's not due there until February, but we'll be there in December to start house-shopping, and we're thinking about coming for Thanksgiving."

"Damn, girl," Alexis said. "You act like Florida is right around the corner."

"Close enough," Brenda replied. "You'll probably be seeing a lot of us before we actually move there. I have to find a job, we need a place to live, Elizabeth needs a school, and that's the big one. You know most of the schools in the city shut down."

Alexis nodded. "I hear you. I might be able to help you with that. I'll talk to some of my patients' parents."

Actually, Alexis understood that point all too well. Her own elementary and high schools seemed to be nowhere near a reopening, and many of her patients were forced to attend private schools their families couldn't afford because of the closures. Those who went to public schools had to travel miles away in their quests for a decent education.

Alexis glanced at her watch. As if on cue, the doorbell rang. "Well, sister-cuz, I gotta go. My date is here. I'll call you tomorrow so we can start planning."

"Do your thang, sis. We'll talk soon. Love you."

"Love you, too," Alexis replied. Once she replaced the receiver, she clapped her hands joyfully and trotted to the door. Now she had a real reason to celebrate!

"Lex, when are you going to stop giving me such a hard time and let me be your man?"

Alexis rolled her eyes and blew out some air. If she had a dollar for every time Jamar asked that dumb-ass question, she could probably get her Beemer fixed and still pay it off. She'd already explained to him a million times that it was too soon to get into a relationship after her breakup with Tony, and she really needed to focus on her practice. Jamar was sweet and considerate, but he wasn't about to break her down.

"Jamar, can't we just have a good time tonight?" she asked as they pulled up to Sweet Lorraine's Jazz Club. Why did it seem that so many people were intent on ruining her good day? The weekend was coming, she had treated ten patients, and her favorite cousin was coming back home. She really just wanted to end the day with some good food, good music, and maybe some good sex. However, the way this night was starting, she'd just have to settle for good food and good music.

"Baby, you know I'm always going to show you a good time, and I understand about your practice, but it's time to get over that fake-ass nigga in Houston,"

Jamar said as he pulled into a parking space near the back of the restaurant.

Alexis waited for him to turn off the car. "Let's not go there tonight. I had a really good day today."

"Then let me make it better," Jamar suggested. "You know we're good together. I'm a lawyer, you're a doctor. We can be like a reverse Huxtable family."

Alexis laughed. "You stupid."

"Whatever, but you know I'm right," Jamar said, smiling. He got out of the car and walked around to the passenger side. Once he opened the door for her and she got out, he met her with a kiss. Before she could protest, he told her, "Just keep what I said in mind. I'm not going to push you, but you know how I feel. Let's go get some food and enjoy the show."

She wanted to tell him off, but when she opened her mouth, nothing came out. It was amazing how a good kiss could render a woman speechless. She decided to leave the issue alone and silently followed him into the restaurant.

The truth was, as much as she hated to admit it, part of her still wanted Tony to call and tell her he'd made a mistake. She still held out for the day when he would tell her he was coming back to New Orleans to claim what was his. Then once he did that, she'd crush his plans by letting him know that she'd moved on and that he'd made the worst mistake of his life.

Although she still harbored feelings for Reggie, Tony was the only man who had made her place those feelings on the back burner. There was a time when Tony made her feel as though nothing else mattered. Many people thought of them as the perfect pair, and were shocked when they'd heard about the breakup.

"Girl, I just knew we'd be eatin' wedding cake in a few months," a girlfriend had told her once.

Tony was also a doctor. They'd met while doing

their residency at Touro. They worked in two separate wings of the hospital, but had locked eyes while eating lunch in the cafeteria. After sharing a brief conversation, they exchanged numbers and, after a year of dating, shared an apartment in New Orleans East. Katrina had hit eight months later, but by the time the winds touched ground, Tony and Alexis were already staying with his cousin in Houston.

Houston just wasn't the place for Alexis. Although she easily found a job treating the evacuees at the Houston Astrodome, she longed for the familiarity of home. Houston was just too big and busy. It didn't have the same laid-back feel that the Big Easy had. She missed the beauty shops that didn't close until the last customer left, even if it meant they would be there until midnight! She missed her family, who had scattered all over the country. She missed the streetcar she sometimes rode to work. She missed the Superdome. She missed the food. The portions weren't big enough outside New Orleans, and she couldn't find a decent shrimp po'boy to save her life! She also missed her creamy Hubig's lemon pies and Big Shot pineapple sodas. But most of all, she missed the old men and women who used to sit on their porches and wave at everyone who walked past. Those people were the original neighborhood watch. They knew what happened, when it happened, and whose son or grandchild did it!

Unfortunately, Tony didn't share her yearning for her beloved city. He was born a Houston man, and once he returned home, he was convinced he would die a Houston man. He would never feel the same attachment to New Orleans that Alexis felt. He'd begun enjoying being with his family again, and instantly fell back in line with the faster pace of the bigger city. He got a job at the Houston Medical Center, where he joined the hospital's neurosurgery program. There was no way he would give all of that up to go back to the corrupt, broken-down swamps of New Orleans, and he made that clear to Alexis when she brought up the idea. A verbal altercation ensued, one that Tony's cousins enjoyed as they sat on the couch and listened to every word. Alexis wanted to slap them across their heads as they looked back and forth at her and Tony as if watching a tennis match.

The last straw finally came when Alexis threatened to go back without him, and an angry Tony shouted, "Well, go the fuck on, then! I'm on the come-up! I don't need you! It wasn't like you were going to give me any kids, anyway."

Alexis could have gotten past all of the venom he spewed, but when he threw her inability to have children in her face, she knew she had to go. So early the next day, she packed her small suitcase into the trunk of her BMW and, with tears streaming down her face, made the long, lonely drive back to New Orleans.

"May I take your order?" asked the young, attractive waitress, derailing Alexis's painful trip back down memory lane.

Forever the gentleman, Jamar ordered white wine for them both, then asked for a little more time to choose their entrees.

"You okay, sweetness?" Jamar asked.

Alexis smiled, pushing the memories to the back of her mind. "I'm good. I was just trying to decide between the crawfish pasta and the chicken breast."

"Well, the pasta would go well with the wine," he suggested.

"Then pasta it is!" Alexis announced, placing her menu on the table.

Jamar chuckled. Once the waitress brought them their wine, he placed their orders, then took a sip from his glass. The next ten or fifteen minutes were filled with strained small talk as Alexis struggled to push her thoughts of Tony to the back of her mind and concentrate on having a good time. She knew Jamar meant well, but she wished he would never have brought Tony into the conversation. She tried to convince herself that she was still happy and better off without him, but her mind wouldn't accept the justification.

"So you said today was a good day, huh?" Jamar asked after a moment of silence.

"It was," Alexis replied, taking a sip of her wine. "Today was beautiful. I sat on the lake today and enjoyed some of this weather."

"You should have called me," he said. "I actually had a slow day. I only had a couple of clients."

"Any new people?"

"Same old folks. But I have a client coming in tomorrow to talk to me about getting a divorce."

Alexis cocked her head back in surprise. "Must be serious. You ain't cheap."

"And you know this," he replied with a wink. He popped his collar and took another sip from his wine.

They laughed.

"Well, good luck with that," Alexis said. "Is it a man or a woman?"

"A man, but that's all I can tell you."

"I know. I wasn't going to ask anything else."

Alexis knew Jamar took his job very seriously. He was by no means Perry Mason, but he was well known in New Orleans. Actually, if she could ever get over her breakup with Tony and her secret infatuation with Reggie, she would probably consider taking her relationship with Jamar to another level. She really did care about him, more than she cared to admit. She just didn't want to get into a relationship with him knowing that she couldn't give him all of herself. That wouldn't be fair to either of them.

Alexis had come a long way since college. There was a time when she would have strung a guy like Jamar on until she was bored with him. Once she'd dropped him, she would move on to the next victim. The Gulf Coast was probably strewn with the hearts of men who had tried and failed to make her love them. Reggie and Tony were the only men who'd come close, and she was determined not to mess things up with Jamar the way she had with Reggie.

Not only that, but she would curse anyone out, man or woman, without a single thought. No one was going to mess over Alexis White, at least not without a fight. She kicked many an ass back in her day, and refused to let anyone, including Reggie, think they'd gotten the best of her.

She couldn't put her finger on it, but she thought her growth stemmed from becoming a doctor. There were so many children who looked up to her that she couldn't bear to make a bad impression on them. With everything going on in the world, she wanted to be one of the few local minority women her kids could look up to. She wanted them to know that every attractive black woman they saw wasn't a glorified porn star or a gold digger like in the videos. She knew not every woman in New Orleans portrayed that image, but she also knew that not all of her patients—especially the teenagers—had a good woman to look up to.

Her affair back in college also contributed to her growth. Even though she continued to do her share of dirt after her breakup with Reggie, it was mostly an effort to relieve her pain. It was embarrassing enough having broken up with Reggie and not being able to explain why, but she really couldn't handle the pain she'd caused Brenda. Having her cousin sleep with her best friend's husband was a lot more than Brenda could swallow. Even after they'd begun speaking again, it was a long time before the two of them could speak comfortably with each other. That was something Alexis never wanted to experience again. She looked forward to Brenda's arrival in New Orleans because it meant the two cousins would grow even closer.

"So how's life in la-la land?"

"Huh?" Alexis asked, realizing she hadn't listened to anything Jamar had said in the past five minutes. Embarrassed, she quickly shoved a forkful of pasta into her mouth. She had barely noticed when the waitress brought it to the table.

"I figured I would visit you in your world since you don't give a damn about mine," Jamar said, shaking his head. He stabbed three shrimps with his fork, one by one, then held the fork midair, awaiting a response.

"I'm sorry, Jamar," Alexis said. "I was just thinking about my cousin Brenda. She's moving here in a few months."

Jamar loosened the muscles in his face. "Interesting. She's the one you told me about? The one who's like a sister?"

Alexis smiled, glad that Jamar was such a good listener. She could only mention something once as an afterthought, but Jamar would waste no time committing it to memory. It felt good that a man took an interest in everything she had to offer. "That's her."

"Nice. Do I get a chance to meet her?" he asked, finally eating the shrimp he'd stabbed earlier.

"Eventually. First, my cuz and I have to catch up."

"No, first you have to dance with me. The show's about to start."

Alexis laughed. Jamar was too smooth. As much as she hated to admit it, he was definitely the right match for her.

# Chapter 3

# It's All Over

Reggie stared in disgust at the shriveled-up piece of latex. He wasn't shocked. He'd always known Nikki was cheating on him. Hell, it was common knowledge that she was sleeping with half the NFL. Most of New Orleans knew what she was doing. She'd even been seen with a couple of the players from the New Orleans Hornets basketball team. He'd grown so used to her transgressions that he really didn't care anymore. But why did she have to do her dirt in his bed?

He couldn't understand why she hated him so much that she couldn't even respect him enough to keep her men out of their bedroom. Or out of their house, for that matter. Furthermore, did she think he was such a fool that she didn't even have to hide it anymore? She could at least *pretend* to have some courtesy, if not for him, then for their son.

Reggie had met Nikki right after the Saints drafted

him ten years ago. They'd dated for nearly two years before he worked up enough nerve to propose. It wasn't that he was afraid she'd say no, but he was afraid of women wanting him for his money. Being a rookie, he didn't make the millions that some of the more experienced players made, but he knew there were a lot of women in the city looking for "potential." And being a Tulane grad and a second-round draft pick, he definitely had potential.

He also hadn't had much luck with relationships. He didn't date much in college because he was tired of women seeing his face and status and treating him like a trophy. Why did young girls act as if he couldn't see that gloating look they wore whenever they were in public? It was the type of look that said, *yeah, bitch, look what I got!*

Alexis, his last real girlfriend before Nikki, had never treated him like a prize, but she cheated. And she cheated bad. To him, she was just another bad chapter in his life that he had to get over. Once he met Nikki, he thought he'd found the answer to his prayers.

Although the Saints had had their ups and downs over the years, he did well with the team, earning countless awards, including Rookie of the Year, MVP, and Defensive Player of the Year. He'd even made two trips to the Pro Bowl. He had yet to achieve his ultimate dream of making it to the Super Bowl, but Nikki was his other dream come true. Every time he played a game, accepted an award, or made a speech at a local school, she was right there in the front row cheering him on. During the Saints' not-so-good seasons, like the one they were having now, she was there to rub his back and reassure him that despite the score, he played well. She was his angel.

It wasn't until he began thinking about retirement that the infidelity began. He'd been wrestling with the idea for about a year, but he'd made the decision final after preseason. Nikki was incensed! He guessed she wasn't ready for him to give up their celebrity lifestyle. It wasn't just about money for her. As an NFL wife, she had *status*. She'd lose some of that if he was no longer in the limelight.

He just couldn't understand when she stopped loving him. Everything had been perfect for so long. How could she have spent ten years with him if she never loved him? Who could keep a charade going on for so long?

Then again, he remembered her attitude change once she found her name on a Web site as one of the NFL's hottest wives. Her behavior remained the same, but Reggie could tell that her head stood higher when she walked into a room. Soon, she no longer had time to volunteer with the team wives' club. Instead, she made it her business to be everywhere Reggie was, apparently to get more face time. She'd been invited to pose for small magazines all over the country. When the two of them walked into a room, fans clamored for both their autographs. But when Reggie began talking about retirement, he guessed she could see the beginning of the end of her own stardom.

Were her feelings just that conditional? Apparently so, he thought as he threw the covers back over the condom. He looked in the nightstand and found a pen and paper. He wrote her a note, laid it on top of the covers, then picked up his gym bag and left the house.

"What's wrong with you?"

Reggie continued bench pressing, trying to take out his silent rage on his already-burning pectorals. Each push into the air was a feeble attempt to calm his anger. He wanted to ignore his best friend and teammate, but he knew his face gave him away. He and Levi had been friends since their first day of training camp ten years ago. They knew each other too well not to know when something wasn't right.

"What makes you think something's wrong?" Reggie asked. Levi knew him too damned well. He clanked the three-hundred-pound barbell back on the stand and sat up.

"Man, if you were any slower during those walk-throughs, we mighta had to call them *crawl*-throughs," Levi joked, sitting on a nearby weight bench.

Reggie shot him a weak smile, then rubbed his bronze-colored bald head. He brought his hand back to his lap slowly, his muscular body already starting to feel the strain from the punishment he'd just subjected himself to. "Your ass never was funny."

"But I speak the truth," Levi replied, smiling.

"Whatever, man."

"Besides, you know you're not supposed to be liftin' this heavy the day before a game," Levi pointed out.

Reggie shrugged. Before he could reply, a chime came from his pocket. He fished out his cell phone, looked at the incoming number, and sucked his teeth. "Hold up, Lee."

He pressed TALK and barked, "Yeah."

"I got your little note," said an angry woman's voice.

"And?"

"That was real fuckin' funny, Reg. How you gonna write 'clean this shit up' and leave it lying around? What if our son saw it?"

"You weren't worried about Shawn finding that fuckin' condom you left in our bed," Reggie snapped. He stole a quick glance at Levi, who tried to turn away to hide the shock that had registered on his face. Reggie looked down and avoided eye contact for the rest of the conversation.

Nikki remained quiet for a few seconds. "Well, uh, you still didn't have to play games like that. If you have a problem, confront me like a man."

"If you think—you know what? I'm not even going there with you," Reggie said. He bit his lip and rubbed his bald head, an action he always did when he tried to think of what to do or say next. "You know that nigga you fucked last night? Stay with him tonight. As for Shawn, I'll be home at seven. He better be there."

"You kickin' me out?"

"Not yet, but the way I'm feeling, if I see you tonight," Reggie mumbled, pausing to shake off the evil thought that ran through his mind, "I don't know what I'll do."

"That sounds like a threat. You can put a hand on me if you want, but—"

"Shut up, Nikki."

A quick flick of the thumb cut off Nikki's tirade of shouting and cursing. He shoved the phone back in his pocket and glared at Levi. "You see the shit I gotta put up with? I've been nothin' but good to that woman, and this is what I get in return. If it wasn't for my son, I woulda *been* gone. I shoulda fucked around on her like most of these guys do on the road."

Levi looked his friend right in the eye. "You sure it's worth going through all this?"

Reggie shook his head. "I don't know."

"Let's go get a beer after dinner. I heard Wendell is throwin' down tonight."

Wendell was the team's chef. It was well known in the Saints organization that Wendell fed the team well the evening before a game. Although the team's season had started off rocky, everyone refused to believe it was because they were too full. They'd just have to work harder. A win was sure to come.

"I can't, Lee. Shawn's gonna be with the babysitter."

"Reg, you ain't gonna be no good to that boy if you walk in the house lookin' like that."

Reggie nodded. "You're right. Let's eat."


A beer turned into about *five*. Levi couldn't convince Reggie to go to a bar, so they bought a twenty-four pack from a package store and went back to Reggie's house. After kissing DeShawn and putting him to bed, the two friends turned on SportsCenter and fed themselves liquid courage to prepare themselves for the heavy conversation they were about to share.

"You know Coach is gonna kick our asses tomorrow if we show up like this," Levi slurred. He wasn't drunk, but he definitely felt good.

"Shut up, nigga," Reggie said with a laugh. "The game's not until one, and you know I always come with my game."

"True, but your mind's not right tonight," Levi said.

"I'm good, and as soon as I find a way to get Nikki out of my life, I'll be even better!"

"I hear you talkin', baby boy, so whatcha gonna do?"

Reggie looked at his friend through slit, buzzed eyes. "You think just because you traded in your wife that everybody gotta do it?"

"No, but when yours is showin' her ass the way she is, you gotta do something," Levi said seriously. "Besides, this is about business. If you play tomorrow the way you practiced today, we might as well just gift wrap the damned game and hand it to Carolina!"

Reggie met his gaze and nodded, placing his beer on the table. "I feel you. On that note, I'ma call it quits."

"I hear you," Levi agreed, placing his own can on the table.

They paused and listened as Stephen A. Smith discussed the Saints' game against the Carolina Panthers tomorrow. This had definitely been a rough season, but it seemed the folks on ESPN had faith that the losing streak wouldn't last forever. They'd need that faith going into tomorrow's game. Losing was getting old.

Once the show went to commercial, Levi turned to his friend. "You ready to go to war tomorrow?"

"You better believe it," Reggie replied, meeting his friend's gaze.

"Good. Then you go on the field tomorrow and do the damned thing. We'll worry about what to do with Nikki Monday."

"You got a plan?"

"No, the question is, do *you* have a plan?" Levi corrected. "She's *your* wife, and this is *your* life."

Reggie nodded. "I know. I wanna get rid of her ass, but I'm not ready to give up my son. How the hell am I gonna convince a judge that I can be a good single parent with my schedule? I travel every other week, practice every other day, and live in two different cities. Shit, I thought when I got drafted I was living the American dream. Nobody told me it would be like this."

"You can do it, bro. It's just going to take some sacrifices. Besides, you still thinking about retiring?"

Reggie nodded again. "I still love football, but I just can't see leaving the game after I'm too old to do anything else. I have an MBA from Tulane! It's time to put that shit to use!"

"I hear you. That shit don't come easy."

"You ain't lyin'," Reggie said. "If Nikki could understand that, I'd be all right. You know how hard it is to get a master's degree while you're playing for the NFL? From fuckin' Tulane, at that?"

Tulane University was one of the most prestigious colleges in the state of Louisiana. Located on the historic St. Charles Avenue, next to equally prestigious

Loyola University, Tulane boasted a demanding curriculum as well as a successful sports program. The school took both aspects seriously, requiring all athletes to attend study halls to maintain their grades. Reggie had been fortunate enough to pursue his undergrad education there on an athletic scholarship, and after graduation, worked for five years to achieve his graduate degree. He was determined to show his son and all the kids who looked up to him that the concept of the dumb jock was the exception, not the rule.

"Yeah, I watched you do it. Between that and running to Atlanta every summer, I don't see how you even had a chance to *make* Shawn!"

"Oh, I had time," Reggie replied with a laugh. "That's something I *made* time for. Nikki may be no good, but that woman is fine as hell!"

Levi laughed with him. "Well, if you really wanna keep Shawn, I'm sure you can, but it's going to take a lot. Most judges give the child to the mother."

"And that's fucked up," Reggie said, pounding his fist into the arm of his recliner. "Any judge who would let a woman as scandalous as Nikki raise a child on her own must be on fuckin' crack."

"Then you know what you're up against. You got a lot to prove," Levi said, digging through his jacket pocket. He pulled out his wallet and handed his friend a business card. "This is the lawyer I've been dealing with."

Reggie took the card and read it. "Jamar Duplessis, huh? He any good?"

"One of the best in our little ghost town," Levi replied. "I don't have kids, so my case is a little different from yours. But I still think he can help you."

Reggie tapped the card against his leg. "All right. I'll give him a call Monday."

"Cool. In the meantime, get that shit out of your mind and concentrate on this game tomorrow."

"Don't worry about me, baby boy," Reggie said as he walked his friend to the door. "I'ma *be* all right. You all right to drive?"

"I'm good," Levi replied. "I'ma see you tomorrow."

The friends gave each other a soulful pound and shook hands like fraternity brothers, then Reggie closed the door. Neither of them had ever joined a fraternity, but over the years, they'd grown as close as any two frat brothers could be. Reggie was glad they'd become friends, because he wasn't sure if he could make it through this mess with Nikki without someone whom he trusted to vent to.

After turning out the lights and TV, he trotted upstairs and into his bedroom. He contemplated whether or not to sleep in his bed. Knowing another man had been there didn't feel right. Then again, he needed a good night's sleep to get the alcohol out of his system and concentrate on the game. He pulled back the covers slowly and was relieved to see fresh sheets.

"At least she had that much decency," he said aloud.

"Whatcha say, Daddy?"

Reggie looked up to find his six-year-old son, DeShawn, standing on the other side of the bed. He wore his favorite pajamas consisting of shorts and an oversized T-shirt bearing his daddy's name. A stocking cap covered his cornrows, the hottest hairstyle for young boys in the South.

"Boy, what are you doing up?" Reggie asked with a smile.

"I was asleep, but I heard you come upstairs," Shawn replied, rubbing his eyes. He looked around the room. "Mommy's not back yet?"

Reggie almost laughed, but held back for the sake of his son. "No, she's gonna be out late."

"She's always out late," Shawn whined. "Can I sleep with you tonight?"

"What's wrong with your bed?"

"Nothing. I just wanna sleep with you."

Reggie glanced at the bed, images of the faceless man still lying between his sheets. He reminded himself that the sheets were clean. Besides, his days with his son could be numbered. "Yeah, lil' man. Jump in."

# Chapter 4

# Game Day

*I shouldn'ta had that last beer.*

That was the only thought that went through Reggie's mind as his body collided with the unforgiving Astroturf, knocking the wind out of him. He was supposed to be making an easy tackle, but his reflexes just weren't agreeing with him. On top of that, his arms were still tight, courtesy of the hard workout he'd subjected himself to after practice.

"I'm never gonna hear the end of this," Reggie mumbled as he picked himself up. Once he got to his feet, he heard the referee's whistle blow. He looked toward the sideline and saw Coach Jim Haslett signaling for him to come to the side. "Shit!"

He trotted to the sideline and automatically took a seat. He knew the deal. He'd seen it too many times before with other players. He'd be lucky if he returned before the fourth quarter. He glanced in the direction of the skybox, where he knew DeShawn was watching. He never wanted his son to see him play badly. At least not *this* badly.

His defensive coordinator came and sat next to him. "You all right today?"

Reggie shook his head. He knew honesty was the best approach for his lackluster performance so early in the game. "Got things on my mind."

"You better shake that shit off, Morgan," the coordinator ordered. "These people didn't pay to see you lose your mind on the field."

"I know."

"And you missed an interception in the last play. You could barely lift your arms. What's the problem? Didn't we tell you guys about those hard workouts before games?"

"Look, I'm just not playing right today. I'll sit out."

"You're damn right, you will, but don't get comfortable," the old coach said. He then looked at him intently and softened his tone. "Look, Morgan, I know you have things going on. We all do. But you gotta zone that shit out when you hit the field. You've been around too long not to know that. I need you to set the example for these rookies."

Reggie nodded again, refusing to meet his coach's gaze.

"You can sit out this quarter, but I'm putting you back in at the third. Get your mind together and get a massage when we go back at halftime. I need you in this game. We have a chance to win this thing."

Reggie looked at his defensive coordinator as he walked away. He always appreciated his coach giving it to him straight. Although his situation with Nikki ate him alive, he knew his coach was right. No one paid to watch him wallow in self-pity. And there was no way he would show his team that he'd slowed down because he still felt the effects of the alcohol. He'd never drunk that much before a game, and he never would again.

"Looks like they took your friend out of the game," said Mary, Alexis's mother.

"I see," Alexis replied.

She, Roman, and their parents, all dressed in their favorite Saints jerseys, sat around their living room, watching the game on their big-screen television. This had been their tradition for years. Like most of New Orleans, die-hard Saints fans ran in the White family. Fortunately, they also ran in the Wilson family. If they hadn't, Alexis was sure her mother would never have married Frank. It was just that serious in New Orleans. They'd loved the Saints through the "Who Dat" years, and the bag head years, into the "we just might go to the Super Bowl" years. Their team had given them heart flutters and heartaches, but through it all, they'd always stood behind them.

"They needed to," Roman remarked. "He's playing like shit! How in the hell did he miss that easy tackle?"

"Watch your mouth, son," Frank interjected.

"As much as I hate to admit it, you're right," Alexis said. "I don't know what's wrong with him today."

"Maybe he misses you," Frank said with a laugh.

Alexis rolled her eyes. She knew Frank was just playing, but he never knew the whole story about Reggie and her. He just didn't know the stake he drove through her heart when he made such comments. One day she would have to tell him, but she didn't feel like reliving ancient history.

Fortunately, Mary caught on to Alexis's slight mood change and quickly said, "Frank, that was a long time ago. Leave it alone."

Frank waved his hand toward his stepdaughter. "Aw, that girl knows I'm just playin'."

"Awww, Daddy, Lex doesn't need that buster," Roman jumped in. "As many men who like her, she could have a man who makes twice as much as Reggie Morgan."

"Hello!" Alexis shouted. "Alexis is still in the room! Now, Roman, I'll get a man when I'm ready. And, Frank, Reggie probably doesn't even remember me. I haven't seen him since we graduated from college."

Frank and Roman both threw their hands up in defense. "Excuse us," they said at the same time.

Everyone laughed. Alexis blew out a sigh of relief once they changed the subject. The truth was, she had seen Reggie a few times since their breakup, but they'd never spoken to each other. Their paths had crossed at a couple of clubs after he was drafted by the Saints, but she never had the nerve to go up to him and speak. She was still ashamed of the way things had ended between them. She'd finally gotten over her shame after a while, but by then, she'd found out he'd gotten married a few years earlier. Soon after, she'd met Tony and had all but forgotten about Reggie. It wasn't until the demise of her relationship with Tony that thoughts of Reggie returned to her mind.

She and her family continued watching the game with only momentary squeals of joy when Olindo Mare booted in a twenty-eight-yard field goal in the second half, tying the game at 6. During the halftime, they chatted more, careful not to bring up Alexis's love life again.

"Oh, oh, oh!" Mary shouted, pointing at the television screen.

Everyone shouted with her as they saw Mike Karney fight his way into the end zone, giving the Saints their first touchdown of the game.

Unfortunately, that would be the closest the Saints

would come to a win. During the fourth quarter, the Panthers came back, scoring ten unanswered points and sealing a 16–13 victory.

"Damn," Roman said. "We're oh and four. What the hell is wrong with the Saints this year?"

"I guess they shoulda never had that funeral last year," Mary commented, referring to the day when the team buried all their awards from the prior season in traditional New Orleans style, complete with a brass band and a preacher. The Saints had come one game shy of the Super Bowl last year, which was their first season back in the Superdome after that tumultuous day in August. Jim Haslett explained that he didn't want last season to be a distracter for the team, and wanted them to focus on "the here and now." The way this season had started, many thought the plan had backfired.

"Yeah, they need to dig them things back up and remind themselves of what they used to be," Roman remarked.

"Don't say that," Alexis said. "Our team will pull it together. Just watch."

Meanwhile, Reggie wished *he* could pull it together. He'd missed another tackle, one that led to the Panthers' fourth-quarter touchdown. He knew he couldn't blame himself totally for the loss, but he hated that he hadn't performed better. He was the one who always brought his A game. The man the younger players admired. The unshakeable one.

He sat on the bench in front of his locker and stared at his feet. He knew he was a damned good football player, but he didn't show it. It wasn't as if this was his first bad game, but if he had played better, there was a chance that his team could have marked their first win of the season. This game meant something!

"Shake it off, man," Levi said from behind. "We got another game next week."

"I hear you, Lee," Reggie said, almost in a whisper.

"We all had our bad moments on the field, but together, we played our asses off," Levi said, trying to encourage his friend.

"I know what you're tryin' to do, Levi," Reggie said, raising his head to look at his friend. "It's not necessary. Everybody mighta played bad, but I know what *I* did to play bad, and that's not me."

"Well, ain't no use beatin' yourself up over it. Shit, I was right there with you."

Reggie chuckled for the first time all day. "I hear you, man."

Although most NFL teams carried a roster of forty-five to fifty-three people, many players were hard-pressed to find a teammate they could click with. They might laugh and talk with other players, but rarely did they get very close to more than one or two people, especially if they were star players. Reggie and Levi were fortunate; they became instant friends the day they joined the team. Even when they broke out into a little noteworthiness, they remained close, never letting their stardom overshadow their friendship.

"I know one thing, though," Reggie said, rising from the bench. He pulled his street shoes from his locker. He never walked in his game shoes. "I've got some changes to make. A brother like me won't be drinkin' before a game again."

"So that was the problem!"

Levi and Reggie looked around suddenly and found their defensive coordinator standing there with his hands on his hips. There was no mistaking that he wasn't happy.

"Look, Coach, I—" Reggie stuttered.

"Save it, Morgan. The only explaining I want from you is when you're gonna bring me that thousand-dollar fine you owe me," he snapped, storming back to his office.

"See that shit?" Reggie asked Levi. "I don't need to deal with that every week."

"You don't deal with it every week," Levi said. "This was your first time."

"First and last," Reggie said, slinging his gym bag onto his shoulder. "Like I said, I've got some changes to make. Catch you later, baby boy."

The friends gave each other their familiar fraternity pound, then Reggie headed out of the locker room. He walked upstairs to the skybox to pick up DeShawn, who had been sitting with some of the team wives and girlfriends. They loved DeShawn almost as much as he did, and were always happy to take care of him when Nikki wasn't at the games. Unfortunately, when he reached the skybox, it was empty.

Confused and worried, Reggie wandered around the area, hoping DeShawn had gone to the restroom. Besides a few loiterers, the hallways were empty. He finally saw a janitor he recognized.

"Hey, Dre," he called. Once the janitor looked up, Reggie walked over to him. "You haven't seen my son, have you? Six years old, comes up to my waist, has corn-rows? He was wearing a Saints jersey with my name on it."

Dre laughed. "Man, you lucky I've seen your son before. You just described every lil' black boy in New Orleans!"

Reggie laughed as well, realizing how silly he sounded. He had to admit that he'd seen two boys who fit DeShawn's description on his way up to the skybox.

"But on the real, he walked out a few minutes ago

with his mama," Dre said. "Light-skinned lady with long hair? She was wearing a black leather suit."

Reggie wasn't sure what Nikki was wearing since she didn't sleep at home last night, but the description definitely fit her. He planned to choke her when he saw her for taking DeShawn without telling him. He stormed out of the Superdome with a mission on his mind and death on his face. He had no idea where Nikki had gone, but when he found her he was going to make her wish they'd never met.

When he reached his car, he sighed with relief when he found his estranged wife leaning against his silver Mercedes. He then grimaced, wondering how much worse his day would turn out.

"May I help you?" he asked Nikki. She looked good in that black leather, but the anger he felt wouldn't let him appreciate her looks. She was about to hear about herself in a bad way.

"Hi, Daddy!" DeShawn greeted, stepping from behind the car. "Good game. You'll get 'em next time."

Reggie's demeanor instantly softened, and he smiled in spite of himself. He thanked God that he would always be a hero in his son's eyes.

"Your son wants to go to Golden Corral," Nikki said without smiling. "You up to it? I figure you should be well rested, as much time as you spent lying on the ground during the game."

Reggie wanted to say, "about as much time as you spend lying on your back," but refrained since his son was listening. He really didn't want to eat with Nikki, but decided to make the best of the situation. Besides, Golden Corral was where the locals ate, and New Orleans wasn't a very starstruck city, so he didn't have to worry about a lot of people interrupting his meal. They might point or wave, but very few would ask for an autograph.

"Very funny," he said. "Where's your car?"

"I rode with some friends over here. They were coming to the game, so I figured I would save my gas."

Reggie shrugged. "Well, hop in. I'm hungry."

DeShawn cheered and jumped in as soon as he heard the door locks pop. Once everyone was settled, Reggie started the engine and pulled out of the parking lot.

"And before you ask, I tried to call you on your cell, but it went straight to voice mail," Nikki said quickly.

"You know I don't keep my phone on during games," Reggie mumbled.

"I know, but I thought you would have turned it on after the game."

"I guess I wasn't fast enough."

"Guess not," Nikki said, looking out of the window.

Reggie wanted to tell Nikki that he was filing for divorce, but he wasn't prepared to have to do it so soon. On top of that, DeShawn was in the car, so he would have to wait. He still wasn't sure how he was going to pull this off without losing his money and his son, but he knew he had to end this. His doomed marriage wasn't worth his sanity or his career.


"Another loss," Roman said, rising from his spot on the floor in front of the sofa. "What is going on with the Saints this year?"

"I don't know," Alexis said. "It's like they can't even *buy* a win."

"Don't worry, kids," Mary said, ever the optimist when it came to the Saints. "It ain't gonna last forever."

"If you say so," Roman said as he and his father broke out in laughter.

"Y'all hungry?" Frank asked, clapping his hands to get everyone's attention. "Let's go to Golden Corral."

Mary grimaced. "That place is gonna be crowded as hell. Besides, you can't think of somewhere closer to go eat?"

"Awww, come on, Mary," Frank pleaded. "You know I love Golden Corral. I need to get me a steak."

"Yeah, Ma," Roman agreed. He had already begun snacking on barbecue potato chips. "I *am* kinda hungry. If we go to Golden Corral, y'all won't have to pay for me gettin' seconds."

"Greedy tail," Alexis said, rising from her own position on the recliner. That spot was usually reserved for Frank, but since he'd chosen to take the sofa with Mary, she'd snagged it while she had the chance.

"Aw, girl, don't act like you ain't hungry, too," Roman snapped. "Doctors gotta eat, too."

"That's true," Frank agreed. "You are gettin' a little on the skinny side."

"I don't know what you're talking about," Alexis said, turning her nose up at her stepfather. "I'm fine."

Everyone laughed as they gathered their belongings and prepared to leave.

Fortunately, when they arrived at Golden Corral, the parking lot had cleared out. A good number of cars were still there, but it was nowhere near the madhouse they would have found if they had come right after church. Although the restaurant was located in Metairie, it was a popular location for most of the city. This restaurant was one of the bigger locations in the area, so even when it was crowded, customers could still find a seat. Unfortunately, the amount of time they would have to wait in line sometimes made them wonder if it was really worth the wait.

This was a decision Alexis and her family wouldn't have to worry about. Since much of the crowd had cleared out, they easily got through the line and found a table for four near the salad bar. Once they each made their way through the buffet, and Frank got his much-desired steak, they sat down and dug in.

"This hits the spot!" Roman exclaimed. He mixed his collard greens in with his rice and prepared to take in another mouthful.

"I know what you're saying!" Alexis agreed, finally admitting to herself that she was hungry. She took a momentary break from her healthy diet and shoveled as much food as she could fit on one plate. She didn't plan on going back for seconds, so she would have to make that one trip to the buffet work. However, she did plan to go back for dessert. There was a slice of chocolate cake she'd been eyeballing since she walked in.

"I'm going to get some more of that dressing," Roman said, rising from the table.

"That boy is greedy," Mary told Frank. "I'm surprised he's still skinny."

"Don't worry about Roman," Frank said. He slapped his chest proudly. "He's got good genes."

"Man, what are *you* talking about?" Mary asked with a laugh. "You're gettin' a little pudgy yourself."

Alexis snorted, trying to hold back a laugh. She sipped some of her lemonade and continued eating. Mary and Frank had the cutest relationship, and Alexis was happy that Mary had found happiness after being alone for so long. Alexis had never met her real father, who'd died in a car accident before she was born. Frank, who had divorced his wife when Roman was still a child, didn't come into her life until her college years. Until then, Mary had raised her basically by herself with the help of Brenda's mother, who was also a single parent.

Most people thought Mary was a mean, bitter woman who said exactly what was on her mind, no matter whose feelings it hurt. Many of Alexis's cousins loved

Mary, but knew better than to cross her. She would hug you one moment, and then curse you out the next.

Because Mary was a no-nonsense woman, if a man misstepped only once, she would walk the other way. She had a child to take care of; she had no time for men who didn't have themselves together or were only trying to get their thrills. Some things didn't change with age.

When Frank came along, Mary put him through a hard time, but he hung in there. He seemed to be the only man who could handle her mean streak. He then did something no one else had ever had the chance to do. He put a light in her eyes and a glow in her skin that Alexis had never seen before. It was almost as foreign as the look Roman wore when he returned to the table.

"What's up with that silly look on your face?" Alexis asked.

"Sis, you ain't never gonna guess what I just saw on the other side of the dining room," Roman replied as he took his seat at the table.

Mary looked worried. "What? A rat?"

Roman laughed. "No, Ma, nothing like that."

"Then what, boy?" Frank asked, looking annoyed.

Roman wanted to keep the suspense going, but the look his dad gave him made him think better of it. "Reggie Morgan is here."

Alexis's heart jumped, but she refused to show it. Instead, she ate the last of her meat loaf and sipped her lemonade. "That's nice."

"He was with his wife and son," Roman pushed.

"Good for him," she replied.

"He's only a few feet away," Roman said. "Go over there and say something."

Alexis slapped her glass onto the table. "Roman, you're so worried about me and my relationships. Why don't I go over there and talk to him after you tell Tameka all about how you're running around with Sheila?"

Roman's mouth hung open in shock. He took a quick glance at his parents, who ate their dinner nonchalantly. They'd seen this episode before. "You didn't even have to go there, Alexis."

"Well, you need to stop it with Reggie," she snapped. "That was a long time ago, so leave it in the past. I'm going to get some cake."

She rose from the table and stormed off in the direction of the dessert table. As she chose her slice of chocolate cake, she couldn't help but sneak a peak toward Reggie's table. She wasn't sure where he was sitting, and didn't want to look obvious. Fortunately, she found him on the first try. Unfortunately, he was looking right in her direction. She grabbed her cake and quickly walked back to her table.

"Enjoy the show?" Roman asked once she sat back down.

"What?"

"You talked all that noise, but you couldn't help looking over there, could you?"

"I don't know what you're talking about."

"Okay, you two," Mary said, slapping her hand on the table. "That's enough. Can't we have a peaceful dinner?"

"Tell your son to get out of my business," Alexis snapped.

"Like you're not all up in mine," Roman retorted.

"All right, now," Frank said, trying not to be loud. "Shut up, both of you."

Alexis rolled her eyes and continued eating her cake. These were the days when she wished she could afford to move out.

* * *

"Are you listening to me?" Nikki asked, waving her hand in front of Reggie's face.

Reggie blinked. "Yes, Nikki, I'm listening to you. I just thought I saw somebody I knew."

Nikki sucked her teeth. "Well, you need to be concentrating on *me* right now."

"How can I not? You always make sure your presence is known."

"Very funny."

"Mommy, can I get some ice cream?" DeShawn asked.

Nikki gave her husband a hard stare, then replied, "Come on, baby."

They rose from the table and walked hand in hand to the ice cream machine.

Reggie watched as Nikki played the doting mother. If she weren't a cheater, she would be the perfect parent. But she was cheating. And not with just one person. She didn't deserve to be rewarded for that. He needed a plan, and he needed it fast.

He smiled slightly at the thought of the person he thought he saw at the dessert table. She looked just like a girl he had dated back in college. She hadn't had braids then, and she was dressed more conservatively than his college sweetheart, but the face was definitely the same. There was a time when he would stop at nothing to get her back into his life. But once he met Nikki, he felt he'd finally found the one. Now he had to wonder if he'd made the right decision.

He looked toward the door just in time to see the woman walking out with what appeared to be her family. She and a younger guy looked directly at him and left without as much as a smile. It had been a long time, but it was definitely—

"Excuse me, Mr. Morgan," said a little boy wearing a Saints jersey and holding a pen and small notepad.

He wore Drew Brees's jersey, but oh well, he was still a fan. "Can I get your autograph?"

Reggie smiled. "Of course, buddy."

The boy smiled and gave him the pen and pad.

"What's your name?"

"Willie."

"Willie who?"

"Willie Thompson."

"Okay, Willie Thompson," Reggie said, scribbling his autograph on the pad. He gave it back to the boy and smiled again. "There you go. Be good, now."

"I will. And don't worry. I know you guys will win next week."

Reggie laughed as Nikki and DeShawn returned to the table. "I'll let the team know you said that."

Once Willie returned to his table, Reggie turned to his own family. He scrunched his eyes at the mountain of ice cream his son had brought back to the table.

"You think you have enough sugar there?" he asked.

"I brought back enough to share with you," DeShawn replied, handing him a spoon.

"Got it," Reggie replied, nodding. He looked at Nikki. "You going to join us?"

Nikki shook her head. "You two have fun with that. I'm stuffed."

"Your loss," Reggie said with a shrug. He then shoveled a spoonful of vanilla ice cream with fudge sauce and candy sprinkles into his mouth. He smiled at his son. "Deeee-licious!"

DeShawn nodded in agreement.

Before he knew it, he'd begun to relax and have a good time. He and Nikki had even managed to have a civil conversation. DeShawn, oblivious of the tension, was just happy to have an outing with his parents. Maybe tonight would turn out to be a good night after all.

# Chapter 5

# Memories

"Baby, did I tell you how excited I am to be moving back to New Orleans?" Brenda asked as she laid her head across Darnell's lap.

Darnell took his eyes from the movie they were watching and checked his watch. "Not in the last few hours."

Brenda giggled and sat up. "Sorry. I know I've been talking your ear off about this, but I can't help it. I just feel like I'm going back there for a reason."

"You are. Your husband's about to be stationed there."

"No, baby, it's more than that," Brenda pleaded. "I've been praying for a way to help rebuild my city. I get so tired of listening to people here talk about New Orleans." She scrunched her face in mock disgust. "*Why didn't they leave? What's taking them so long to rebuild? The crime is so bad in New Orleans.* They get on my nerves. Florida gets hit by hurricanes every year, and these people keep coming back. You'd think they'd understand what New Orleans went through."

"Well, sometimes it's easier to judge when you're not the one going through things," Darnell surmised.

"But that doesn't make it right," Brenda replied. "I'm so tired of people and their criticisms. When is the last time any of them tried to rebuild an entire city? I wish they could have seen what I saw when I went back to New Orleans. All those people homeless, sick, and distraught. One guy helplessly watched his wife get washed away with the current. This one little girl, couldn't have been any older than six, watched her grandmother die in the hot sun outside the convention center."

"Yeah," Darnell said. "I remember you telling me about them."

"And then people ask why it's taking so long? Ask those damned insurance companies. My grandmother is still waiting for her settlement. Some of those people were living in dilapidated wooden houses before the flood. How do you expect them to afford to clean off their property with no financial help? Yeah, a few churches helped some people, but they can't help everyone!

"And then all those people got mad at Mayor Nagin for his 'hole in the ground' comments," Brenda continued, her arms flailing about. "I admit he didn't say it right; the man has never been known for his tact, but both of those events were tragic. And you can't expect to rebuild an entire city in a year or two."

"Baby, calm down. You're gettin' all swoll up in the chest," Darnell laughed.

Brenda smiled in spite of herself. She knew she couldn't help but get emotional when she thought of her beloved city. It just pissed her off when her coworkers and neighbors asked her those stupid questions about New Orleans. New Orleans had never been a prosperous city. Poverty had ruled the streets even before Katrina hit. So many people, including her own mother, sat home broke, wondering what to do and where to go the day before the hurricane hit. Had she not sent her mother two hundred dollars and begged her to leave the city, Brenda might have seen another familiar face in the Superdome.

Her cousin Lena had actually refused to believe that the hurricane would even reach New Orleans. So many storms had threatened the city and then turned at the last minute. Lena, as well as countless others, opted to stay and not spend the money to relocate because of another false alarm. At first, even Brenda had thought people were being unreasonable when she saw all the people on the news leaving the city, but as she watched the weather reports, reality hit her hard. The storm was coming, and it wouldn't be pretty.

"So what do you think you're going to do when you get there?" Darnell asked. "You know you can't save the world."

"I'm not trying to, but I do plan to do my part," Brenda vowed, stretching her legs across her husband's lap. "Just the fact that we're moving there is going to help the economy. And when we buy a house, we'll be adding to the infrastructure. But I haven't figured out where I'm going to work. Working at your hospital is a guaranteed paycheck, but I want to try to help as many people in the city as I can, like my little cousin is doing."

"Well, you said yourself that Alexis isn't making a lot of money because a lot of her patients can't pay her," Darnell pointed out.

"Yeah, but if it weren't for people like her, a lot of poor people wouldn't have anywhere to go for quality medical care," Brenda countered. "Those doggone free clinics are overcrowded and filled with people seeking cures for STDs. And if they're struggling to get their house insurance payments, I'll bet you a dollar to a doughnut—my grandmother used to say that—that they probably can't afford health insurance."

"You say that now, but I bet you Alexis is getting pissed with people coming in for treatment and not paying her."

"I'm sure she is, and I'ma tell you, she's a better person than me because I don't think I could put up with it that long," Brenda remarked. She relaxed a bit at the thought of her younger cousin. "I can't wait to see Lex again. We haven't hung out in years."

"I can see why," Darnell replied, taking a deep stretch with both his arms and legs spread as far as they would go. "That girl has been busting her tail lately trying to get that practice off the ground."

"I know. I wish I could help her."

Darnell snapped his head toward his wife and glared for a moment. "Brenda, don't even think about going over there and working for her for free. We gotta eat, too."

Brenda's mouth dropped open in surprise. "What makes you think I was thinking that?"

"Because as much as I love you, you try to take everybody's problems on as if they were yours. I wouldn't put it past you to go work for her, thinking you were just helping her out. Alexis is a grown woman who can handle her own business."

"I know that, but—"

"But nothing. Now money is going to be tight enough as it is with property values going up and us sinking money into this move. Volunteer work isn't going to help us pay the bills."

"Darnell."

"On top of that, I'm talking about retiring in

two years. We need to start saving for that. My little retirement fund isn't going to put food on the table forever."

"Darnell."

"And don't forget most of the schools down there are still closed down, which means Elizabeth might be going to private school. That's another few hundred a month, plus buying uniforms. And don't even mention Christmas—"

"Darnell!"

"What?"

"Give me some credit," Brenda retorted, folding her arms. "Don't you think I thought about all of that? And what would make you think I would want to work for my little cousin? There are other ways I can help her, you know."

"I know there are, but I wanna make sure *you* know," Darnell replied, pointing at his wife. "You and that Mother Teresa complex is gonna get us in trouble one day."

"You're gonna stop with that Mother Teresa mess. You used to say that's what you loved about me."

"I do, but damn! It's gotta stop somewhere."

Brenda held a brick-wall hand up at her husband. "You know what? I'm not even gonna argue with you about this. You're just assuming things and I'm not gonna let you suck me into that."

Darnell laughed so hard he had to hold his stomach. "I'm assuming things? Okay. Look me in the eye and tell me you didn't consider working for Alexis."

Brenda moved closer and looked into her husband's dark brown eyes, determined not to blink. She knew he was right, but there was no way she was letting him win this discussion. "I did not, and will not, consider working for my little cousin."

Darnell smirked and nodded. "Yeah, right. Tell me anything."

"I'm not even thinking about you, Darnell Jordan," she pouted, tossing a pillow at him.

"Don't get mad at me," he said with a laugh. "I'm almost forty years old. I ain't no new fool."

"Shut up!"

Darnell continued laughing. Once he finally calmed down, he smiled at his wife, who was still pouting. "Come here, baby."

"Umm-umm."

"Girl, get over here," he coaxed, pulling her by the arm until she was nearly on top of him. Her face remained hard, her body rigid. "You know I'm only playing with you. I love the fact that you care for your cousin, but promise me you'll find another way to help her. We just can't afford for you to work for free."

"I know," Brenda said, softening her disposition. "I promise."

He hugged her tightly until she finally hugged back. "Thank you, baby. I love you."

"I love you, too. Just don't call me Mother Teresa anymore."

# Chapter 6

# Moving Forward

"Let's go to the casino," Shalonda suggested.

"Why not?" Alexis agreed. They had been sitting at Shalonda's house for the past couple of hours with nothing to do. Shalonda's husband, Robert, was with his weekly bowling league, and Alexis didn't feel like being bothered with Jamar that night. They'd had a date the night before, and it was the same old thing—him not understanding why she didn't want a relationship right now.

"But you know how I am," Shalonda said with a laugh. "Fifty dollars and I'm through. I have better things to do with my money than to give it all to Harrah's."

"I hear you," Alexis agreed, although she knew her friend had nothing to worry about. Shalonda worked as a production engineer at WWL TV, one of New Orleans's oldest TV stations. Robert was a high school teacher and an army Reservist, but with their combined incomes, Alexis knew they could afford to blow more than fifty bucks at the casino. But with rising gas prices and a fluctuating economy, she could understand why they chose to be a little more frugal than they normally would.

"But watch," Alexis said. "How much you wanna bet I'll see one of my patients' parents in there spending the money they should be paying me?"

"I don't have to take that bet; I *know* it's the truth," Shalonda agreed.

Shalonda and Alexis had been best friends since their days at the University of New Orleans, known to many in the city as UNO. During college, Shalonda practically lived at the White house, as they affectionately called Ms. Mary's home, but these days, with Shalonda married with an eleven-year-old daughter and Alexis still single and living with her family, it was the other way around.

Alexis appreciated her and Shalonda's friendship because she'd never had many female friends. In college, many girls didn't trust her enough to let her in their circle. She couldn't blame them because back then, she was known for taking what she wanted, no matter who was in the way. After college, she became involved in her work, and therefore didn't dedicate much time to getting to know new people.

The two women easily had more fun together in their thirties than they did in their twenties. That whole "been there, done that" mentality that women are known to get in their thirties actually held some truth to it. Although they were only thirty-two years old, they'd both experienced enough to know how to have fun without putting up with much of the bull that went along with it.

Alexis attributed much of that to their being professional women. They each took their careers seriously.

With the city's population significantly smaller than what it was two years ago, they understood that every move they made could be magnified one hundred times.

Alexis also credited Mary for their new attitudes. Growing up, neither of them wanted to listen to Mary's ranting and raving, but as they got older, they realized that Mary actually knew what she was talking about. She never sugarcoated her words, but she spoke the truth. And the more they listened, the smarter they got.

"You think Mama Mary will watch Brianna for us till we get back?" Shalonda asked, rising from the sofa to get herself ready.

"I'm sure she won't mind, but lemme ask," Alexis replied, pulling out her cell phone.

The phone rang three times before Mary picked up. "Whatcha need, Alexis?"

"Why you think I need something?" Alexis asked with a laugh.

"Because you're calling me out of the blue, and you're out with your friends."

Busted! You couldn't pull anything over on Mary. "Well, I was wondering, well, Shalonda wanted to know if you could watch Brianna for a couple hours while we go to Harrah's."

"Umm-hmm," Mary replied. "I knew it was something. How you know I ain't got plans for tonight?"

"Do you?"

"No, but you don't need to assume that I'ma always be home when you two need a babysitter."

"I'm sorry, Mama. I'll tell you what—I'll bring you a strawberry daiquiri on the way over there."

"Make it a large and you got a deal," Mary said. "And bring Frank a Crawgator."

"Thanks, Mommy," Alexis sang with a smile. "We'll be over there in a few with Brianna and your drinks."

"All right," Mary agreed, "but don't do this no mo', Alexis."

"I won't, Mama."


"Once again, it's packed," Alexis observed as Shalonda drove past Harrah's Casino in search of a parking space.

"Well, it's Wednesday," Shalonda said. "Captain Charles is playing tonight."

"Oh yeah!" Alexis exclaimed. "I forgot about that. Tonight should be fun."

Captain Charles was the most popular DJ in New Orleans. His repertoire was a mixture of old and new school soul and R & B that always pulled people to the dance floor. A couple of years before the hurricane, Alexis saw Captain Charles rock the house at the Louisiana Superdome during the Essence Music Festival, and half of those tourists didn't even know the songs he played! The music was so good, they didn't even care.

The crowd at Harrah's was no different. They rocked to Frankie Beverly and Maze's "Before I Let Go" as Alexis and Shalonda walked into Masquerade, the circular bar that sat in the middle of the casino. As they walked closer to the bar, the crowd became denser, forcing the two women to inch their way into the area. Shalonda leaned close to Alexis and whispered, "Girl, this is hopeless. Let's just go find a slot machine. We can hear the music from there."

Alexis agreed, and they found their way back out of the crowd. The casino was alive with activity. The card tables were full, even the ones in the high-limit areas. Bells and computerized music from the various slot machines rang all around them.

Being the thrifty women they were, they immediately

searched for the quarter red, white, and blue machines. They'd leave the fifty-cent and dollar machines for the real ballers. Unfortunately, there wasn't an empty quarter machine in sight.

"Actually, 'Londa, let's walk around for a while," Alexis suggested. "It's ridiculous in here."

"Yeah," Shalonda said.

They hadn't walked long before they ran into Renee, one of Alexis's friends from high school. Renee had also attended the University of New Orleans for a while, but began working at Harrah's as a slot attendant once family demands became too much.

"How you doing?" Renee asked. "You still working over there at Touro?"

"Yeah, I'm still there," Alexis replied. "I'm not going anywhere."

"I'm gonna have to bring my son over to see you," Renee said.

"You don't live in a FEMA trailer, do you?" Alexis asked cautiously.

"Girl, no," Renee replied, waving off the thought. "We have one, but I'm about ready to give that thing back. I got my house fixed months ago."

"Good, because I have enough patients in those trailers," Alexis said, breathing a sigh of relief.

"No, you don't have to worry about that. I'm just ready to switch doctors. Mine is too damned slow, and he never sees his patients on time."

"Oh, girl, well, that's easy." Alexis then remembered Shalonda standing next to her. "I'm so rude, I'm so rude. This is my friend Shalonda. We went to college together."

"It's about time," Shalonda remarked. "I thought I was invisible for a minute."

"Don't worry, girl," Renee said, shaking Shalonda's hand. "Alexis has always been a mean bitch."

The three ladies laughed; then Alexis and Shalonda made their way around the casino floor. The entire casino was a colorful circle that resembled the French Quarter during Mardi Gras. There was even a parade that rolled through the crowd twice a night complete with a brass band and a krewe that tossed beads at the patrons.

Harrah's hadn't always been this crowded. Captain Charles used to perform at Bally's, a riverboat casino in East New Orleans. The casino moved to Lake Charles, Louisiana, after the flood. There was another casino on the West Bank of New Orleans and another in neighboring Kenner, Louisiana, but when Harrah's reopened, it regained much of the East Bank crowd who refused to drive that far just to gamble.

Many people didn't care for the casino industry, but as far as Alexis was concerned, they were a much-needed source of income for New Orleanians. She would never forget how many people returned to New Orleans when Harrah's promised to rehire all its former employees after rebuilding. They'd also hired a number of new employees, many of whom had traveled back and forth from Baton Rouge every day looking for work.

"How are you ladies doing?" asked a familiar male voice from behind.

Shalonda and Alexis turned quickly and nearly jumped when they found Jamar standing there. He looked as if he'd been at Harrah's all evening. He wore a pair of slacks that Alexis was sure went with a vest and jacket he'd probably left in the car. The cuffs of his crisply starched shirt displayed shiny blue and white cuff links, and his tie was loosened at the neck. His smile told Alexis that he'd had just enough hurricane drinks to feel good, but he definitely wasn't drunk.

"Not as good as you," Alexis remarked. She didn't

know whether to smile or run. Jamar was looking good, but she didn't want him trying to pull her away from her evening with her girl. "What are you up to?"

"Just showing a client a good time," he replied, eying Alexis hungrily. "How are you doing, Ms. Shalonda?"

"Very well, thank you," Shalonda replied. She took a step back and waited for her friend to finish speaking.

"Is this client male or female?" Alexis asked, folding her arms. She knew she shouldn't care since Jamar technically wasn't her boyfriend, but she couldn't help feeling a twinge of jealousy at the thought of him working closely with another woman. The way she figured, if he wanted her so badly, no other woman should even stand a chance of getting close to him. She knew it was selfish, but it was the truth.

Jamar winked at her. "Why do you always ask me that? You know my heart only belongs to you."

Alexis and Shalonda looked at each other and laughed.

"That was smooth, Jamar," Shalonda remarked.

Jamar popped his collar. "You know me. I can't help but be smooth."

"Okay, if you say so," Alexis said, patting his chest. "I'll let you get back to your *client*. Give me a call tomorrow."

Jamar backed off slowly. "I'll definitely do that."

Once he disappeared into the crowd, Shalonda turned to Alexis and asked, "Why do you make it so hard on that man?"

"I couldn't even tell you," Alexis replied. She watched intently as an older man played three fifty-cent progressive slot machines at once. If even one of them hit, he would walk out of Harrah's eight thousand dollars richer. She silently wished him luck. "I mean, I like him and all, but deep down, I'm not ready to commit to him."

"Why?" Shalonda asked, moving forward just in

time to avoid being knocked over by a pack of college kids. "You don't trust him?"

Alexis shrugged. "That might have a little to do with it."

Shalonda waited for her friend to elaborate, but when she didn't, she joined her in watching the old man feed the three one-armed bandits. He still hadn't managed to win more than a couple hundred dollars, and judging from the six twenties he slid into the machines, she was sure there was some bill he probably wouldn't be able to pay next week.

Shalonda never could understand people who had trouble paying their bills but never failed to hit the slots. She'd even seen people walk into Harrah's, and Bally's during its heyday, still wearing their work uniforms. That urge to quickly make a dollar out of fifteen cents was stronger than many could handle.

Bored with watching the man spin his life away, Alexis turned to see what other sights the casino held. Her eyes locked in on a young woman wearing a T-shirt and jeans with a scarf covering her head. She tapped Shalonda on the arm and pointed at the woman. "What the hell did I tell you? I shoulda made you take that bet."

"Awww, that's messed up," Shalonda said, shaking her head. "She have an appointment with you this week?"

"No, she owes me for two other visits, and then brought her son in last week and claimed she couldn't pay me until payday."

"I guess that's today."

"I should go collect my money now."

"Alexis, don't you cause no scene in here," Shalonda warned.

Alexis sucked her teeth and glared at her friend. "You know me better than that."

The woman looked up, frowning once she caught

Alexis and Shalonda looking at her. Her eyes resembled those of a child whose mother had caught her sampling the private stash. Alexis just rolled her eyes and walked away.

"Let's go see how the high rollers are doing," Shalonda suggested.

"Yeah, because this chick is depressing me," Alexis agreed. "With all the money she put into that machine, I could have paid for three weeks' worth of gas."

The two women chuckled and walked over to the high-limits section. No one was allowed in this area unless they were playing, but they enjoyed standing near the separation rail and watching the reactions from the rich people who bet hundreds like one-dollar bills. They really liked it when Shalonda's friend Pam dealt in that area. She'd been known to make grown men cry with her baccarat skills.

Fortunately, they weren't disappointed. Just as they walked up, a yuppie wearing a cheap suit and a loosened tie had hit the card table and whined, "You're killin' me, Pam!"

Pam laughed and smoothed her ponytail. "Hey, that's the way it goes sometimes."

"I see your girl is hurtin' them, as usual," Alexis said to Shalonda.

As if on cue, Pam looked up and waved at them. She couldn't talk because the hungry rich men demanded her attention. She quickly looked down and dealt the cards. Just as quickly, one man cheered while the yuppie groaned again. He rose from the table and tipped her fifty dollars.

"You got me tonight," he said, backing away. "I'll see you next week."

She waved at him. "All right, Tom. Be safe tonight."

He waved and walked out of the area. No one dared

take his place, but Pam didn't miss a beat. "Bets up," she announced, running her hand across the table.

Alexis glanced around the area to see how the other patrons were doing. She nearly lost her breath when she saw a very handsome, muscular bald man sitting at the blackjack table. "Not again," she mumbled.

"Huh?" Shalonda asked.

"Reggie's over there," Alexis explained, pointing toward the high-limit blackjack table.

"What's he doing here? I thought the Saints had an away game this weekend."

Alexis shrugged. "I guess he hasn't left yet."

"You going to say hi?"

"Hell, no!" Alexis snapped.

Shalonda laughed. "You're going to have to face that man one day."

"No, the hell I won't," Alexis said, moving away from the area to avoid being seen. "You know this is the second time this week I've seen his ass?"

"When was the other time?"

"At Golden Corral Sunday."

"Did you speak then?"

"No, and Roman got on my nerves about it."

"Girl, that mess happened between you two over ten years ago," Shalonda said, shaking her finger at her friend. "You need to get over that. You're not the same person you were then."

"I know, but every time I see him, all those bad memories come back," Alexis said, folding her arms.

"Now, Lex, you know you're stronger than that. What happened to the girl who had the world wrapped around her finger? You earned a medical degree, survived a hurricane, broke off an engagement you should never have had in the first place, and opened a big-time private medical practice. And you mean to tell me you can't face an ex-boyfriend?"

"Laugh if you want," Alexis snapped, smiling in spite of herself. She knew it sounded silly. She was a thirty-two-year-old woman running and hiding from her college sweetheart. But he wasn't just anyone; he was the only man who'd ever completely had her heart. She could be strong and coy with anyone else, but with Reggie, she'd never be able to find the right words.

"Well, I'm going to say hi," Shalonda said, walking back toward high limits.

"Oh no, the hell you're not," Alexis snapped, grabbing her friend's arm.

"What? I like Reggie. Can't I at least wish him good luck Sunday?"

"No! He has enough fans to do that for him. And remember," Alexis said, finally letting go of Shalonda's arm, "you were *my* friend before you were his."

Shalonda couldn't help but laugh. "That was real adult of you."

Alexis smiled again. "Shut up."

"Well, let's go sit at the bar," Shalonda suggested. "It looks like it's clearing out in there."

"Okay," Alexis agreed, relieved that her friend had let up. They walked back to Masquerade and took seats at the bar. Just as they were about to order, Jamar walked up on them again.

"We meet again," he said, placing his arms around both their shoulders. "Can I buy you ladies a drink?"

"How about two hurricanes?" Alexis suggested.

"Sounds good," Shalonda agreed.

"As you wish," Jamar said, signaling for the bartender. He made small talk with them until their drinks arrived, then bid them farewell. "I gotta get up early tomorrow, so, Lex, I'll see your pretty self tomorrow. Shalonda, you take care. It's always a pleasure."

"He's so sweet," Shalonda purred once Jamar left the bar.

"Don't start!" Alexis snapped. She took a sip from her hurricane, wondering why everyone but her seemed to know what and who was best for her.

"There you are, Dr. White!"

Alexis turned to see the lady she'd seen earlier feeding the slots. The shock on her face spoke volumes to the lady.

"I've been lookin' for you since I saw you a while ago," the lady continued.

Alexis and Shalonda looked at each other curiously, then looked back at the lady, who looked very much as if she were only a couple of weeks out of high school.

"What's up, Ms. Lincoln?" Alexis asked, nonchalantly taking a sip from her hurricane.

"I know this is the last place you thought we would bump into each other, but I'm actually glad I saw you tonight," Ms. Lincoln said quickly. "I hit big on the slots tonight. I was gonna use some of the money and pay you tomorrow, but since you're here tonight, I thought I would save a trip and give you your payment now."

Alexis looked back at Shalonda and tried to suppress a grin. "You don't have to do that now."

"Yes, I do! You've been good to me and Dante, so the least I can do is make sure we make good on our bills. So take this money."

Ms. Lincoln pulled out a wad of twenties and hundreds. She'd definitely hit a jackpot sometime tonight. She peeled off three hundreds and handed them to the shocked doctor. "And here's another twenty. You and your friend have another drink on me. I'm sorry we made you wait so long. It won't happen again."

Before Alexis could even utter a thank-you, the lady disappeared into the crowd almost as quickly as she had appeared. Alexis raised the money at Shalonda, then quickly put it away before any desperate, unlucky gamblers could take notice. "Ain't that some shit?"

Shalonda laughed. "I guess guilt can do some strange things to people."

"Yeah, well, I'll bet she won't be late with another payment now that I've peeped her game."

"Well, you know what they say—anything goes in the casino."

# Chapter 7

# Get Happy

"How you doing, Jamar?" Reggie greeted, walking into Jamar's office Wednesday afternoon.

Jamar looked up and smiled. "Well, if it isn't the champ! Congratulations on that game the other day."

"Thanks, man," Reggie said with a proud smile. "It's about time."

The Saints had finally won their first game of the season, 28–14, over the Seattle Seahawks. The entire team had played with a new fervor. Although they went scoreless in the second half, they held the Seahawks to only two touchdowns the entire game. Reggie had never felt better about his performance. He was focused. He was loose. And most importantly, he was sober!

"Thanks for taking me out the other day," Reggie said, taking a seat in front of Jamar's desk. "I really needed to get my mind off of things. I should be giving *you* my game ball."

"Don't mention it," Jamar said. "From what you told me, a night at the casino was long overdue."

"You ain't never lyin'," Reggie said, stretching his feet out in front of him.

"So, you think about what I said?"

"Yep, and I already put it into motion."

Jamar looked harder at his client. "You did? You don't waste no time, do you?"

Reggie shook his head. "Jamar, you just don't know how much I need to get this behind me."

"I feel you, but you know the hard part is yet to come."

Reggie nodded sadly. "I know, but I'ma do what I gotta do. Shawn means the world to me."

"I understand," Jamar said, placing his hands on his desk. "But you know cheating isn't exactly grounds for losing your child."

"Shit, it should be. Especially since every fuckin' body in New Orleans and parts of Atlanta knows what she's doing. How is that supposed to affect a child?"

"Hey, you don't have to preach to me," Jamar said. "I know where you're coming from. I'm just saying it won't be easy. You've not only got to prove that the cheating actually happened, but you've also gotta prove that her actions are bringing harm to your son."

"I will, you can trust that," Reggie said, punching his fist into his left hand.

"Have you told her you want a divorce yet?"

"No. I was trying to see where our plan goes first."

"You might want to move quick," Jamar advised. He pulled out some paperwork and handed it to Reggie. "The waiting period for a divorce changed this year. Because DeShawn is six years old, you two have to be separated for twelve months before you can file for a divorce."

"Damn," Reggie mumbled when he saw Jamar's

words in black and white. "This is going to take longer than I thought."

"The only way you cut that time short is to prove without a doubt that she cheated," Jamar explained. "Just because she spent the night out doesn't mean she was sleeping with someone. She can easily say she fell asleep at a friend's house."

"Aw, come on, Jamar," Reggie whined. "You know that's bullshit."

"I know, but many a case has been won because the petitioner couldn't prove anything."

"What about the condom I found in my bed?"

Jamar shrugged. "It could have been a couple of her friends who used your bed while you weren't home."

"That's bullshit, and you know it."

"I know, but I have to give you every possible argument."

"What if I get witnesses?"

"As long as they're people who can prove without a doubt that Nikki's been creepin'."

"Shit, I know for a fact people who actually slept with her, but I don't know if they would help me."

"Well, if you can get them to help you, you can easily get a fault divorce and you won't have to worry about that separation period," Jamar said, reclining in his chair. He paused and took a breath. "In the meantime, you can go ahead and file for separation to get the ball rolling, but DeShawn will probably go with Nikki until after the divorce proceedings."

"Shit!"

"Hey, don't kill the messenger, but you haven't proven that she shouldn't raise him," Jamar explained. "But it's not all bad, Reg. During that time, you'll have time to settle any joint debts and you can terminate community property so you won't be liable for any debts she incurs during the separation."

"What about Shawn?"

"There's no reason you can't still see Shawn on a regular basis," Jamar assured him. "You're a good dad, I'm sure. Besides, this is football season, so you don't have a lot of time, anyway. And if Nikki is doing her thing like you say she is, she'll probably have Shawn spending nights with you when you're in town."

"I doubt that," Reggie said, sucking his teeth. "She's gonna want Shawn just as badly as I do. She's not going to want me spending too much time with him. He might mess around and say he wants *me* instead of *her*."

Jamar nodded. "There's a chance of that. But there's a chance of a lot of stuff. That's the risk you take in a high-profile divorce. My job is to make it as painless as possible without it making the local news."

Reggie looked his attorney in the eye. "Can you do that?"

"Yes," Jamar replied. "Are you willing to do this, knowing the risks involved?"

"Yes," Reggie said without blinking.

Jamar looked at his client harder without saying a word. He needed to make sure Reggie meant what he said. Once he was satisfied, he turned to his computer. "Then let's get started with this separation paperwork."

Reggie felt as if all of the life had drained out of him once he arrived at his Chateau Estates home. Chateau Estates was located in Kenner, a suburb of New Orleans. Reggie, Nikki, and DeShawn had moved there once the Saints returned to New Orleans the year before. Their original home in Eastover had been destroyed.

Eastover, located deep in New Orleans East, used to be the premier residential area, home to many of the New Orleans African-American elite. Once Katrina hit, Reggie traveled with the team until the off-season, when he returned to his hometown of Atlanta. He'd already moved Nikki and DeShawn to his second home there.

Although Reggie loved his new home, which was completely on the opposite side of the city from his original one, he missed Eastover. The community was quiet, and many of the neighbors knew each other. It was a predominantly African-American community, unlike the mostly Caucasian area where he now lived. However, he knew he would probably never go back to Eastover, although the area had shown great signs of revitalization. He'd just grown comfortable in his new surroundings.

Most days, the commute from Kenner wasn't so bad because he didn't have to drive through the morning and evening rush-hour traffic. The drive between home and the Saints' training facility was much shorter than it used to be. Many times, he could even make it home before nightfall.

That night, the traffic was heavier than usual. The cars on both sides of Interstate 10 seemed to move only a couple of inches every few minutes. As Reggie got closer, he found the cause of the gridlock—a five-car pileup! He groaned and slammed his head back against the headrest. His babysitter was definitely getting overtime tonight. He pulled his cell phone from his pocket and called home.

"Hey, Necee," he said once he heard her pick up. "I'm on the way home, but there's a real bad wreck on I-10. I'll probably be another forty-five minutes."

"No problem, Mr. Morgan," she replied. "Your wife just got here, so I'm about to leave. I have an early class in the morning."

"Nikki's there?" Reggie asked.

"Yeah, she got here about ten minutes ago."

Reggie tried to hide his disgust. He'd hoped to have the house to himself before Nikki arrived, but he couldn't say that to Necee. A twenty-year-old babysitter didn't need to know all his business. "That's good. Did she pay you yet?"

"Sure did," she replied. "I got a nice tip, too."

Reggie chuckled. "That's what I'm talkin' about. Make sure you don't spend that all in one place."

Necee laughed and bid her boss farewell. Reggie folded his phone shut and stared blankly at the unending line of red lights ahead of him. He didn't seem to be going anywhere. He glanced at the Popeye's chicken box sitting on the passenger seat. His mouth watered as he thought of the buttermilk biscuit inside. He looked back at the gridlock, then tore into the box. Might as well enjoy the traffic jam the best way he could.

"'Bout time," Nikki remarked once Reggie walked through the door. She was dressed in a nightshirt and was curled up on the sofa watching a movie.

Reggie groaned and dropped his gym bag near the door. He silently walked into the den where Nikki sat and flopped onto his recliner. "Where's DeShawn?"

Nikki sucked her teeth and winced. "And hello to you, too. Your son is in his room playing PlayStation."

Reggie rolled his eyes and looked at his wife. "Nikki, don't act like you rolled out the red carpet when I walked in."

"Well, it's not like you've been acting like you want me around these days," Nikki replied, sitting up and pulling her feet underneath her.

Reggie gave her a sideways smile and sat up. The timing couldn't be more perfect. "Nikki, tell the truth. You don't wanna be married to me anymore."

Nikki stared at him with a blank expression. When she didn't reply, Reggie continued. "You gave up on me a long time ago."

Her expression softened slightly. "I never gave up on you, Reg. You gave up on yourself."

He looked puzzled. "What are you talking about?"

"Reggie, you're one of the best defensive ends in the NFL," she said, scooting closer to him. "You have at least three more good years in you, and you're ready to give all of that up. I know the team is having a bad season this year, but you're not even keeping your eye on the big picture."

Reggie pursed his lips. "What's the big picture?"

"If you're not happy with the Saints, why not move on like Joe Horn did? Try finding a team you can get a Super Bowl ring with."

"What makes you think I'm not happy with my team?"

"Why the hell else would you want to retire at thirty-two years old?" Nikki snapped, waving her hand in the air.

"Nikki, if you took as much time to talk to me as you did fuckin' around on me, somebody might actually mistake you for someone who gave a shit about me," Reggie said, leaning back in his chair.

She stared at him, shock written all over her face. "Excuse me?"

"You heard me! You think you know everything, but you don't know shit!"

Nikki sat up straight, placing both feet on the floor. Reggie couldn't help but notice her freshly pedicured toenails, each adorned with a rhinestone. Even in her at-home, comfortable state, she never failed to look stunning. "Reggie, I'm not going to have you cursing at me. You need to watch who you're talking to."

Reggie opened his mouth to light into her, but thought better of it. Instead, he rose from his chair, walked to the bar, and calmly made himself a gin and orange juice. Once he was satisfied with his drink, he leaned against the wall and took a sip. "You're right, Nikki. I don't need to be cursin' at you."

Nikki looked surprised that he'd calmed down so quickly. "Thank you."

"I filed for separation today," Reggie said quietly after taking another sip from his drink.

"Excuse me?"

Reggie set down his glass and retrieved his gym bag from the doorway. He pulled a brown envelope from the top of the bag and handed it to his wife. "See for yourself."

She took the envelope from him and opened it slowly. She read over the papers with scrunched eyebrows. She was so quiet that Reggie nearly grew nervous as he awaited her reaction. He refreshed his drink in an effort to calm his nerves.

"You sure about this?" she finally asked, placing the papers next to her on the sofa.

"As a heart attack," Reggie said quickly.

She shrugged her shoulders and rose from the sofa. "If you like it, I love it."

"What's that supposed to mean?" he asked, following her out of the den.

He stayed hot on her heels, receiving nothing but silence until she reached the steps. Suddenly she turned around and put her finger into his face, her rhinestone-adorned nail nearly scratching his nose. "You think you're hurting me with this? Did you expect me to fuckin' cry about this? Hell to the naw! I've been ready to leave this damned marriage for years; I was just waitin' for *your* ass to say something."

Reggie knocked her hand away from his face and glared at her. "I never held a gun to your head and made you stay with me. That door works just fine. And you coulda left it whenever your heart desired."

"Don't give me that shit, Reg," Nikki hissed. "You think you made it as far as you did by yourself? I was with your ass when you were strugglin' to make it past third string. I gave up my dreams so I could follow your narrow ass from city to city and make you feel good about yourself even when you played like shit! Now you wanna leave me? Who the hell else do you think wants to be stuck with some washed-up football player who gave up on himself before it was time?"

"So because I want to use the degrees that I worked damn hard to earn, you think I'm giving up on myself?" Reggie asked. "I guess you can't understand that because the hardest decision you ever made was whether the fuckin' wives' meeting should be held at the zoo or the French Quarter. When is the last time you even had a damned job?"

"Before I met your funky ass, that's when!" Nikki snapped. "You think being president of that club is easy? Who the hell do you think is responsible for your endorsements? How the hell do you think you've gotten most of those awards from the city? Because you're such a wonderful football player?"

Reggie doubled over in laughter. "You're right. I guess you slept your way to the top for both of us. Thanks for *really* taking one for the team."

His laughter suddenly stopped when a flash of lightning struck his left jaw. He rubbed his face, realizing Nikki had just knocked the daylights out of him.

"I fuckin' told you to watch who you're talking to!" she shouted. "I ain't one to be messed with. You mighta forgot, but that's *my* neighborhood you see on the news every night. And you know the Ninth Ward don't play."

Reggie glared at her through squinted eyes. "And neither does Bankhead. Try that shit one more time."

Nikki drew her hand back to take him up on his offer, but he caught her wrist just as she began to swing. He twisted it behind her back and sandwiched her against the wall. "You need to get out of this house before I hurt you."

"You must be out of your fuckin' mind if you think you're going to kick me out of this house again without my son," Nikki shouted, struggling to regain control. "This is my house, too! I ain't goin' nowhere!"

"Oh, you're goin' somewhere," Reggie hissed in her ear. "And you're going to keep your voice down before Shawn comes down here."

"Then let me go!"

Reggie snatched his hand back, forcing Nikki to fall to the floor. She rubbed the pain from her wrist, but refused to cry. Reggie had to admit that she truly was a tough woman who took nothing from no one. He knew she'd be better off without him.

"Let me tell you something, Mr. NFL," she said, her voice finally lowered. "I'm leaving, but not because you think you're throwing me out. I was with you when you signed the deed to this house. This is my house, too, but I refuse to live here with you anymore. You're right; I don't want to be married to you anymore. I fell out of love with you a long time ago. I only stayed with you because it was expected. Now that you're walking out on your career, I don't need to feel bad about walking out on *you*. But don't get it twisted. DeShawn is coming with me."

Reggie stood over her and nodded. He knew this would happen. He would have to get used to seeing his son when he could. He just prayed that one day he would get DeShawn back. "You don't need to leave tonight. Let him sleep. Just find a place when you can."

"You must think I'm stupid," Nikki sneered. "I've had a place for the last year. You think you're the only one in this family who can have two houses? Where do you think I stay when you're not here? Or when I have a 'late meeting'? Yeah, Shawn can stay the night, but I'm going to my place and get some rest."

"I knew it had to be something," Reggie said, walking away from her. "Whatever, Nikki. Carry your ass on out of here. Just give me some time with my son."

Nikki softened a bit and followed her husband into the den. She watched him sit in his favorite recliner and stare at the television screen. "You playing here this weekend?" she asked.

Once Reggie nodded, she said, "I'll just pick him up Sunday evening so he can go to the game with you."

He nodded again. An awkward silence passed. "Sorry it had to end like this," he said, nearly in a whisper.

"Yeah."

"I'm going to take a shower," Reggie announced after a few minutes. "Take your time packing your stuff."

He grabbed his bag and headed upstairs without looking back. As he reached the top of the steps, he heard scrambling near DeShawn's room. When he looked through the cracked door, he could just see his son climbing into bed. Sadly, Reggie trudged into the master bedroom and closed the door. He walked into his bathroom and turned on the shower.

As he pulled off his clothes, he replayed the night's events in his mind. He'd gotten the results he wanted, but never expected it to be this painful. He'd begun the process to divorce his wife, but it ended with a wrestling match that his son had the unfortunate displeasure of witnessing.

Once he climbed into the shower and the steam enveloped his body, he finally let go of the pain. As the tears rolled down his face, he vowed to put all of this behind him as quickly as possible. It wasn't going to be easy, but he knew tomorrow would be a brand-new day.

# Chapter 8

# Three Times

"Hey, Jamar," Alexis greeted.

"Hey, yourself," Jamar replied.

"We still on for tonight? I'm in the mood for some jazz."

"Long week?"

"Nothing you can't help me fix," Alexis said with a smile.

"I like that. I'll see you at seven."

"All right, now," Alexis said to herself as she hung up the phone. She looked around her little office and smiled. "I just love it when a plan comes together."

She was between patients and had decided to give Jamar a call. They'd grown closer over the past few weeks. She had to admit that the good lawyer was slowly breaking down her defenses. She felt it was time for them to get closer, although she still wasn't sure how close they should get. She definitely wasn't ready for marriage, but she knew there was no use stressing over Reggie, and Tony was obviously not coming back for her. The old her would never have racked her mind over men. She felt she was losing her edge. She was losing the Alexis that she used to be. Something had to be done.

Jamar made things interesting. He was professional, but he wasn't a nerd by any stretch of the imagination. He had a street edge that kept him sexy. He knew how to make a joke. And he actually listened to what she had to say. Yet, at the same time, he had a tender side that only she was allowed to see. He constantly sent her flowers, and always made it a point to make her feel like the queen she knew she was.

There weren't many men who could appreciate an attractive woman with a career. Many thought a beautiful woman was only good when her legs were open, but Alexis was only too happy to show them differently. Even in her young, wild days, she knew she had a plan for her life. She made straight As in high school, even while going out every Friday night. Things started off a little rocky in college, but once she found her flow, she knew there was no way anything would stop her from being a doctor.

Unfortunately, that drive was what caused her to get an abortion when she realized her wild days had caught up with her. It was amazing. In all the sexual escapades she'd had, she'd never contracted an STD. Yet she seduced a married man who cared nothing about her and got pregnant. It was amazing how things worked. She'd only gone to Virginia Beach that Christmas to spend time with Brenda. Yet, when she saw Christopher, she thought she'd have a little fun as well, despite the fact that he was married to her cousin's best friend, Andrea. Little did she know that that fun would change her life forever.

She'd never even thought twice about dealing with her pregnancy and having the baby. All she could see was a speed bump in her quest to become a doctor and a roadblock to her one day marrying Reggie. She'd had the abortion and thought she was in the clear until something happened. She'd fallen in love. It was a new feeling for her. Until then, love had never really been a part of her vocabulary. So when it happened, she thought it only right that she tell him what she did. Unfortunately, she wound up losing him in the process. So here she was today. She'd become a doctor, but lost her first love. On top of that, the complications from the procedure would never allow her to have another child.

It was a long time before she could accept the fact that she was sterile. Some nights the thoughts would bear down so hard that she would cry herself to sleep. She could never talk to anyone about it because talking about it would mean admitting her reality. Not even Shalonda knew about her inability to have children, although she was the one who had accompanied Alexis to the clinic.

Alexis couldn't even tell her sister-cousin Brenda. The entire affair had nearly torn the two cousins apart. Once things had finally gotten back to normal between them, Alexis couldn't bear to bring those bad feelings back. Brenda and Andrea were again as tight as ever, and from what Alexis knew, Andrea and Christopher were stronger than ever after undergoing months of therapy. It was just best to let things be.

A knock at the door shook Alexis from her thoughts.

"Yes," she called out.

"Dr. White," Ms. Kay said, after poking her head into the office. "Your two-thirty is here."

"Okay," Alexis replied, checking her face in the small mirror on her desk. "You get her vitals yet?"

"I'm about to, but I just wanted to let you know she was here."

Alexis smiled. "Thanks."

Ms. Kay had been a major blessing to Alexis since she'd opened her clinic three years ago. She'd originally met her during her residency at Touro. Alexis looked up to Ms. Kay because she was an older woman who'd been a registered nurse for the past twenty years, and had no plans of retiring any time soon. During her residency, Alexis had struck up a friendship with her and had often sought Ms. Kay for advice. When she got ready to open her clinic, Ms. Kay shocked her by saying that she would gladly work for her and help her get started. Alexis nearly cried at the thought of someone she admired believing in her so much.

Once Ms. Kay left, Alexis checked her face again and powered on her computer. She searched for her patient's electronic records to get updated on what she would be dealing with. Latisha Delachaise. Nine years old. Generally healthy, but was scheduled for a checkup. Alexis grinned. There would be no drama with this patient. She might even get paid today. Things were looking up.

"Brenda, what time are you two driving in tomorrow?" Alexis asked, balancing the receiver between her shoulder and her ear as she searched her closet for her teal sandals with the two-inch heels. She had to find them because they were the only shoes she had that went perfectly with her teal linen strapless tunic and matching pants. Black pumps just wouldn't do tonight.

"We should get to my mama's house around five o'clock in the evening," Brenda replied.

"Oh, okay," Alexis said, retrieving her desired shoes

from the back of the closet. "I should be off work by then."

"That's good. Then I'll give you a chance to get home and we'll stop by your house around seven."

"Perfect. Mama said she's making gumbo because she knows you ain't had none since the last time you came home."

Brenda laughed. "She ain't lyin' about that. Now, are we coming to your house or staying at mine for Thanksgiving?"

"Auntie Ernestine didn't tell you?" Alexis asked, running her fingers through her long curly hair. She'd removed the braids two weeks ago, and enjoyed the softness of her natural hair.

"Apparently not."

"We'll be at my house. You're in charge of the collard greens."

"How did I get tasked with cooking? I'm the visitor!"

Alexis laughed. "Girl, you know that visitor stuff doesn't work in New Orleans. I don't care where you're coming from; if you're family, you're cooking. Shalonda's sister just got back from Iraq and she's making potato salad for their dinner, so you know your little trip from Florida doesn't mean anything."

"That is so wrong," Brenda said.

"No, that's family. You're lucky Darnell doesn't have to cook."

"Believe, me, Lex, I love my man with all my heart, but you don't want that man anywhere near the kitchen."

"Yeah, I remember you telling me about that surprise dinner he tried to cook for you."

They both grew silent, reminiscing on the runny instant potatoes and tough pork chops he had served. Brenda had told Alexis that she had to eat it so she wouldn't hurt his feelings, but she ended up in the bathroom the rest of the evening. Since then, she'd been brutally honest about her husband's cooking, and praised God that he had countless other talents to make up for it.

"Well, sister-cuz, I've gotta get off this phone. I'm going out with Jamar tonight."

"That's cute. You two getting serious?"

"I don't know, but I decided to let him get a little closer. We'll see where it goes."

"Well, I hope it works out for you. You could use a good man in your life."

Alexis froze in her tracks. "What's that supposed to mean?"

"Just what I said. You know I was never all that crazy about Tony, and I wanted to go to Texas myself and whip his tail for how he treated you. You're my girl, and I know you deserve better."

Alexis softened a bit. "I hear you. I'll get engaged again when the time comes."

"I'll leave it at that," Brenda said, retreating. "Go get ready for your date. Darnell's calling me."

"Okay, sis. I'll see you tomorrow night."

The doorbell rang just as Alexis hung up the phone. She turned to her full-length mirror and checked her appearance once more.

"I got it!" Roman called out. A few minutes later, he called out again, "Alexis! Jamar's here."

Alexis rolled her eyes upward as she emerged from her room. Why did her brother have to be so silly? She wished he would act like normal people and speak without shouting all over the house. She would definitely have to start looking for her own place soon. She grabbed her purse and coat and waltzed into the living room, where the rest of the family sat watching TV.

Jamar couldn't hide his delight when he saw Alexis enter the room. "Damn, you look good."

"Tell me something I *don't* know," she replied, twirling around so he could see the entire package. She stopped and took in his cream-colored sweater, which he matched with a pair of coal-gray slacks. "You're looking good yourself."

"Did you expect anything less?" he asked with a smile.

"Oh God," Roman groaned as he lay on the floor. "Can you two old people please go so I can watch TV in peace?"

Mary and Frank laughed.

"You can learn something, boy," Frank said. "A lady likes being complimented."

"And she likes a man that looks good with her," Mary added. "That's how your daddy was able to get me. He always looked good."

Roman groaned again and rose from his spot on the floor. "I really don't need to hear this."

Everyone laughed again as Roman sulked to his room. Mary waved him off. "Don't worry about him. He's just mad because both of his girlfriends had to work tonight and he ain't got nothin' to do."

"I'm not thinking about that boy, Mama," Alexis said with a chuckle. "One of those chicken heads will be calling him before the night is over. Watch."

"Yeah," Frank agreed, smiling. "He reminds me of myself when I was younger."

Mary sucked her teeth and looked at her husband as if he were crazy. "Alexis, you two better go before your daddy gets hisself in trouble."

"On that note . . ." Jamar said, guiding Alexis to the door.

"We'll see y'all later," Alexis said as they left the house.

"Okay, have fun," Mary replied as Alexis closed the door.

Once they were settled in Jamar's gray Acura, Jamar said, "Your dad is a trip."

"Yeah," she agreed.

"It must have been fun growing up with him."

Alexis looked at him curiously. "I never told you? Frank's not my real dad. They just got married after the hurricane, but they've been living together for about five years. Roman is Frank's son. He moved in with us when he started going to Dillard a couple years ago."

"No, I didn't know that. Your parents are divorced?"

Alexis pursed her lips. "No, my dad was in the army. He died in a car accident before I was born. My mother raised me by herself."

"I'm sorry to hear that," Jamar said as he turned the car onto Elysian Fields Avenue. "Do you know much about him?"

"A little," Alexis replied. "I know he was a recruiter for the army and that he was from Panama. He was older than my mother by a few years, but from what she tells me, they were very much in love and planned to be married before the accident."

"Wow," Jamar said. "That's sad. Do you ever go to Panama to see his family?"

Alexis shook her head. "I don't know if he had a chance to tell his family about me. I'm sure they knew he had a child, but they never stayed in touch after he died. The army had a memorial ceremony for him here with his friends and coworkers, but his body was shipped back to Panama to be buried. His family wrote her a couple of times, but then the letters stopped coming. She never heard from them again."

"I'm sorry. It's like you have a whole part of your history that you've never had the chance to learn."

"I know. I wouldn't mind going there and meeting them one day, but I wouldn't even know where to start."

"Yeah, that would be hard, but I'm sure there's a way to make that happen," Jamar assured her.

Alexis shrugged. "Yeah, probably, but it's been so long that I'm not really worried about it. If I do, I do, if I don't, I don't. My mama's the one who's been there for me since day one. It's not like I never had anyone in my life. I know who my real family is. If I went to see them, it would just be out of curiosity. I don't see them adding anything to my life."

"I hear you, sweetie," Jamar said, patting her thigh. He turned onto St. Claude Avenue, which would lead them to Sweet Lorraine's Jazz Club. The club had become a favorite hangout for them. Neither of them liked the hip-hop club scene. It was much too loud and busy for either of their tastes. Sweet Lorraine's provided them with a more relaxed atmosphere that allowed them to both eat good food and socialize.

The club was more crowded than usual for a Tuesday night. It wasn't jam-packed, but nearly every table was filled, forcing them to have to sit near the back of the restaurant.

"I guess we should have gotten here earlier," Alexis said, looking around.

"Damn that," Jamar replied. "Stay here for a minute. I'll find us a better seat."

He walked farther into the restaurant as Alexis sat down. A few minutes later, he returned with a smile on his face. "Who's the man?"

"You got us a table?"

"Uh-uh. First you gotta tell me who's the man."

Alexis chuckled. "Okay, you're the man, baby. Now where are we sitting?"

"Right by the stage, sweetie," he said, holding his hands to the side, presentation-style. He offered his hand to Alexis and helped her out of her seat. They then walked in grand fashion to the front of the restaurant, where a table for two awaited on the right of the stage.

Alexis smiled. "You definitely are the man."

"I told you to stop playing me short," Jamar said proudly. "You just don't know who you're dealing with."

"I don't think you know who *you're* dealing with," she corrected.

"Oh, I know," Jamar replied, pulling out her chair. He then took his own seat and picked up his menu. "Whatcha in the mood for tonight?"

Alexis smiled, impressed with Jamar's confidence. "You keep acting like that, and I'll be in the mood for you."

Jamar looked up, surprised at Alexis's flirtation. "You better stop that."

She just smiled and read her menu. After they placed their orders, Jamar excused himself to go to the restroom.

"Don't take too long," Alexis said with a smile just as the waitress placed her cosmopolitan in front of her. She tasted it and looked up at Jamar as he walked away. For the first time since they'd met, she was actually starting to see real possibilities with him. Maybe they could actually make this thing work.

"I thought that was you out there."

Jamar looked into the mirror and found Reggie standing behind him. "Man, you know you don't sneak up behind a black man in this city."

Reggie laughed. "My bad, man. I just wanted to speak."

Jamar dried his hands and shook hands with his client. "It's all good. How's everything going?"

Reggie shrugged. "It's okay. Nikki still has DeShawn. I get to see him on weekends when I'm in town. She's keeping him for Thanksgiving since we're playing Carolina Sunday."

"Sorry you can't spend more time with him. How you holding up?"

"Good. I mean, it's quiet with Nikki and DeShawn gone, but at least I have peace of mind."

"Cool. Come see me after you get back from Carolina so we can move the plan forward."

"All right. I'll call you later so we can set up a time. I won't hold you long. I saw you were with somebody."

"Yeah, that's my girl. She's fine, huh?"

"Yeah, I gotta give you that. She in law, too?"

"Naw, man, she's a doctor."

"Impressive. Go do your thing," Reggie said, shaking hands with his lawyer again.

"All right, baby boy. You here with somebody tonight? Because you know you have to be careful with that."

"Relax, man. I'm with one of my boys. My babysitter wanted me to hear her poetry tonight, so I dragged him over here with me. This ain't really my type of place."

"I hear you. My girl likes coming here, so I've kinda gotten used to it."

The two men laughed together.

"Well, I won't hold you up," Reggie said. "We'll talk soon."

"All right, bro. Take it easy."


Once Jamar left the restroom, Reggie leaned over the sink and stared at himself in the mirror. He couldn't believe the way life worked sometimes. Eleven years ago, he'd broken up with the one woman in college whom he'd truly loved. She'd cheated on him and broken his heart. He had to leave her.

He'd always vowed to get her back, but over the years, his vow seemed more like a distant memory.

He'd hardly seen her since they broke up, and the few times he did, she always turned the other way. Once he married Nikki, he thought less and less about her.

Now lately, it seemed as if Alexis was everywhere. It was one thing to see her at Golden Corral, and another thing to see her at Harrah's, even though she pretended not to see him, but now here she was on a date with his lawyer! His grandmother had once told him that many good things happen in threes. Tonight was his third time. But he couldn't confront her in front of Jamar. Jamar was his lawyer. Besides, what good would it do to create an awkward moment for all of them?

Yet he knew he had to talk with Alexis. Even if it was just to get closure and get her completely out of his system. He needed a plan.

# Chapter 9

# Face Your Fears

Reggie sat nervously behind the wheel of his convertible Lexus coupe. He had been parked in front of Touro Infirmary for the past twenty minutes, wrestling with himself as to whether or not he should go in.

He felt like a stalker. Who else would stare from afar at a woman all night, get jealous when she left with her date, then spend two hours on the phone the next morning calling every hospital in the city until he found her? If she called the NOPD on him, he wouldn't even be able to blame her.

He turned up the radio, hoping Soulja Boy could calm his nerves and give him the courage he needed to walk into that office. He had no idea what he would say when he saw Alexis. Judging from their last unintentional encounters, she definitely remembered him, but did she even care to talk to him? She never made a move to talk to him before. But then again, it wasn't as though he'd made any move to speak to her, either.

He chuckled at the memory of the fight she tried to start over him back in college. They were at the now-defunct Tabu Nightclub on St. Charles Avenue. They'd already broken up, but when she saw him on a date with another girl, she nearly had a fit. Drinks were thrown, curses were shouted, and Reggie wound up having to carry Alexis out of the club. He yelled at her during the entire drive home that night for being childish, but the truth was he would have done the same thing had the shoe been on the other foot.

Although Reggie broke up with Alexis when he found out about her affair with Christopher, he never fell out of love with her. However, he couldn't bring himself to take her back. It had taken a lot for him to admit that he loved a girl who was known as the town whore. Everyone had told him to leave her alone, but he rebutted them all by telling them there was something in her that they never took the time to see. He had to eat those words when she cheated on him. Although no one knew about the affair because it happened while she was out of town, it didn't take away from the embarrassment he felt. There was no way he could take her back. What if she slept around again?

So instead of taking her back, he casually dated until graduation. He even used his college celebrity status to sex every one of his dates and a few girls who'd developed starstruck crushes. Eventually, he'd developed his own A Team, many of whom followed him until after he was drafted. Nikki was part of that team until she proved herself worthy of his seemingly misplaced love. They began dating exclusively, then eventually married.

Now, for the first time since college, he wondered if he'd made the right decision. It wasn't that he thought Alexis was the one who got away, but he had to wonder if Alexis really had loved him the way she claimed to. Did she really learn her lesson from that affair? One thing was for sure—he'd never know until he talked with her.

A wave of guilt swept through him as he exited his car. How could he even think about approaching a woman who was dating the man who was helping him divorce his wife? Jamar had been good to him. If it hadn't been for him, Reggie would still be at home wondering what to do about Nikki's indiscretions. Now he felt freer than he'd felt in three years. Whatever happened with his impending divorce, he would be happy, and he owed that to Jamar.

He tried rationalizing that he wasn't trying to date Alexis. He only wanted to talk with her. He'd seen her three times in less than two months. That had to mean something. Besides, even if there was a chance, he wasn't sure that he wanted to take it. How many times could he be hurt? He wondered if unconditional, faithful love was even in the cards for him.

"Here goes nothing," he mumbled as he stepped into the elevator. He pushed the button that would take him to the third floor, then took a deep breath. He twisted his college ring around his index finger, which reminded him that he was still wearing his wedding band. He quickly slipped it off and put it into his pocket. No need in complicating things—it wasn't as though he would ever reconcile with his wife.

Once he reached the third floor, he wandered around, searching for office number 320. There it was. Dr. Alexis White. *I wonder why she never got married?* he thought.

He took another deep breath and turned the knob. Inside, he found two women sitting with their children, and a young-looking woman sitting behind the reception desk. He swallowed and walked confidently up to the desk.

The receptionist looked up and smiled. She looked him up and down slowly before asking, "May I help you?"

"Uh, yeah," Reggie replied. He searched for her name tag. "Latonya, is Dr. White in?"

"Yeah, but she has a patient," she replied. She looked him up and down once more. "Can I help you with something? You need to make an appointment for your child?"

Reggie smiled, catching on to Latonya's flirtation. She couldn't care less if he needed an appointment. She was just testing the waters to see if he was married or had kids. He needed to put an end to this charade quickly. "No, nothing like that. I just wanted to say hello to Alexis."

"Alexis," she repeated, almost in a whisper. "Okay. Have a seat and I'll let her know you're here. Can I have your name?"

"Reggie Morgan, but can you please not tell her who it is?" he requested. "We haven't spoken in a while and I want it to be a surprise."

Latonya perked up a bit. "Reggie Morgan from the Saints?"

"Shhhh," he shushed, placing his finger in front of his mouth. "Yeah, that's me."

She smiled, although Reggie could still note a bit of jealousy. "I'll just tell her someone needs to see her, but it might be a while because she has two patients waiting."

"That's okay, I'll wait," Reggie said. He took a seat near the reception desk. He tried passing time by reading a magazine, but both children ran up to him, obviously overhearing his conversation with Latonya.

"Can I have your autograph, Mr. Morgan?" the little girl asked. "Good luck Sunday."

"Yeah, y'all gonna kick the Panthers' butts!" the boy added.

"Quon!" his mother snapped.

"Thanks, kids," Reggie said with a laugh. "Just because you said that, we're gonna make that happen."

"That's cool, Reg," the boy said, drawing both shock and awe from the adults in the room.

"Quon!" his mother called again. "You know better than that!"

The boy looked at his mother, seeming to hate the fact that she was interfering with his gangsterlike disposition. He turned back to Reggie with a disgusted look on his face. "Sorry, Mr. Morgan."

Reggie smiled. "I feel ya, lil' man. Just make sure you listen to your mama."

The boy's mother gave him an appreciative nod as Latonya called her son's name. Reggie nodded back at her and quickly signed both the children's pieces of paper, just as a nurse came out and called Quon's name. The boy ran behind his mother and disappeared behind the examining room door.

"That was very nice of you," the girl's mother said. The girl sat beside her mother and looked in amazement at the autograph.

"Hey, if it wasn't for the kids, where would we be?" Reggie replied.

"Well, their parents appreciate all you do, too," she said, placing her arm around her daughter. "You guys have done a lot for the city since you've been back. I'm glad you didn't stay gone for good."

"Me, too. New Orleans has been good to us."

The lady smiled and nodded, then continued reading the book she was holding. As Reggie watched her, he wondered if he had really done enough for the city of New Orleans. He would never forget the letters the team received, begging them to stay in New Orleans once rumors surfaced that the team would move to San Antonio. He also would never forget the cheers they received during their historic first game back in the Superdome when they dominated the Atlanta Falcons. During the good and the bad times, this had always been a city who loved their team. He just wished he could return half that love. He would start with Sunday's game against the Panthers.

Another half hour passed before Latonya informed Reggie that he would be able to speak with Alexis.

"You didn't tell her who wanted to see her, did you?" he asked, the case of nerves rapidly returning.

"No," she assured him. "I just told her she had a visitor in the waiting room. She'll be here as soon as she finishes with Xanthipia."

"Zan what?" Reggie asked, his faced contorted in confusion. Where did these parents get these names? He then remembered that he never asked either of the kids their names before signing their autographs. He just wrote his standard kids line, "Stay in school, Reggie Morgan, #27."

Latonya just smiled and shrugged, as if hearing his thoughts. "It'll be just a few more minutes."

"Zan-tip-eee-ah," Reggie whispered to himself. He thanked God that he never asked the kids their names. He wasn't sure if he would have been able to hide his shock. He then thought about the girl's mother. She seemed so educated. Where in the hell did she come up with a name like that?

Xanthipia came through the door holding her mother's hand with her right hand, and a lollipop with her left. She turned to Reggie and waved the lollipop at him. "Bye, Mr. Morgan."

"Bye," he replied, refusing to even try to say her

name. Her mother smiled at him and continued
walking out of the door.

"I'm sorry I kept you wait—" Alexis said a few minutes later as she came through the examining room
door. She froze in her tracks, nearly dropping her
stethoscope when she saw her mystery visitor. She
opened her mouth to continue, but nothing came out.

Reggie was also momentarily speechless, but quickly
got over his apprehension. "How are you, Alexis?"

"F-fine," she stammered, still staring at him as if she
were staring at death itself.

"I was hoping I might be able to talk with you for a
minute," Reggie said.

Alexis stole a glance at Latonya and her nurse, both
of whom were staring from across the reception desk
as if watching a black romance movie. She turned and
walked back through the door, stating over her shoulder, "Come to my office."

As Reggie followed close behind, Alexis shot Latonya
a glare and said, "Don't forget that Brenda's coming
over tonight. We gotta be outta here no later than four
thirty."

"Okay," Latonya replied, waking up from her nosy
trance. Even the nurse caught on to the message and
began fingering through the patients' files. "You not
going to French Riviera tonight?"

"No, I don't have time for aerobics today," Alexis
replied. "Tomorrow's Thanksgiving and we have too
much to do."

"True," the receptionist replied, pretending to
write something in the appointment book.

Alexis continued walking until she reached her
office. She held out her hand toward the doorway
and invited Reggie to enter first. Once he was seated,
she closed the door and gave him the same glare
she'd just given her receptionist. "May I help you?"

Her demeanor caught him off guard. Although they hadn't spoken in years, he wasn't expecting the chill he felt as she spoke. "I, uh, wanted to talk with you about this pain I've been feeling in my ankle."

Alexis folded her arms and leaned against the door. "You do know that I'm a pediatrician, right?"

"Yeah, but since I was in the neighborhood," he stammered, "I figured I would talk to you."

"Bullshit, Reggie," Alexis snapped, shooting him an even meaner look. "I don't work that close to your training facility and if I remember correctly, the Saints have their own doctor."

Same old Alexis, Reggie thought. She always could smell bullshit from a mile away. He sighed and rubbed his bald head. "Okay, Alexis, the truth is I tracked you down so we could talk."

"At my job, Reggie? Couldn't you have called instead of embarrassing me in front of my patients and employees?"

"Now, Alexis, would you have agreed to speak to me if I had called you?"

She paused for a second, considering his question. "Probably not. It's been a long time. Why now?"

"Truthfully?"

"No, lie to me. I like that."

Reggie laughed in spite of himself. "Same old Lexy. You always were a smart-ass."

Alexis rolled her eyes at that comment. "What do you want, Reggie? I'm still working."

"Okay," he said, retreating, "it's like this. I know you saw me at Golden Corral last month. And you saw me at Harrah's. But what you don't know is I saw you last night at Sweet Lorraine's."

Alexis gasped. "You were there? I didn't see you."

"I know. I made sure of that. You were having a good time and I didn't want to ruin that."

"Wait," she said, holding her hands in front of her like a wall. "How did you know where to find me?"

"I, uh, had heard you were a doctor and I tracked you down."

"From who?"

He shrugged. "You know this is a small town. It's not hard to find people. I kinda tracked you down."

Alexis pursed her lips and looked out of the window. There wasn't much of a view, but it seemed to provide a temporary escape from her present reality. "Why would you do that?"

"Lexy, we've run into each other three times in the past couple months," Reggie said, rising from his chair. "Don't you think that's too much of a coincidence?"

Alexis shrugged. "This is a small town. It happens."

"I think it's more than that," Reggie replied. "I'm not saying there's something still between us. I'm sure you've moved on, and so have I, but maybe this is God's way of saying we need to talk."

"I'm not sure there's anything we need to talk about."

"Let's find out," he replied. He glanced at her clock. "What time are you taking lunch? Can I take you to get something to eat?"

Alexis sighed and again looked out of the window. She then rolled her eyes and faced Reggie for the first time since he arrived. "What about Houston's?"

If anybody was paying attention, they would have sworn that Alexis and Reggie were strangers on a blind date. Every move they made, from picking up their silverware to their feeble attempts at conversation, was an awkward mess.

Alexis mentally kicked herself for getting into this situation. This was the moment she'd dreamt of for years. She'd always loved Reggie, and seeing him this close made her love him even more. But she just wasn't ready for reality to hit her so quickly.

Where did Reggie get off showing up at her job like that? If he tracked her down the way he said he did, he should have known that she was the *boss*, not an employee. She had an image to uphold. Of course, Latonya was her younger cousin and Ms. Kay was a longtime family friend, but he didn't know that. As far as he knew, he'd embarrassed the world out of her. What kind of boss brought that type of drama to her job? She knew Latonya had heard her college stories, so she needed her cousin to know that she'd come a long way since then. She felt that was the only way Latonya would take her seriously.

And why did he think he could just pop back into her life after all these years? If he cared so much about talking to her, why hadn't he approached her sooner? That damned Reggie always did have control issues. He was probably waiting for the moment when he could have the upper hand. He needed to wait until she *wasn't* ready, which made him even *more* ready. Selfish bastard. She wished her glare could melt him where he sat.

"So you just going to sit and stare at me all day?" Reggie asked. He took a sip from his water and folded his hands on top of the table.

"You invited me here to talk," Alexis muttered.

He nodded. "You're right, I did. But we're not doing much talking."

"Guess not," she replied, looking down at her barely eaten meal. "What did you want to talk to me about?"

"I don't know," Reggie admitted. "Our paths have crossed so many times over the years, but we've never said anything to each other. I just figured it was God's way of saying we had some unfinished business to discuss."

Alexis sucked her teeth. "I don't think so. If I remember correctly, you didn't want anything to do with me after we broke up. I practically begged you to give us another chance, but you treated me like shit."

"I wouldn't say I treated you like shit. I just needed time to think."

"And your thoughts led you to marry somebody else. And don't think I didn't hear about all those women you slept with before you married the chosen one."

"Now, be fair, Alexis. We hadn't spoken in three years by the time I married Nikki. Truthfully, I would have loved for the woman walking down that aisle to be you, but it didn't look like it was going to work out that way."

Alexis shook her head sadly. "You didn't even try."

"I did try, but all I kept seeing was you getting pregnant by a married man. That was too hard to swallow."

She again glared at him. "You're never going to let me live that down, are you? Do you even care how much shit I went through after that? I had an abortion, Reggie. I also almost lost my cousin over that shit. My mother took forever to trust me again, and—"

"And what?"

She shook her head and snapped, "Nothing. You didn't care because all you were worried about were your own feelings. You knew how hard that whole time was for me, but you let me go through it alone. I loved the shit out of you, and all I wanted was to get you back. But you know what? I hate myself even more for letting myself let you make me out to be a fuckin' fool!"

The look on Reggie's face spoke volumes. "Alexis, I'm sorry, but be real. You didn't really think it would be that easy to forgive and forget, do you?"

"Well, why now is it okay to forgive and fuckin' forget?"

"Because we're older now. It's time to move on."

"What do you want, Reggie?" Alexis asked, exhausted from the entire conversation. She wasn't sure why she was so upset, but the entire ordeal just didn't feel right. Why would he track her down like that? Why would he wait ten years to talk to someone who'd lived in the same city as him all along? "You trying to remind your-self of the trash you left to marry your precious wife?"

His head jerked back as if Alexis's words had given him a Mike Tyson jab. "Lexy, if you would just listen to me—"

"I don't have to listen to shit!" she snapped, trying hard not to cause a scene. She snuck a peak to ensure that no one was listening to them. "And stop calling me Lexy! My name is Dr. Alexis White. No one calls me Lexy anymore."

"Fine, *Dr.* White. But just so you'll know, I didn't ask you to come here so I could take you back to our col-lege days. I didn't even come here to date you. I just thought we might be able to be friends. We're adults now. Can't we leave the past in the past?"

Alexis bit her lip and looked away, embarrassed at the venom she'd just spewed all over Reggie. Should she have let him speak his case before she began curs-ing his very existence? Was he really trying to extend an olive branch?

Reggie continued. "Too much time has passed for us to go through life like this. How can two people live in the same city, go to the same places, and pre-tend not to know each other? You're a good person, and I'm proud of all you've accomplished. I've always told you that you had a lot to offer the world."

Alexis nodded. He had told her that. In fact, he re-minded her of that the night he told her he loved her.

If anyone believed in her, it was Reggie. Even when everyone thought she would do nothing more than drop out of school or contract an incurable STD, Reggie was there to encourage her.

But that was the very reason she couldn't get past the way he'd left her. She knew what she'd done was wrong. She'd cheated on him with a married man. But she thought they were under the understanding that they weren't serious and could date whomever they wanted. And he also knew that it took a lot for her to admit to herself and him that she loved him. He witnessed the pain she went through when the reality hit her that she'd taken her own baby's life. But he left, anyway. And on top of that, he never spoke to her again. Until today. Just the thought of it tugged at her tear ducts.

"I'm not sure I can be friends with you," she said in a voice barely above a whisper. She took a sip of her fruit juice and stared at the table, awaiting his reply.

To her surprise, he only nodded. "I understand. A lot has happened between us, and too much time has passed."

Alexis blinked and looked at him. Had she been that successful in hiding her true feelings for him? He couldn't see through all her anger that she'd never fallen out of love with him? *Wow*, was the only word that came to her mind.

She picked up her fork, ate some couscous, and began pushing the rest of her food around her plate. The nervousness returned as she asked, "So what now?"

"Alexis, I still want to be your friend," Reggie pushed, reaching across the table and taking her hand. "I refuse to let another ten years go by without us speaking to each other. I know all of this came as a surprise. I'm sorry if I embarrassed you earlier. All I ask is that you think about what I said. I'm here if you need me."

Alexis scrunched her eyebrows. "What do you want from me?"

"For you to stop being so suspicious of me," he replied, looking into her eyes. "I've never taken anything from you. I know it's too late for us to be together. I'm not asking for that. I just want my friend back."

He pulled out a business card from his jacket pocket and handed it to Alexis. "You can call me anytime."

She took the card from him and gave him a sideways smile. "Won't your wife have a problem with that?"

He looked away for a second, then faced Alexis again. "Let me worry about that."

They sat in silence for a few more minutes, neither of them eating much of their lunch. Finally, Alexis looked at her watch. "I'm sorry. I need to get back to work. I have a patient in thirty minutes."

Reggie raised his hands in resignation. "I understand. I have to get back to the Dome, anyway."

He signaled for the check, then left his payment and a sizable tip on the table. He then walked to the other side of the table and pulled out Alexis's chair. Once they were out of the restaurant, he asked, "Can I at least get a hug from my old friend?"

She hesitated for a moment, then decided to loosen up. They embraced, but she cut it short after a few seconds and walked to his car.

"Well, at least I got that much," Reggie commented, following her to the car. He chuckled. "You're a hard woman."

She couldn't hide her smile that time. "I didn't totally change."

Reggie dropped Alexis off in front of her building, then drove off. Once he was completely out of sight, she reached for her cell phone.

"Hey, how's it going?" she asked once she received an answer. "That's good. Look, I know you're going to be tired later, but can you please meet me at French Riviera? I really need to talk."

"Alexis, this had better be important," Brenda fussed as she pulled on a pair of shorts. "I've been driving for almost nine hours, and you ask me to go to the gym? I don't know who the bigger fool is—you for asking, or me for agreeing to it."

"I'm sorry, sis," Alexis said, pulling her hair back into a bun, "but I really needed to talk, and I can't do it at home. Roman is nosy as hell."

Brenda grew concerned. "What's wrong?"

Alexis remained silent until they reached a heavy bag in the workout room. "You don't have to exercise, but can you hold the bag for me?"

Brenda obliged, and Alexis backed up and assumed her best karate stance with her right foot behind her. She didn't know a lick of karate, but had learned enough from her kickboxing class to let out some aggression. Once she was ready, she swung her right foot forward and kicked the bag with all her might. "Reggie came to see me today."

"Reggie who?" Brenda asked, bracing herself for the next kick.

"Reggie Morgan, my ex-boyfriend from college," Alexis replied, taking another kick. This one was harder than the first, nearly sending Brenda stumbling back.

"Dag, girl," Brenda commented, trying to keep her balance. "Oh, I remember him now. The football player. You never mentioned him before. I didn't know you two still kept in touch."

"We don't!" Alexis proclaimed, changing her stance. This time, her left foot went flying into the heavy bag. "He just showed up at my office with no warning. Talkin' 'bout can he take me to lunch?"

Brenda laughed. "Did you go?"

"Hell, yeah, I went. When have you known me to turn down free food?"

Brenda laughed again. "Well, what did he want? It's been a long time."

Alexis rolled her eyes and took a swing at the heavy bag. "He *claims* he wants to be my friend."

"Is that what you want?"

"Nope," Alexis snapped. She dropped onto an exercise mat and began doing crunches.

"Why not?" Brenda asked, kneeling next to her cousin.

Alexis remained silent until she reached forty, then sat up and looked at Brenda. "It's been more than ten years and he hasn't said two words to me. How is it that all of a sudden he wants to be friends?"

Brenda smiled. "Maybe he still loves you."

Alexis dropped back down for another set of crunches. "That bastard is married."

"Maybe not happily."

"Either way, he's still married."

Once she finished her second set, she sat up again and pointed out, "Besides, even if he's not happy, that's what his ass gets. I tried for two years to get him back. I pretty much begged his ass, and you know Alexis White doesn't do that. And he still went for that tramp."

"Do you know her?" Brenda asked, widening her eyes.

Alexis dropped back into her crunches. "No, but she looks like a tramp."

Brenda fell back in laughter. "Girl, you got issues. Tell the truth—you're jealous because he married somebody else."

Alexis sucked her teeth as she finished her last set.

"What I got to be jealous of? I'm sexy as hell! I can date any man in here if I wanted to!"

"Sure in the hell could," commented a muscle-bound man who happened to be passing by. He stopped at a treadmill and smiled at them as he climbed on.

The two cousins looked up, then looked at each other and laughed. "See?" Alexis asked.

Brenda lowered her voice once she got over her laughter. "That might be true, but you know you still want Reggie."

Alexis pulled her knees under her chin. She just wasn't ready to accept the truth—at least not after today. "That might have been true at one time, but not now. And even if I did, he said he only wants to be friends. What good would that do me?"

Brenda nodded. "I hear you. It's hard to just be friends with a man you've always been in love with. But you never know what will happen in the future. Maybe you should pray on it."

Alexis shook her head. "That wouldn't do any good. I don't do married men."

Brenda lifted her eyebrows and tilted her head slightly. Alexis knew what she was thinking. Inadvertently, they'd brought back terrible memories.

"What time do we need to get back to your place?" Brenda asked.

"We'll get there around six," Alexis replied, grateful for the change of subject. "Mama should have the gumbo ready by the time we get there."

"Okay, I'll just go straight to your house and have Darnell and Elizabeth ride over with my mama."

Alexis smiled. "How is Elizabeth? She drive you crazy on that ride?"

"You know it," Brenda replied, smiling. "She had to use the bathroom every hour. Then she complained about being bored. She was too hot. Then when we turned on the AC, she was too cold. We didn't get any peace until she dozed off!"

Alexis laughed. "I can imagine. I hear about my patients all the time from their parents."

"Girl, you just don't know how good you have it."

Alexis's smile dropped a bit, but not enough for her cousin to notice. "No, you're the lucky one. You have a beautiful daughter."

"Yeah," Brenda admitted. "I am blessed. I thank God for her every day."

Alexis looked at her cousin admirably.

"What?" Brenda asked, feeling the weight of Alexis's gaze.

"Nothing. I just really admire how you've been a Christian all these years. I think you've been saved all your life."

"Yeah, well, it hasn't been easy, especially since I married a man who hadn't been to church in five years."

"Well, he's going every Sunday now," Alexis noted, intrigued. What could her cousin possibly have done to change a man? She'd always been the passive, quiet type. "How did you change his mind?"

Brenda rolled an exercise ball toward them and sat on it. She did a few crunches before replying, "I prayed about it. I used to try to force him to go with me, especially when we first got engaged. I wanted a Christian marriage whether he liked it or not! We'd fight every Sunday.

"Finally, I stopped bothering him about it. I would just get up and go. I had to realize that I wasn't perfect, so I couldn't expect him to be. Eventually, I guess I started setting the right example because one day he offered to go to Bible study with me. He liked what he heard, so he went back. Pretty soon, we began going to church together every Wednesday and Sunday."

"So he just up and went?" Alexis asked, leaning

back. She began doing frog kicks. Her midsection was her favorite part of her body, and she felt frog kicks chiseled it to perfection.

"Not right away," Brenda admitted. "It was probably almost a year after we were married before he started going regularly."

"What made you marry him if you didn't think you would have a Christian marriage?"

"Because I knew I had a good man. He didn't hang out in the streets and he showed me every day in different ways how much he loved me. After I prayed about him going to church with me, I left it alone. If he was the man for me, God would reveal it. It wasn't easy, but he finally revealed it to me."

Alexis contemplated her cousin's words. "Is that what it takes?"

Brenda nodded. "You never know when the right man will come along. He may not be perfect when you first meet him, but if he's the one, you'll know if you're patient enough."

Alexis nodded. "So I guess you're saying I shouldn't be so hard on Reggie."

"If he's married and trying to mess around with you, then yes, you should be hard on him," Brenda replied. "But from what I remember of him, I don't think that's the case. Just give him a chance to show you what he's about."

"I'll think about it," Alexis said.

"That's all I'm asking."

# Chapter 10

# Be Thankful

"I love you, baby."

"I love you, too."

"You know you're what I'm most thankful for today, don't you?"

"And I thank God for you every day."

"Damn all that love shit," Mary shouted as she walked into the living room. "You need to check on them greens, 'cause if they burn, that's gonna be your ass!"

Brenda looked at Darnell and laughed. Alexis, who had been watching the nauseating lovefest from the sofa, laughed, too. "I told them, Mama."

Brenda's head snapped toward her cousin. "You didn't tell us nothin'. Don't hate because my man loves me."

Alexis snorted. "Please, I ain't gotta hate. You musta forgot who you were talkin' to."

"Well, I didn't forget," Mary interjected. "Both y'all asses need to get into this kitchen."

Brenda pretended to pout as she walked into the kitchen. "I'ma tell my mama you talkin' to me like this."

"Go 'head and tell her," Mary challenged. "She'll be back in a minute. And I'ma tell her how you almost let the greens burn tryin' to be Cupid's lil' cousin."

At that, everyone broke out in laughter. Alexis smiled at Darnell, glad that he'd learned to accept her mother's brashness.

"Is there anything I can help with, Aunt Mary?" he asked.

"Just stay your ass out of this kitchen," Mary said quickly. "This here is women's work."

"Besides, you know your ass can't cook," Alexis added as she followed her mother into the kitchen.

"I've been taking lessons!" he yelled back.

Brenda pursed her lips and shook her head at her cousin, silently telling Alexis that Darnell was still banished from the kitchen.

"Wooo," sighed Brenda's mother, Ernestine, as she walked through the door. "We had to go to three different stores to find this shit."

Frank and Roman followed her through the door. "Next time, you won't wait to buy corn bread mix on Thanksgiving Day," Frank scolded. "You know better than that."

"Well, some of us have a job, Frank," Ernestine snapped. "I don't have time like everybody else."

"Then next time don't be so quick to promise shit you can't deliver," he retorted.

Alexis and Brenda leaned on the kitchen counter and watched as their parents argued back and forth. It wouldn't be a family event if Frank and Ernestine didn't fight at least once. They cared about each other, but couldn't stand to be in the same room as each other. Ever since Mary and Frank met each other, he and her sister Ernestine mixed about as easily as oil and water.

"You glad to be home?" Alexis asked her cousin.

"Thrilled," Brenda replied.

"Hey, Uncle Frank," Darnell called from the sofa. "Come watch SportsCenter with us."

"Yeah, I'm comin'," Frank replied, glaring at his sister-in-law. Once he took a seat next to Roman and Darnell, he mumbled, "That woman just makes me wanna punch the shit outta her."

Ernestine had begun walking to the kitchen, but suddenly froze in her tracks and turned toward the sofa. "I heard that, Frank. Go on and try it and see if I don't knock your black ass back to the Third Ward."

"All right!" Mary shouted, clapping her hands. "That's enough of all that. I ain't gonna have all this on Thanksgiving."

"Well, you better tell your husband to stop messin' with me," Ernestine mumbled as she walked into the kitchen. "You know I don't play that."

Brenda and Alexis looked at each other again and laughed. Their parents meant what they said, but it was no less funny. This was what made them family.

"You check on them greens?" Mary asked.

"Yes, ma'am," Brenda said quickly. She speed-walked back to the stove and stirred the collard greens, which had already begun to fill the kitchen with their fresh aroma. The ham hocks and seasonings had blended perfectly with the leaves. She spooned out a small leaf to ensure that they were tender enough to remove from the fire. Satisfied with the consistency, she turned to Alexis and asked, "Can you hand me a bowl please?"

Alexis obliged, and Brenda promptly poured in the greens. Alexis then pulled the baked macaroni from the oven and placed it on the counter next to the greens.

"We're done, Mama," she announced.

"Good, now y'all go sit down so Ernestine and I can finish up in here," Mary said.

The cousins did as they were told and took a seat in the living room with the men, who had become engrossed in the pregame shows on ESPN. Neither woman was interested in sports, especially since the Saints weren't playing until Sunday, so they entertained each other.

"So you thought any more about what we talked about?" Brenda asked.

"We talked about a lot of stuff," Alexis replied. "What are you talking about?"

Brenda sucked her teeth. "About Reggie, girl."

"No," Alexis snapped. "There's nothing to think about."

"You are a hard woman."

"No, just sensible. He popped back into my life all of a sudden yesterday, and now I'm supposed to jump through hoops? I don't think so."

"I think he made the first move," Brenda pushed. "At least see what he wants."

"He told me," Alexis snapped. "He wants to be my *friend.*"

"Alexis!"

"What?"

"Stop being so difficult," Brenda scolded. "At least talk to the man."

"What do you want me to do, Bren? Invite him over for dinner?"

"I'm not saying all that, but at least be cordial. You know you still have feelings for him. Why not talk with him and see if there's anything worth pursuing?"

Alexis shook her head no, then folded her arms across her chest. This just wasn't the way things were supposed to happen. *She* was the one who was supposed to be in control. Not Brenda. And definitely not Reggie.

What would she look like acting as if she'd been waiting on Reggie all these years? She had, but *he* wasn't supposed to know that.

She was so glad that Roman wasn't paying them any attention. He was always trying to get into his big sister's business. She sighed with relief that the TV was up loud and he and the other men were talking so much that they barely noticed Alexis and Brenda sitting in the room.

She glanced at the telephone, wondering whether she should take the plunge and call Reggie. However, as quickly as the thought entered her mind, it left. There was no way in the world she would add another awkward moment to her holiday. It was bad enough Frank and Ernestine were fighting, and she was sure she and Roman would fight before the end of the night. Mary was sure to curse everyone out sooner or later. Why add to all that drama with her famous ex-boyfriend who might or might not want her back?

"Okay," Alexis said suddenly. "I'll call him, but only when I know I'm ready to talk to him. And it won't be today. You seem to forget that I already got a man."

"Who? Jamar?" Brenda scoffed. "You just started liking that man three hours ago."

"He's still my man," Alexis retorted, rolling her neck.

Brenda laughed. "If you say so. Where is he, anyway? Is he coming over?"

"No," Alexis snapped. She looked at her cousin as if she should have known better. "He's not ready for all that yet."

Brenda laughed again. "You mean *you're* not ready."

Alexis pursed her lips and looked at the television. "Take it how you wish. Anyway, he's out of town."

Fortunately for Alexis, her cousin stopped pushing the issue. Why did Brenda want her to call Reggie so badly, anyway? She didn't even know him that well.

How did she know he was as nice as she thought he was? And even if he was, how could she be sure that he hadn't changed over the years? As far as Alexis knew, she'd avoided him this long, so there was no need in rushing a reunion now.

Then on the other hand, if he wanted to talk with her so badly, why hadn't *she* heard from *him*? He could have called her just as easily as she could have called him. Yet she hadn't heard from him since their lunch yesterday. There was a time when he wouldn't have waited for Alexis to make a move; he would have made it for her. She guessed those times had come and gone. Maybe he really was happily married.

He knew he was wrong, but his game wasn't for three more days. Besides, his coach knew his situation and should understand that he needed a short escape from reality. That was the blanket Reggie wrapped around himself as he staggered toward the bar to make himself another drink.

His glass was about three-quarters full before he stopped pouring the Hennessy. He then picked up a nearly empty can of Coke to add a bit of color to his drink, but only a few drops trickled out. He just shrugged and threw the can to the side. It hit the floor with a clang and bounced a few times before nestling itself against the wall.

"Ain't no sunshine when she's gone," Reggie sang, swaying back and forth in a small, lonely circle. "That's what the hell I need—some music!"

He walked over to his CD player and searched for something that would fit his mood. He didn't own Bill Withers, but he did have something that would make a suitable replacement. The soothing sounds of Al Green filled the room.

"Yeah!" he shouted, dancing and holding his drink in the air. His song sounded like a drunken plea for help. "I'm so in love with you. Whatever you wanna do is all right with meeeeeeeeeeee."

In his mind, he really didn't know who he was singing to. Until tonight, he was sure he didn't love either Nikki or Alexis anymore. Both of them had cheated on him. Hell, to him, neither of them was worth his love. But the more he thought about it, Nikki was the mother of his child. She'd been there through the good and the bad. The past couple of years excluded, she'd been a perfect wife and a great mother. She was the one who had taught him how to love again.

Alexis was his first real love, so when she cheated, even though she admitted it when she didn't have to, it tore him up. He wanted to believe that, despite her past, she only wanted to be with him. But she cheated with a married man, got pregnant, then had an abortion to hide the entire thing. Yet, through everything that's happened in her past, she'd made something of herself. Even after all her mistakes, she'd proven that she really *was* the shit. Who'd ever have imagined that she would become a doctor? With a private practice on top of that!

He thought back to their uncomfortable lunch. She'd really let him have it. She came at him with her guns blazing, nearly making him want to melt into his seat. Yet, as he looked into her eyes, he could still see the hurt she had felt so many years ago. He couldn't believe it, but she actually still loved him. Was it possible?

"That girl don't love me no more," he said aloud. He took a long sip from his drink and fell back into his favorite recliner. "If she did, she never woulda fucked around on me. She ain't no better than Nikki. Don't nobody love me but my mama and my son."

He looked sadly at DeShawn's picture, positioned prominently on the mantel.

"I'ma get you back, boy," he told the picture. "We still got stuff to do together. And maybe one day I'll find you a new mama." He took a sip from his drink and smiled. "It just won't be today. You gonna learn, Shawn, that every woman that says she loves you don't mean you no good. Sometimes all they want is money!"

He slammed down his glass, spilling some of his drink onto the coffee table. He looked at the small puddle of alcohol and shook his head. "Alcohol abuse."

The telephone rang, nearly making him jump from his seat. "Who the hell?" he asked aloud.

He rose from his seat and walked over to the phone, trying to compose himself. Everyone didn't need to know he was celebrating Thanksgiving with Hen Dog. Before he could even pick up the phone, the blaring sounds of hip-hop greeted him. "Who dis?"

"What's up, baby boy?" Levi greeted.

"I can't call it," Reggie replied, clearing his throat. "Whatcha up to?"

"Chillin'."

"Man, come on out. You don't need to be sittin' there alone. I'm at 7140 and the place is on fire!"

Reggie shook his head. There was no way he felt like being around a bunch of superficial people who would only see his status and paycheck. Besides, even if he did go out, with the amount of alcohol he'd had at home, the police would have a field day with him if he tried to drive.

"Naw, man, I'm good. I'll catch up to you tomorrow when we get ready to fly out."

"You sure, bro?"

"Positive."

"All right, but you better not be over there thinkin'

about your problems. That shit's gonna be there. You better live your life."

"I hear you, man," Reggie replied. Even through the phone line, he knew his friend could see right through him. Everyone knew how much he loved Nikki. "Trust me, I'm fine. Happy Thanksgiving, baby boy."

"Same to you, bro," Levi said. "Let me know if you need anything."

"I'm good. Just make sure I wake up in enough time to make the plane tomorrow."

Levi laughed. "I should be telling you that. I got two fine sistas sittin' with me. But don't worry. I got you."

Reggie laughed, too, then bid his friend good-bye. He wished he could put his problems behind him as Levi did. Levi had divorced his wife a year ago, and didn't seem to be going through the pain Reggie was currently suffering. How did he do it?

"'Cause he's a fake ass!" Reggie said aloud. "He knows he loved that woman. Why he gotta front for me?"

*The same reason I'm frontin' for him,* Reggie thought. Not many men had the strength to express their real feelings in front of their boys. While a woman can cry to her girl about how she's been dogged out, a man will try to stay strong and will only mutter, "She's a trip."

Reggie chuckled in spite of himself. He didn't have the same friends he'd had back in college. No one would understand how he felt about Alexis, and no one would understand why he wanted so badly for his marriage to Nikki to work.

He sighed as he took his seat again and downed his drink. Was he doomed to have every woman he fell in love with cheat on him? Had he not proven that he was good for more than a handsome face and a few dollars? Why couldn't the women he met see past that?

He couldn't wait to leave the NFL. At least once he joined the working world he would meet women with jobs who had gained their status on their own. Women like Alexis. Why did she keep invading his thoughts? He'd gone years without worrying about her, and now all of a sudden he couldn't get her out of his mind.

Why? Why, after all these years, did they keep bumping into each other? Why did he show up at her job? And why the hell did she have to be dating his lawyer?

He wrestled with whether he should tell Jamar he knew Alexis, but decided against it. There really wasn't much to tell. All he and Alexis shared these days were a couple of close encounters and a failed lunch date. There was no need to report that. And she'd already made it clear that she didn't want to speak to him, and frankly, he didn't want to lead her into thinking he wanted anything more than friendship. The best thing for him to do, Reggie decided, was to leave the entire situation alone.

# Chapter 11

# Make Up
Your Mind

"Where did this come from?" Alexis asked, eying the mile-high bouquet of roses sitting on Latonya's desk. She'd just finished examining a young girl who was trying desperately to get over the flu.

Latonya rolled her eyes toward Alexis and shrugged. "They're for you. They got here a few minutes ago."

"Bye, Dr. White," the little girl said, giving Alexis's knees a tight hug.

Alexis laughed, momentarily taking her eyes off the mystery flowers and returning the hug. "Bye, Danisha. Make sure you drink your juice and take a hot bath tonight."

"I will," Danisha said, releasing her doctor's legs. She grabbed her mother's hand and followed her to the door.

Her mother smiled as she opened the door and led her daughter out. "Thanks again, Dr. White. Hopefully we won't have to see you tomorrow."

Alexis laughed. "Let's both keep our fingers crossed."

Once the mother and daughter left the office, another mother entered. This time, it was a young woman with a baby boy. Renee followed behind them with her own son, who appeared to be about five years old.

"Hey, Alexis," Renee greeted. "I hope you have room for me today. I woulda called first, but Marcus's doctor was overbooked as usual, and Marcus just hasn't been eating well at all."

Alexis cut her eyes at the roses, knowing she would have to wait at least another hour or two before she could get a closer look at them. "Don't worry about it, Renee. Just let me give David his shots and I'll be right with you. In the meantime, you can give Latonya your insurance information."

"Take your time, girl," Renee said, taking a seat. Marcus immediately walked over to the toys Alexis had set up in the waiting room. "I got everything you need. Harrah's takes good care of their full-time employees."

"All right, then," Alexis said, taking a sigh of relief and turning to the woman with the baby. A large smile spread across her face as she bent down toward the baby. "Hey, Davey, you ready?"

"Now, you know he ain't ready for no shots," the mother said with a laugh.

"I know, I was actually talking to us," Alexis replied. "Come on back."

The mother shifted David into a more comfortable carrying position and followed the doctor into her small laboratory. Ms. Kay, always one step ahead, was already there waiting for them.

"Ms. Kay, please get the hep-B, diphtheria, type-B

influenza, polio, and pneumococcal conjugate ready,"
Alexis requested.

"Uh-oh," Ms. Kay said with a smile.

"Yeah," the mother groaned. "This should be fun."

Alexis smiled. Although she knew how much agony
the procedure would bring to little David, working
with babies was what she enjoyed most about her job.
"Don't worry. We'll make it quick."

"And we have the suckers ready," Ms. Kay assured
the mother.

"I might need one, too," the mother joked.

The ladies laughed as they prepared little David for
his shots. An ear-piercing, infantile scream let everyone in the office know that the procedure had begun.
It took both Alexis and the young mother to hold
David down to finish the shots, but as promised, the
procedure went by quickly.

Alexis picked up the baby and rubbed his back.
"It's all right, Davey. It's all over now."

The baby's cries immediately turned into whim-
pers, as if he understood everything his pediatrician
told him. Alexis smiled wistfully as she felt his arms
squeeze her neck and his head find a comfortable position on her shoulder. Ms. Kay passed her a lollipop,
which she maneuvered into the baby's hand as she
gently bounced him into a slumber.

"I can tell you been workin' with babies for a while,"
the mother said, watching in awe. "It takes me forever
to calm that monster down. "You got kids?"

"Unfortunately, no," Alexis replied, leading the
mother to the front of the clinic. "Maybe one day, but
not *to*-day."

"You married?" she asked.

"Nope."

"Wow," the mother said. "Well, when you do make

that step, you ain't got a thing to worry about. You're good with kids."

Alexis smiled as she carefully handed the baby to his mother without waking him. "Well, I guess we'll have to see about that."

The mother shifted her eyes anxiously around the room, and then looked at the pediatrician without making eye contact. "D-Dr. White, is it okay if I pay you Friday? My check don't come in till then."

Alexis pursed her lips, struggling not to show her frustration. Friday was in another four days, and she knew it would be at least another two weeks before she saw David's mother again. "Ms. Mason, last time you told me that, I didn't see you for almost a month. Why didn't you just come in when you had the money?"

"I didn't know I could wait that long, Dr. White," the mother pleaded. "I don't want my baby gettin' sick because I can't afford to get his shots."

Alexis wanted to scream, but held on to her professionalism for dear life. "Then you should have talked to me before you let him get these shots. Vaccinations are expensive."

Ms. Mason looked down in shame, obviously aware that she'd been caught in her lies. "I promise you I'll be back here Friday as soon as I cash my check."

Alexis rolled her eyes and stole a glance across the counter at Renee, whose attention was completely on her son. She thanked God no one else was there to witness the travesty that was taking place. She was so tired of being taken advantage of. "Ms. Mason, if you're not here Friday, you can forget about bringing David back here. I love your son, but I have a business to run."

The mother looked at Alexis as if she'd lost her mind. "You would just do that to David? It's like that?"

"Don't put this on me," the doctor said quietly, her anger growing. Today just wasn't the day for another person to take advantage of her kindness. "I don't want to stop treating David, but you seem to think quality care just grows on trees. Go out there and see how many doctors take IOUs instead of money. None of them! So you keep taking advantage of me, and you and your son will be assed out! See if I'm lyin'!"

The shame on Ms. Mason's face turned into a snarl. "You know what? I ain't gotta take this shit! You'll get your fuckin' money Friday, and then you don't have to ever worry about seein' my black ass here no more!"

"Do what you have to do, Ms. Mason."

With that, the young woman took her baby and stormed out of the clinic. The entire performance didn't faze Alexis in the least. She knew Ms. Mason would be back. Not only did she put up with the Mason family's money problems, but she knew no one would care for David the way she could. And as much as Ms. Mason hated to admit it, Alexis knew *she* knew it, too.

"You all right, cuz?" Latonya asked.

"Yeah, I'm good," Alexis mumbled, leaning against her hallway wall and folding her arms. "Tell Renee to come on back."

"All right," Latonya said. "You want Ms. Kay to get her vitals?"

"Uh, yeah," Alexis snapped as if the question were the silliest one asked all day.

"You ain't have to get all smart," the receptionist mumbled as she returned to her desk.

Alexis rolled her eyes at her cousin/receptionist and walked into her office. She was definitely losing her edge. There was a time when no one dared to talk to her the way she'd been talked to that day. Back in the day, she would have introduced her fist to Ms. Mason's mouth for cursing at her for no reason. Latonya would still be picking her face up off the ground once Alexis

124        *Rhonda M. Lawson*

was through with her. Why did she feel she had to take everyone's shit now?

"Because I'm a doctor!" Alexis said out loud once she closed the door behind her. "I'm living the American dream. I'm the pride of every black girl in the hood and all that other shit."

She had to laugh in spite of herself. It was sad, but true. She was a professional woman, so there had been, and there always would be, times when she would have to swallow her first inclination and pretend the customer was always right. She'd nearly failed at that with Ms. Mason, but she pulled it together quickly. She couldn't let people like her lying patient get the best of her, because as much as she hated to admit it, she really was the pride of the hood.

*Knock, knock.*

"Yeah," Alexis answered dryly.

"Dr. White," Ms. Kay said through the door. "Your patient is ready for you."

"Thanks. Tell her I'll be there shortly."


Alexis enjoyed Renee and Marcus's visit for a variety of reasons. First, it was short and sweet. Marcus was just being a picky eater. Since he was still gaining weight, she suggested that Renee prepare smaller portions of healthier foods until he got used to eating them. If, after a month, his eating habits still hadn't improved, she told Renee to bring him back so she could test him for anemia.

She also enjoyed the visit because it gave her a chance to catch up with her high school friend. They only saw each other when Alexis visited the casino, so it felt good to talk with an old friend without competing with bells, whistles, and screams.

"Girl, we gotta catch up more often," Renee said, as Alexis walked her back toward the waiting area.

"I know," Alexis agreed. "It's been too long. I can't believe you have three kids!"

"Yeah, but I'll be damned if I have any more. I already told my husband that."

"I don't blame you, but I can't say I'm not jealous."

Renee waved her off. "Girl, you better enjoy your freedom while you have it. Right now you have a good job running your own business, and you can go when you wanna go, and do whatcha wanna do without some man askin' you when you're gonna be back. You don't have to worry about diapers, day care, or babysitters. When you take a nap in the middle of the day, no one wakes you up and tells you they're hungry, and I'm not just talkin' about the kids! And you ain't takin' time off work to take your child for a checkup! Believe me, you're good."

Alexis smiled and nodded. "I hear you, girl."

The friends gave each other a hug and Renee headed for the door.

"She seems cool," Latonya said once Renee left.

"She is," Alexis agreed.

"So, you gonna find out who these flowers are from?" she asked anxiously. "Maybe they're from that fine-ass Reggie Morgan."

Alexis snorted. "I highly doubt that. I told him he better not ever show up at my job like that. And you didn't help anything cheesing at him the way you were."

"Please," Latonya said. "I do not cheese."

"I'll let you tell it," the doctor said, picking up the bouquet and heading for her office.

"Where you going?"

"To mind my business. Now get *you* some!"

Alexis had to laugh once she was safely behind her office door. Latonya was too nosy for her own good.

Alexis would tell her later who the flowers were from, but in her own time. Besides, if they were from Reggie, she didn't want her little cousin to see the goofy grin she was sure would spread across her face. As far as everyone was concerned, Alexis wanted nothing to do with Reggie Morgan, and she planned to keep it that way.

Yet there was something romantic about the thought of getting roses from the one who got away. She really wanted Reggie to keep pursuing her. What if he actually still loved her after all this time?

She took a deep whiff of the red roses. Whoever sent them definitely had taste. Each rose had been picked just before full bloom. The stems were green and sturdy and stood in a tall crystal vase. These flowers definitely hadn't come from Walgreens!

The purple envelope stood conspicuously among the buds. She could no longer stand the suspense, and promised herself that if they were from Reggie, she'd play it cool for the rest of the day and would consider calling him that night. Finally, she plucked the envelope from its holder and pulled the card from inside.

*Hey, Sweetie, I know it's been a while since we've seen each other. Call me tonight so we can catch up.*

*Love you,*
*Jamar*

Jamar! How in the world had she let herself forget just that quickly that she had a boyfriend? Both guilt and embarrassment rolled through her body. He'd only been out of town for a week. Obviously, he was back and thought a bouquet of roses was a romantic way to let her know he was back.

*Stupid!*

How could she let the thought of Reggie get her so riled up? Yes, she had definitely lost her edge, but she was determined to get it back! Reggie had no power in the White household!

She smiled as her eyes traveled to her phone, which sat expectantly at the edge of her desk. Quickly, she hit the speaker button and dialed Jamar's number. She took a long whiff of her roses as she listened to the rings.

"Hello?"

"Hey, you," Alexis greeted, the smile still plastered across her face.

"Hey, yourself."

"When did you get back in?"

"Late last night," he explained. "I didn't wanna call you that late. I was going to call you this morning, but I got an early call and had to run in to the office."

"Understandable. I've been working like a dog all day." She paused for a moment, taking another whiff of her roses. "I got your gift."

"You did, huh? You like 'em?"

"What you think?"

Jamar laughed. "Just makin' sure."

"You love me, huh?"

"I think you know that by now," Jamar said seriously.

"I believe you. I care about you, too, but I'm not sure I'm ready to fall in love again."

"It's all good, but I know all that's gonna change soon."

"You sure about that, huh?"

"I *know* that," Jamar said confidently. "You know you can't resist me."

Alexis laughed. "You're really feeling good about yourself today, aren't you?"

"Let's just say absence makes the heart grow fonder.

You gonna come over tonight so I can show you how much? You have a full body massage waiting for you."

Alexis parted her lips to respond, but another knock at her door stopped her.

"Yes!" she shouted.

"Dr. White, you have a walk-in sitting in the examining room," Ms. Kay said through the door.

She rolled her eyes upward and glanced at the clock. It wasn't quite five yet. She was really through with the day, but she'd already instructed Ms. Kay and Latonya that it was okay to take walk-ins as long as all of their scheduled appointments had been taken care of.

"Give me a minute," Alexis mumbled.

"I guess you gotta go," Jamar surmised.

"Yeah."

"I feel you. You're the woman."

"Yeah, you know what they say—you gotta pay the cost to be the boss," Alexis said. "What time you want me to come by tonight?"

"I'll pick you up at eight," he replied. "That should give you time to get to the gym."

Alexis smiled again, loving the fact that Jamar had taken the time to get to know her schedule so well. "Eight is good. See you then."


"What are you smiling about so much?" Jamar asked, digging his index finger into Alexis's dimple. He'd always loved her dimples. They made her seem vulnerable and lovable, even through the tough exterior that she always tried to portray. He could never understand why she consistently built a wall between them. In the year they'd been seeing each other, she never allowed him to get too close. Every time he even mentioned being anything more than a close friend, she'd change the subject. Lately she'd softened, but he could tell there was still something standing between them.

He kissed her forehead as she snuggled closer to him and pulled the blanket to her shoulders.

"Nothing," she said quietly. She moved his finger away from her dimple and kissed it absently.

There was that wall again. He understood that she still harbored feelings for her ex-fiancé, but he thought she'd gotten over him once they'd gotten closer. Even with his week in Atlanta, the last month had been good between them. They talked more, and spent quality time together. He could tell there was more between them than just sex, but he needed her to see the same thing. And he wasn't sure how long his patience would last.

"You know, you remind me of this experience I had when I was a little boy," Jamar said, pulling Alexis on top of him.

She shot him a confused look. "Huh?"

"When I was a kid, I couldn't understand my times tables for anything in the world," he explained. He rolled over and placed Alexis back on her pillow, then began stroking her flat stomach. "I didn't figure out how grouping things equated to my tables, and counting on my fingers just made me dizzy."

Alexis laughed, but let him continue.

"My mama told me, 'Boy, if you don't learn them damn times tables, you gonna stay in the fifth grade forever,'" he said in his best mama impression. "'You wanna be a dumb-ass forever?'"

Alexis laughed even harder.

"Go ahead and laugh," Jamar pouted. "That was a hard time in my life. I thought I really was going to be a dumb-ass for the rest of my life."

"How did you get over it?" Alexis asked once her laughter subsided.

Jamar smiled and lifted his eyebrows. "I had to concentrate and apply myself. It took me a while, but I figured it out. Math became my new challenge. And once I figured it out, I was unstoppable. You remember Dwayne Wayne from *A Different World*?"

Alexis nodded.

"By the time I became a teenager, I was the real-life version of him," Jamar announced. "Don't get me wrong. I pulled the women, but I was hell when it came to math. People used to pay me to do their homework. By the time I became a senior, I had a whole tutoring business!"

"All right, now," Alexis said. "So how do I remind you of that?"

"Because for me, you're almost the same kind of challenge," he explained. "You're a hard woman. You got layers on you that I can't even begin to understand. But I'm not going to give up on you. Soon, you're going to see that I care about you, walls and layers and all, and you're going to love me just as much as I love you."

Alexis looked at him and nodded. "What makes you love me so much? I ain't gave you nothin' but a hard time since we met."

"I like a challenge. I overcame math, I overcame law school, I overcame Katrina, and I'ma overcome your mean ass."

Alexis laughed, despite the backhanded compliment. "You can kiss my mean ass."

Jamar shot her an evil smile. "I plan on it."

She smirked at him. "Why you tryin' to be grown?"

"Girl, you better ask somebody. I *am* grown."

Alexis gazed into Jamar's eyes, forcing him to ponder the thoughts that might be swimming in her head. He felt he was breaking down her defenses, but how could he be sure? He'd never had to work this hard to get a woman. What made Alexis so special?

She was beautiful, no doubt about that, but he'd been with beautiful women before. He'd even been with models and a couple of television stars. Hell, being a successful attorney in a city like New Orleans, he could have his pick of any woman who crossed his path.

But there was something different about Alexis. They fit each other. And he meant it when he told her that he was up for the challenge. She'd finally begun to open up to him. All he needed to do was be patient. Eventually, he would get what he wanted—her hand in marriage.

Alexis suddenly shifted her position, propping her head with her hand. "What are you so deep in thought about?"

"Thinking about you," Jamar replied.

"What about me?"

"Nothing in particular. Just glad to see you again. I missed your little mean ass."

"You're gonna stop calling me mean, ya hear?" Alexis snapped, popping him lightly on the chest. "You ain't seen me get mean yet."

"Shit!" Jamar sneered. "Let you tell it."

"Well, if I'm so mean, why are you wasting your time with me?"

He looked into her eyes, wondering why she would even fix her mouth to ask such a question. "If you have to ask that, then you really don't understand."

"Understand what?"

"How much I really care about you. I told you before, I'm not that fool in Texas. I'm different from any other man you ever been with. When I make a promise to you, you can take that shit to the bank and cash it. I'm that brotha that can take care of my job, then come home and take care of my woman. I want you to be that woman."

"Jamar, I *am* your woman."

"Yeah, you're with me, all right, but your mind is somewhere else. We've gotten closer, but there's still a wall you won't let me cross. What's holding you back?"

Alexis looked down, then stared out of the window overlooking Jamar's bed. He wanted to repeat his question, but couldn't bear to interrupt her internal struggle. She couldn't even look at him. Instead, her eyes found solace darting back and forth from the pattern on his blanket to the roofs of the apartment buildings across the street.

Five minutes had passed without a word. Finally, Jamar shook his head and turned his back to her. "Don't worry about it, Alexis."

Almost immediately, he felt kisses slowly invade his neck and earlobes.

"Stop, Alexis," he said without flinching. "That's not what I'm looking for right now."

"You love me, don't you?" she asked, rubbing her hand up and down his arm.

He turned back over to face her, his face remaining stoic. "That's not the point."

She crawled on top of him and rubbed her fingernails down his chest. "That is the point. If you love me, I need you to be patient with me. I'm working out a lot of things right now."

Jamar grabbed her hands and pulled them behind his head. "What things?"

"Things I don't want to discuss right now."

"Well, you need to tell me something because you got a good man right here under you, but you're trying with everything you got to push me away."

"How am I pushing you away?"

"By holding me at arm's length. You act like you're afraid for me to get too close."

"I'm not afraid of anything," Alexis retorted, moving from on top of him.

Jamar rolled over and faced her again. "Then what is it? You holding out for somebody better?"

"No."

"You sure said that fast. A little *too* fast."

Alexis sucked her teeth and moved away from him. "Jamar, I'm not one of your clients. You can stop your cross-examination any time now."

"No, baby," Jamar replied. "When I cross-examine somebody, they usually turn out to be guilty. Now if you stop acting like you've got something to hide, you won't have to worry about being in the spotlight."

Alexis sucked her teeth again and rose from the bed.

"I don't need this shit," she mumbled, searching the floor for her clothes. "I had a hard enough day with deadbeat-ass patients and my smart-mouth cousin. I don't need you trying to pressure me into something I'm not ready for."

Jamar lay on the bed unmoved, watching her get dressed. He wanted to stop her, but at the same time, he knew this was vintage Alexis. When she lost control of the situation, she also lost her temper. There was no use trying to reason with her when she was like this. The best thing to do was wait it out. Once she calmed down, she would be back to her quiet, reasonable self. She just needed time to get out of the situation so she could think without being placed on the spot. He'd seen it too many times before.

"You know what, Jamar?" she snapped, pulling on her tank top. "I'm not one of those women who jumped when you said jump. Just like you said you're different from the men I was with, I'm damn sure different from the bitches you dated. I have my own mind and I move at my own speed. You can't make me fall in love just because you decided you were in love with me."

Jamar rolled onto his back and put his hand over

his forehead. "Alexis, I'm not trying to make you do anything you don't want to do."

"You say that, then you jump on me for not moving as fast as you."

"That's not the point. The point is, you are holding back and you can't even be honest with me or yourself and admit why."

Alexis snatched up her purse and headed for the door. "I'm out."

A loud slam that rattled the pictures on the wall followed a minute later. Even Jamar flinched a bit from the force. He shook his head slowly, replaying the argument in his mind. Alexis was definitely going to be a challenge. "But I'm still gonna marry your mean ass."

# Chapter 12

# My Way
or No Way

"Step heel, touch!" shouted Teena, the unrelenting step aerobics instructor.

Normally, Alexis and Shalonda would joke about how crazy Teena was, comparing her to a drill sergeant who hadn't realized she was out of the army. However, today, Alexis attacked the triple-risered step in front of her with a new intensity, still reeling from the argument she'd had with Jamar two days ago.

*No one told him to fall in love,* she told herself as she performed a crossover. He knew the deal when they met. She'd told him from jump that she wasn't ready for anything serious. But now that she'd made the mistake of letting him get a little closer, all of a sudden he was ready to practically walk down the aisle. And then he had the nerve to get mad because she didn't feel the same?

"That boy got me bent," Alexis mumbled, moving into a basic right step.

"Come on, ladies, lemme hear you!" Teena commanded. Alexis ignored her, keeping the intensity all over her face.

She had to admit that Jamar had all of the qualities she wanted, but she wasn't about to be forced into something she wasn't ready for just because *he* thought the time was right. Alexis White had never been the type of woman to let a man dictate anything to her, and she wasn't about to start now. Tony had tried and failed when he tried to punk her into staying in Houston. She even walked away when her boss tried to talk her into working more hours with less pay. She wished she could have seen his face when he found out about her successful, thriving practice. All that business could have been his had he not tried to use her.

She smirked to herself. Even in her wild days, she'd always made her own rules. So why should she start now letting some man tell her what to do?

"All right, ladies, time to cool it down," Teena announced.

"Wooooo," Shalonda groaned, bending over and grabbing her knees. "I thought she would never say those words."

"Huh?" Alexis said, snapping from her thoughts. Once the words registered in her mind, she replied, "Yeah, she worked it today."

Shalonda sucked her teeth as she bent into a standing groin stretch. "Let you tell it. You were right along with her, trying to be She-Ra or some damn body."

Alexis laughed. "Just had some things on my mind, that's all."

"Okay, ladies, take a deep breath, stretching out your hands as far as they'll go, then give yourselves a big hug," Teena instructed. Once the class did as they were told, she smiled, clapped, and said, "Thanks for coming out. I'll see you next week."

Alexis and Shalonda joined the rest of the class in halfhearted, exhausted applause, then left the studio.

"You still trippin' on Jamar?" Shalonda asked once they were back in the locker room.

"Yep, and don't try to tell me I'm wrong, either," Alexis replied as she rifled through her locker. She pulled out a water bottle and took a swig.

"I ain't said a word," Shalonda said, raising her hands in resignation. "You know him better than I do."

"That's right, and I know I'm gettin' damned tired of him thinking I'm still hung up on Tony."

"I know, especially when it's really Reggie that you want," Shalonda remarked with a laugh.

Alexis nearly laughed with her until she realized what her friend said. "Excuse me?"

"You heard me. You're pushing Jamar away because Reggie popped back up."

"Where did you get that from?" Alexis asked, turning to her friend.

"Let's see," Shalonda said, counting on her fingers. "You've been dating Jamar for a year with no problem. Then once you decide to get closer to him, Reggie pops back up and you go right back into your shell."

"Excuse me?" Alexis asked again, dropping onto the bench near her locker.

"You heard me!" Shalonda repeated, laughing again. "Don't get me wrong, Lex, I understand how you feel. I ain't never had all the men you have, but I know how you felt about Reggie back in the day."

Alexis took a deep breath and rolled her eyes. "First of all, Shalonda, I told Jamar from jump street that I didn't want anything serious with him. And if I remember correctly, I cursed Reggie out two weeks ago and haven't heard from him since."

"Lex, we've been friends for almost thirteen years. You think I haven't seen you curse people out before? And you think I forgot how much hell you put Reggie through after he broke up with you?"

"That was then, this is now," Alexis replied, rising from the bench. She picked up her gym bag and began stuffing it with old gym clothes that needed to be washed.

"Okay," Shalonda said, resigned. "You're my sister and all, but I'ma let you keep playing that game with yourself."

"I'm too old for games," Alexis snapped without looking back. She slammed her locker shut and slung her gym bag over her shoulder.

"Baby girl, I'm not gonna fight with you," Shalonda said, following her friend out of the gym. "I think it's fine that you have two fine, successful men to choose from."

Alexis stopped walking and glared at her friend. "Why does everybody seem to forget that one of those fine, successful men is married, and the other one is too damned pushy?"

"Well, I don't condone fooling with married men, because I know I would go off if somebody tried to get with my husband," Shalonda said once they reached her car. She pointed her remote toward the car and unlocked the door. Before climbing in, she added, "However, you never gave the man a chance to tell you what he wanted. If he really does want to be friends, why not get past what happened in college and try it?"

"Because I don't want to be his friend," Alexis admitted.

Shalonda climbed into her car and started the engine. "You're a cold woman. You always did want to have your cake and eat it, too."

"And I ain't changing for nobody," Alexis retorted with a weak smile.

"I wouldn't expect you to; you wouldn't be the Lexy I know and love."

Alexis laughed as her friend pulled out of the parking lot, although she ached on the inside. Secretly, everyone was right. Although every day she grew more and more out of love with Tony, she still secretly wanted him to return to New Orleans and beg her to take him back. And as much as she hated to admit it, she wished like hell that Reggie wasn't married. Yet the chances of either of those wishes coming true was about as likely as her grandmother's flood insurance being paid off. On top of that, she had the feeling that as much as she liked Jamar, she'd only be settling for him because she couldn't have who she really wanted. She couldn't live with that. It just wasn't the Alexis way.

"Hey, big head," Roman greeted as Alexis walked into the house.

"I know your water-head-ass ain't trying to talk about somebody," Alexis retorted. She took her gym bag into her room and headed for the kitchen. "Where my mama?"

"Girl, you didn't learn shit in college, did you?" Roman said, following his sister into the kitchen. "The question is, 'where is my mother?' That's that UNO education for you. If you had gone to a black school like me, they would have taught you to speak."

"Boy, shut up!" Alexis ordered, popping him on the back of his head. "Now, *where is my mother*?"

"She just called and said she's on the way home," Roman replied, laughing and rubbing the sting from his head. He walked back into the living room and flopped back on the sofa. "You just coming from the gym?"

"Yeah."

"Latonya called about an hour ago."

"What *she* want?" Alexis asked, taking a seat on the recliner.

Roman looked up quickly and smiled. "Ooo, sounds like you and your little cousin didn't have a good day at work."

"You just don't know. Her little fast ass be killin' me sometimes."

"Then why you have her working there?"

"Because she does a good job," Alexis explained. "I just get tired of her gettin' smart all the time."

"You knew that girl had a slick tongue when you let her work there. How you gonna get mad now?"

"I don't know, but I'ma tell you this—tomorrow is a new damned day. I'm not putting up with all that drama anymore."

Roman laughed. "I'ma see how long that lasts."

"Watch!" Alexis proclaimed. "Now, what did she call about?"

"She called to say Ms. Somebody called to apologize and that she's bringing your money in the morning."

"Miss who?"

"I don't know. She said it was some lady that came in the other day with a baby who you told couldn't come back if she didn't bring you your money," Roman explained. "Gangster!"

Alexis laughed. "Oh, that was Ms. Mason. I guess her mama made her pay up."

"I guess, but I woulda paid you, too, if you came at me like you was my pimp or somethin'."

Alexis laughed again. "It's not like that, but I have to eat, too. I'm tired of people thinking they can take advantage of me. They're lucky the old Alexis ain't here no more."

"Well, she's not gone forever," Roman remarked. "I hear her pop out every now and then."

"Yep, and she'll be making a few more appearances real soon, so watch your back."

"Why you say that?"

"Like I said, I'm tired of people thinking they can take advantage of me. I ain't been nice all my life."

Roman shook his head. "Some man musta pissed you off."

"Why you think every mood I'm in has to do with a man?"

"Just guessing."

"See, it's stupid mess like that that's gonna make the old Alexis come back to stay."

Roman laughed just as Mary came through the door. "That's nice. My two kids sittin' and talkin' without fightin'."

"That's just because you got here too soon, Mama," Alexis replied, rising from her chair. She walked over and gave her mother a kiss. "Mama, you better remind Roman how mean I used to be."

Mary shook her head. "She ain't lyin'. I swear workin' with them children at that clinic softened her up."

"I know she used to be mean, I was there," Roman said. "I just don't want her to think she's gonna start with me, because I ain't the one."

"Roman, you know I love you," Alexis replied, moving toward her brother with her arms open wide.

He jumped off the sofa and quickly moved into a fighting stance. "Get away from me, girl."

The two women laughed at him.

"I don't see nothin' funny," Roman said.

"That Dillard education must not be paying off," Alexis mocked. "I think you meant, 'I don't see *anything* funny.'"

"Later for you, girl," Roman mumbled, waving his hand at her. He dropped back onto the sofa and continued watching TV.

"What's wrong with him?" Mary asked Alexis.

She shrugged and followed her mother into her bedroom. "He was fine a while ago, then he got serious."

Mary shook her head. "You can never tell with these young people these days."

"I guess, but he just snapped all of a sudden, like right when you came in."

"I'll have his daddy talk to him when he gets in."

"Where is Frank?" Alexis asked, taking a seat on her mother's bed.

"I don't know, but I do know I'ma take advantage of some peace and quiet and get some reading done before he gets here," Mary replied as she stretched out on the bed. She kicked her daughter lightly. "You going out tonight?"

"Nope," Alexis said, taking the hint and standing back up. She leaned against her mother's dresser. "I don't feel like being bothered tonight."

"What's wrong? You mad at Jamar?"

Alexis then realized she'd never told her mother about the fight she'd had with Jamar a couple of days ago. Thinking back to her earlier conversation with Shalonda, she really didn't feel like getting into it again. Although she valued her mother's opinion and knew she would always be real with her, she was tired of Jamar crowding her thoughts. "Not exactly. I just don't feel like being bothered tonight."

"Well, every woman needs some 'me time,'" Mary said, turning onto her side to face her daughter. "I'm 'bout to get mine."

"Okay, Mama," Alexis said with a laugh. She moved toward the door. "You dropped enough hints. I'm gone."

"Close the door on the way out," Mary called after her.

Roman was still sitting on the sofa when Alexis returned to the living room. She sat next to him and patted his leg. "You all right, lil' bro?"

"I'm straight," he replied, his eyes still on the television.

"You're not acting like you're straight," she pushed. The thirteen-year age gap between them didn't allow them to have many heart-to-hearts, but Alexis hoped that the few they did have convinced Roman that he could come to her. When they weren't joking around, they fought, but seldom did they have any true brother/sister moments. Even before their parents married, their relationship was barely more than hello and good-bye. She wasn't young enough to hang with him, and he wasn't old enough to understand life. Besides their parents, they had nothing in common. Yet they genuinely liked each other, and had even developed a familial love for each other. Alexis hoped that love would allow him to open up to her tonight.

"I said I'm straight, Lex, now cool out," Roman snapped.

"That's all right," Alexis said, mimicking his disposition. She slouched on the sofa and folded her arms the same way her brother's were folded. "You ain't gotta tell me nothin'. I'm just an old woman who ain't never been nowhere in life. Hell, I don't even have a life. All I do is go to work, go to the gym, then go home. I have one close friend, and a boyfriend who ain't even called me tonight. I'm tryna help you, and I can't even help myself."

Roman looked at his sister and sucked his teeth. "Shut up, Alexis. Play that role with Jamar or somebody. I ain't the one."

Alexis sighed heavily. "You're right."

Roman tried to maintain his composure, but couldn't help but smile. "You are one silly-ass woman."

Alexis maintained her disposition, although she laughed on the inside. "Now I'm silly. Just add that to the list of my problems."

"Go somewhere, girl!"

"Now my brother's tryna kick me out. I just can't win."

"What is wrong with you?"

"Nothing."

"Stop it!"

Alexis looked her brother in the eye. "You gonna tell me why you snapped on me?"

"I didn't snap on you," Roman said. "I just didn't feel like being bothered."

"You were fine earlier."

"I really wasn't. I just got tired of pretending."

Alexis furrowed her eyebrows in concern. "What's wrong?"

Roman strained his neck to see if Mary's door was still closed, then moved closer to his sister. "You can't tell nobody."

"I won't," she promised. "Now, what's the problem?"

"You know I've been messin' around with Tameka and Sheila, right?"

"Yeah, and I told you you needed to stop—"

Roman cut her off with his hand. "Later, Alexis."

"Sorry."

"Anyway, one of them—"

"Hey, there!" Frank announced as he barreled through the front door.

Roman took a deep breath before turning to his father and greeting him. "Hey, where you been?"

"Me and Harold went to the DAV for a little while," Frank explained. "We got into a bid whist game and time flew."

He looked at Alexis cautiously. "Your mama mad?"

"Please, she is not thinking about you," she replied, waving him off. "You know she doesn't trip on stuff like that. She's in the room reading."

A look of relief washed over Frank's face as he headed for the bedroom. "I knew that."

Roman and Alexis laughed as they watched him creep into the bedroom. It was no secret that Frank feared his wife's wrath, but everyone knew it was her strong will that he loved most about her.

Once he was safely behind closed doors, Alexis turned back to her brother. "Okay, now what happened? Is one of them chickenheads pregnant?"

"Shhhhh!" Roman hissed with his finger held to his lips. "Damn, mouth-almighty! You tryna get my ass kicked?"

Alexis lowered her voice, stealing a glance at their parents' closed door. "Sorry. Now, what's going on?"

Roman pursed his lips and shook his head. "Never mind."

"Aw, hell, no! You done opened the bag, now you might as well let the cat free. Now, what happened?"

He looked again at Mary and Frank's door, then placed his face in his hands. Once he looked up, he found his sister's eyes piercing his inner thoughts. He took a deep breath and let out the truth. "One of them bitches burned me."

"What? Are you sure?"

"Let's put it this way," Roman said, stealing another glance at the door. "When I went to piss this morning, my knees buckled and I had to hold on to the sink. Felt like my dick shot out fire."

Alexis cocked back her head in surprise. "Wow, you didn't have to be that honest. I got the idea."

"What the fuck am I gonna do?" Roman pleaded. "I don't know if it's Tameka or Sheila. You know Tameka is my heart. What if it was Sheila that got me, and I accidentally put Tameka out there? Or what if Tameka has been steppin' out on me?"

"You sure it's just one of them?"

"Sis, I ain't sleepin' with nobody else. I promise."

Hearing the word *sis* made Alexis glow inside. It

wasn't often that he called her that. It reminded her that he didn't just think of her as an older buddy. She was his sister. Not by blood, but there was a bond.

"Well, the first thing you need to do is take care of yourself," Alexis said, taking his hand. "Come by my office tomorrow and I'll take care of you."

"Damn, you sure?" Roman asked, his eyes wet with tears he refused to let fall.

"Boy, you're my brother," she assured him. "You think I'm just gonna leave you out there like that?"

"Thanks, sis. You just don't know how much I appreciate this."

"It's all good, but I told you this would happen. Why do you mess around on Tameka, anyway? She's a nice girl and she loves the mess outta your lil' doggish behind."

"I know, and I love her, too, but everybody I know got a boo on the side," Roman admitted. "Besides, I ain't ready to settle down—I'm just nineteen."

"And now you're nineteen with an STD. You know what you got?"

"Hell, no! I ain't never had this before."

Alexis blew out some air and shook her head. When were these hardheaded teenagers going to learn? But then, who was she to judge?

"Just come to my office tomorrow so I can test you," she said. "I'll try to rush the results, but I can't promise anything."

"But what about Latonya's nosy ass?"

"Just tell her you're there to hang out with me. She doesn't go into the examination area. Ms. Kay will help me out, and I know she won't say anything. She's too professional for that."

"What about Tameka and Sheila?"

Alexis patted her brother's hand, feeling his pain. She had slept with a wealth of men in college, but by the grace of God, she never contracted an STD. However, she remembered the pain of hiding her abortion from Reggie until she could no longer take it. She really had no words that could comfort her brother. "Let's just take care of one thing at a time. Let's get you tested so you can find out what you have."

Roman nodded, agreeing to his sister's plan.

"But you know," Alexis warned, "you will have to talk to both of your girls and make sure they get tested."

His eyes shot open. "How the hell am I supposed to do that?"

"Roman, this is the wrong time to be thinking of yourself. You need to be straight up with those girls, or else you can cause them some serious complications that can affect the rest of their lives. You can either be a man and talk to them face-to-face, or you can be a punk ass and write a letter, but either way, you will talk to them."

"Shit."

"I know, but that's life. In the meantime, no sex."

"Shit, you ain't gotta worry about that," Roman proclaimed. "After this, I don't wanna see no parts of a pussy."

Alexis laughed, knowing that feeling would only last a moment.

# Chapter 13

# Taking Action

"How 'bout this one?"

Reggie stared wide-eyed at the eight-foot regency evergreen standing in front of him. His son couldn't be serious. "Shawn, don't you think that's a little big?"

"No," DeShawn replied, looking confused. "Our tree last year was big."

Reggie knelt down so he could face his son on his three-foot-five-inch level. "Last year, we had more people. It's only going to be me and you this year."

"Can't we still have a big tree?" DeShawn pleaded.

Reggie sighed and looked at the hulk of a Christmas tree. It was so large that he could barely see around it. It was definitely a nice tree, but he could already tell it would be the first of many uncomfortable conversations to come this holiday season. He gazed sadly at his son and smiled. "How 'bout we get a tree just like this one, but smaller? Do you know how long it would take for me and you to decorate this big old thing? Besides, we're going to be doing so much hanging out that we won't even have time to look at it."

DeShawn laughed. "Okay, fine, but that means you owe me two presents."

"Boy, I clothe you and feed you. That should be enough!"

"That doesn't count! You're a daddy; you have to do that."

Reggie laughed, relieved that he was able to lighten the mood. He stood up and led his son around the store in search of the perfect Christmas tree. "No, I don't. I could have left you in the hospital and had some other mommy and daddy take you home."

"Uh-uhhhhhh," the little boy sang. "You would never leave me."

"Yeah, huh," Reggie mocked, letting go of the boy's hand. "In fact, I'ma leave you right now."

He took a quick turn down an aisle and hid behind a spruce tree covered in white lights. He snickered as he watched his son wander through the trees looking for him.

"Daddddyyyyy!" DeShawn whined playfully, once he reached the spruce.

"Awwww, you found me!" Reggie groaned, placing his arm on his forehead.

The father and son played around like two childhood buddies, dipping behind trees and scrambling through the aisles. Passing shoppers probably thought Reggie was the epitome of immaturity, but he didn't give a damn. This was one of the few cherished moments he would share with his son, and he was determined to make the most of it. Lord only knew how many more days like this he would have with DeShawn.

He didn't even expect to have this one. He'd fully prepared himself to sit at home and ring in the holidays with his Hennessy in one hand and his crotch in the other. With Christmas in a couple of weeks and his family no longer in the house, he felt like Scrooge on crack. Outside of beating the Falcons for the second time this season, there truly was nothing to celebrate.

Shocked was an understatement when Nikki called him Monday night and asked if DeShawn could stay with him for Christmas. Aside from making arrangements for Reggie's weekly visits with DeShawn, they hadn't spoken in weeks. Nikki hadn't even mentioned the holidays before then, and every time Reggie tried mentioning any plans, she would change the subject.

He never tried inquiring about the reason for the change of heart. "Be thankful for small blessings" had become his new motto. As far as he was concerned, Nikki may have felt bad about the way things had ended between them, although he couldn't help thinking that maybe she was up to something. Nikki may have been from the streets, but she was smart. After all, what mother would willingly spend Christmas without her only child?

*Later for her*, Reggie said to himself. Only time would reveal his estranged wife's true intentions, and when it did, he would be ready. In the meantime, he was going to enjoy his holiday with DeShawn as if it was his last. Just in case it actually would be.

A vibration coming from his pocket interrupted his thoughts.

"Slow down, Shawn," he said as he fished out his cell phone. The little boy immediately slowed into a walk and began browsing the Christmas decorations farther down the aisle. "Morgan."

"What's up, Reg?"

Reggie exhaled, amazed at his lawyer's sense of timing. "Jamar. Tell me you have good news for me."

"What good news you lookin' for?" Jamar asked.

"The mandatory separation has already started. You have a temporary custody agreement that you both seem to be following. . . ."

"That's the thing, Jamar," Reggie said, following closely behind DeShawn as he wandered through the aisles. "This temporary sh—thing. You find a way to turn the tables my way?"

"I told you before that's an uphill battle. Unless you can prove Nikki's an unfit mother, there's not much I can do for you. Adultery isn't a strong enough case."

Reggie slowed down, letting DeShawn walk farther ahead of him. "What about the fact that she's not even spending Christmas with her son?"

"She's not?"

"She just called me out of the blue and asked me if he could spend Christmas with me."

"Reggie, that could actually mean she's being fair. Didn't he spend Thanksgiving with her?"

"Yeah, but—"

"Then that alone doesn't make her unfit. If anything, it shows she's trying her hand at coparenting."

"I doubt that," Reggie scoffed, sucking his teeth. "But I'll leave it at that since I can't prove anything right now."

"Man, just enjoy your holiday and leave the legal stuff to me," Jamar said with a chuckle. "In the meantime, keep yourself in check. You still retiring after this year?"

"Yeah."

"We're losing a hell of a player, but that's the best move for you. It shows stability. You making all of your visitations?"

"Hell, yeah."

"I figured, but I had to ask. What about the ladies?"

"What about 'em?"

"You know what I'm talking about! You sleeping with anybody?"

"Like I got time to think about that."

"Hell, all pro ballplayers have tight schedules, but that doesn't stop 'em from getting a little ass every now and then," Jamar pointed out.

"Daddy, can we get this one?" DeShawn asked, holding up a box of Proud Family Christmas ornaments.

"Yeah, baby boy, put 'em in the basket," Reggie said, thankful for the momentary diversion. Jamar's question had immediately brought to mind images of Alexis. Thoughts of Levi and his constant coaxing to go out soon followed. He knew Alexis would never be a possibility, but he wasn't sure how long he could hold Levi off. Sooner or later he was sure he would take Levi up on his offer and meet some woman who would get him into trouble. He returned to his conversation with his attorney. "No, I haven't been with anybody."

"Well, if you do meet somebody—and I'm not saying you need to—you need to be careful. Loose lips sink ships, and all you need is for one little chicken-head-ass girl to go around town bragging about how she's sleeping with Reggie Morgan, and your adultery case is gone."

"I hear you," Reggie said, nodding in agreement. "But you ain't gotta worry. I wouldn't be doing any woman any good right now."

"Just make sure you keep that in mind," Jamar warned. "Or at least find somebody who can keep her business to herself."

"Daddy, how 'bout these?" DeShawn called out, holding up a box of multicolored tree lights.

Reggie frowned. Once he came into adulthood, he vowed never to have multicolored lights or artificial snow on his trees. He felt it cheapened the look. "What about all white? I promise it'll make the tree look better."

"If you say so," DeShawn groaned, replacing the box.

He moved over to a box of white lights and placed it into the cart.

Reggie laughed, then returned to his conversation. "Is that what you called me about? To make sure I'm still not gettin' any?"

"No, I also called to say Merry Christmas," Jamar said, a smile apparent in his voice.

"Yeah, okay," Reggie said with a sideways grin. "Same to you."

Once he placed his cell back into his pocket, he caught up with DeShawn and nearly fell over when he realized how many decorations his son had placed into the basket. "Dag, Shawn, you really do think we're gonna buy that big tree, don't you?"

"No, but they have a lot of stuff here," the child answered, his face painted with a sheepish grin.

"Well, we're gonna have to put some of this stuff back. You got enough stuff in here to decorate the whole neighborhood's trees."

"Okay, but I'm keeping these," DeShawn proclaimed, laughing and holding up the Proud Family ornaments he'd asked about earlier.

"Okay, you can have that. Now put some of this stuff back so we can pick our tree and get outta here."


Two weeks before Christmas and three weeks before the new year, and Alexis felt she'd accomplished nothing. Sure, her practice was still busy, and some of her customers' IOUs had been paid, but she felt she needed to be doing more. Maybe if she could find a way to help her patients get on their feet, they might be in a better position to pay her. If it weren't for her living with her parents, she'd only be a couple of paychecks away from being homeless herself. They weren't all like the woman she saw in the casino a couple of months ago.

But what could she do?

Maybe she could do a Brad Pitt and build some houses. But then again, she didn't have a home herself, and although she was doing okay, she had nowhere near the dollars Brangelina had.

What about a neighborhood cleanup?

"Who am I kidding?" she asked herself with a laugh. She didn't even like cleaning her own bedroom and barely washed a dish in her house. How in the world would she pull off cleaning up an entire neighborhood? Besides, she really didn't believe sweeping a street would do much for her patients in the long run. The thugs would probably mess it up again before the day was out.

She lay back on her bed and explored her mental Rolodex, looking for an idea. She stared at the ceiling, wishing the cracks would spell out something for her. A few ideas came, but nothing she thought would be doable. It was obvious she'd need some help, so she rolled over and dialed Shalonda.

"Hey, girl, whatcha doing?" Alexis asked once she heard her friend's voice.

"'Bout to take Brianna to the beauty shop," Shalonda replied. "This girl's hair looks like who did it and got away with it."

Alexis laughed, picturing Brianna looking like Medusa. "You want me to call you back?"

"Give me about ten minutes to get in the car and get my earpiece on and I'll call you right back."

Alexis quickly returned to her thoughts once she hung up with her friend. Thoughts of doing a health fair danced around her mind. It would give her a chance to give free medical care to the many people in the city who desperately needed it, and it could boost her practice at the same time. She could also pull a few other doctors into the mix and help them as well. But how would she be able to do that by herself? How would she get the money? Where could she have the fair? Would people even show up?

Yet, for as many obstacles as entered her mind, a million more reasons came to push forward. Little kids could receive vaccines their parents couldn't otherwise afford. Older people could get their blood pressure and cholesterol levels checked. She could give out more information on the dangers of living in those damned trailers for an extended time. She then thought about Roman and his diagnosis of chlamydia. How many more people could be walking around with STDs and not even know it?

The phone rang, snatching her from her thoughts. Alexis reached for the phone quickly and glanced at the caller ID. "Hey, girl."

"All right, now I can talk," Shalonda said.

"Mommy, can I get curls this time?" Alexis could hear Brianna ask.

"Now, Bree, I know you see me on the phone," Shalonda snapped. "We'll talk about that when we get to the shop."

"Ohhhhkayyy," the little girl groaned.

"So what's going on?" Shalonda asked, turning her attention back to her friend.

"I need your help," Alexis said quickly.

"With what?"

"I have this crazy idea to do some community service, but I have no idea where to start."

"Whatcha tryin' to do?"

Alexis sighed, hoping her friend wouldn't think she'd lost her senses. "Well, I want to do something to help my patients. I know a lot of them can't afford good medical care, and I've always wanted to do my part in rebuilding New Orleans. So I was thinking of putting on a health fair."

"That sounds like a great idea! How can I help?"

"By telling me what to do. I've never done anything like this before. I know it's going to take some money and a lot of time. I want this thing to be big."

"When are you trying to do this?"

Alexis bit her lip as she looked up at her calendar, knowing Shalonda would flip when she heard the answer to that question. The date was right around the corner, but the more she thought about it, the more it made sense. "February tenth, the Saturday before Valentine's Day."

"Damn, girl, why so soon?"

"I just don't wanna wait on this. And I figure it's a good way to bring in Valentine's Day. Think about it: show him that you love him inside and out."

Shalonda laughed. "I like where you're going, but that's corny as shit."

"Forget you," Alexis said, smiling. "I just thought about it today."

"I'm just messing with you. But you know if you're trying to do something that soon, you're not going to have time to put in for a grant. You're going to have to convince some people to come out of their pockets, and that's not going to be easy."

"I know, huh? I was thinking I could get some other doctors to go in with me, but whatever they put in is probably just going to cover their expenses. We're still going to need to pay for vaccines, a location, advertising, all kinds of stuff."

"You think Touro will help you pay for some of it?"

Alexis shrugged. "I can ask."

"You can also ask one of the sororities to help sponsor it," Shalonda suggested.

"I never thought about that," Alexis said, a lightbulb going off in her head. "Those sororities are always looking for a community service project. In fact, the Zetas come to Touro all the time for a program they do with new mothers."

"There you go," Shalonda said. A few seconds went by. "You know, there is another route you can take."

"What?"

"You can get some local celebrities to help you out."

"Like who?"

"I know one you know personally. I'm sure he would help you out. In fact, I know he would."

"Who, Reggie?" Alexis asked, her nose scrunched in disgust.

"Yes, Reggie," Shalonda replied. "And before you say anything, this is about business, not about those little games you two play with each other. You get a few of those Saints to come out, and the kids and women will follow. Not to mention, the Saints organization might drop a few dollars on you."

Alexis knew her friend had a point, but she wasn't ready to admit it. She was no longer mad at Reggie, but she couldn't see herself working with him every day. She'd just gotten to the point where she no longer thought about him on a daily basis. "I don't know about that."

"Lex," Shalonda said. "I'm not saying you have to marry the man or even go on a date with him. But he can help you make this thing a reality."

Alexis let out a deep sigh and shook her head. "I'll think about it, but I think I might be able to pull this off without him. My mind is working now."

"Girl, if I had time to argue with you, I would, but I just pulled up at the hairdresser and I need to get Bree settled," Shalonda said.

"All right, handle your business."

"You do the same," Shalonda said. "And that includes not being so bullheaded."

"Shut up, Shalonda," Alexis snapped. "I told you I'll think about it."

"Think hard."

"I will, but I ain't makin' no promises."

# Chapter 14

# 'Nuff Said

"If you insult my mama with that bullshit offer, I'ma sue y'all asses myself!" Mary yelled into the phone.

The outburst nearly made Alexis drop her newspaper. She looked up at her mother sympathetically. Mary had been fighting this same battle with her mother's insurance company for the past year. While they tried to convince her that her mother didn't have flood insurance and therefore they couldn't pay for water damage, Mary countered that it was the hurricane that caused the flooding, and therefore her mother should be awarded her full payment.

"Mr. Jackson, my mama paid her payments on time every month for thirty years," Mary pleaded. "Even after my daddy died, she never missed a payment. Now, when it's time to return some of that loyalty, this is how you do her?"

Alexis could feel her heart ache as she listened to

Mary. It really wasn't about the money. Once the waters receded and the city regained some semblance of normalcy, her grandmother, Margaret Holmes, had moved into a very well-kept senior home in Metairie. Her monthly retirement check paid the rent, with enough money left over for groceries and incidentals. Margaret wanted for nothing except an occasional visitor. But for Mary, her mother's comfort was no excuse for the insurance company's greed. Even after being threatened with a class-action suit by other New Orleanians in the same position, she felt the company just refused to do right.

In the meantime, Margaret's house still stood as a shell of its former self. The trash had been cleaned away, and thanks to the kindness of a couple of churches, new drywall replaced the molded interior structure. However, limited money and the wait for a decent payment from the insurance company kept the family from moving forward with the construction. She hadn't even received a check from Louisiana Road Home because of the continuous battle with the insurance company. In short, the house, along with everyone involved with it, was in a holding pattern.

"Look, all I'm asking is when the inspector comes to the house next week, to be fair," Mary said. "We've gone as far as we can with the house trying to rebuild. My mother deserves better than this. It's time to put the house back together so we can heal and get past this."

Alexis grew still, thinking she heard a crack in her mother's voice. It wasn't often that she heard Mary cry, but she knew how strongly she felt about Margaret's house. It was her childhood home. All of her memories had been washed away. Photos and trophies were buried deep under mud all over the Lower Ninth Ward. Dolls and old clothing were covered in mold, never to be recovered. And while many other people were resigned to let the state take over their homes because of a lack of funds, Mary refused to give up without a fight.

"Mama, what do you plan to do with that house?" Alexis asked once Mary hung up with the insurance adjuster.

Mary sat next to her daughter and shook her head. "I don't know. I thought about giving it to you, but you're not tryin' to live in that neighborhood once you get on your feet. Maybe Roman, but that boy ain't ready to take care of no house by himself. It's too far from the West Bank for Brenda and Darnell to live in. And Mama already said she's happy where she is."

"You gonna sell it?"

"I don't know, Alexis. I ain't even thought that far. Right now I just wanna rebuild it because I'll be damned if I let my mama's house go to waste."

"I hear you. I don't know what I would have done had this house been damaged that badly," Alexis reflected.

Mary patted her daughter's hand and moved over to the recliner so she could stretch out. "We were certainly blessed. But now that I think about it, I should just go ahead and sell the house. We could put the money in an account for Mama in case she needs anything. Maybe she could use it to take a trip."

"That would be nice," Alexis said with a smile.

"So, how you comin' with that big 'to-do' you're trying to put together?" Mary asked.

Alexis sighed, thinking of all the work she'd put into the last week and a half. She couldn't believe the amount of money she would need to make this thing happen. "All I can say is thank God I have a good relationship with Touro. I decided to have it at the convention center, which cost way more than I had planned. But Touro is sponsoring the room for me."

"Well, congratulations, girl!" Mary exclaimed, sitting up.

"Well, it's not set in stone yet, but my friend Thomas on the board of directors said it's pretty much good to go," Alexis explained. "You know, I told you the Red Cross is going to do a blood drive, and we're going to get people to put their names on the American Bone Marrow Donor Registry. After Christmas, I'm going to send a letter to the Zetas to get their support, and some of my doctor friends at Touro are going to set up their own booths. I think we're going to do AIDS and STD testing, blood pressure and cholesterol testing—"

"Damn, girl, slow down," Mary said with a laugh. "You're makin' me dizzy!"

Alexis laughed, realizing her excitement had taken her words a mile a minute. "I'm just excited! This is coming together better than I thought it would. All I wanted to do was help some people, and it looks like I'll be able to do it."

"You sure didn't waste no time gettin' it started. I'm proud of you for being so focused."

"Thanks, but I have to. I only have a couple of months to put this together and not a lot of money to do it."

"You talk to some of the churches?"

"Not yet, but at this point, I need people who are going to bring some money to the table," Alexis replied, tucking her feet between the sofa's cushions. "I still have to pay for testing supplies, vaccinations, advertising, door prizes, all kinds of stuff. Not to mention paying Latonya and Ms. Kay for overtime."

"Child, you better find some volunteers," Mary warned. "You think two people are going to be able to handle all that?"

Alexis bit her lip. "I didn't think about that."

"You making a list of all the stuff you'll need?"

"Yeah, but I guess I'd better get a little more detailed."

"You'd better. With something as big as you're trying to make this, every little thing counts. And you gotta have a budget and stick to it."

"See, that's why I have you, Mama," Alexis said with a smile. "You always keep me on track."

"That's what I'm here for."


With Mary's words still fresh in her mind, Alexis grew scared for the first time since starting this project. She'd made good headway, but there was still too much more that needed to be done. After making her list, she realized it wasn't just about vaccines, refreshments, and advertising. She'd also need computer equipment and security. And decent door prizes would make her health fair different from the others that seemed to pop up all over the city. Judging from the figures she'd written down so far, she would need at least one hundred thousand dollars on top of the Touro sponsorship in order to make her vision a reality.

*Damn, that's a lot of money*, she thought. *What if it doesn't work?*

Would people really be interested in a one-day health fair? And even if they were, would she have enough medication and testing materials to last the entire day? She'd heard about a weeklong medical fair just last month in which some patients had to wait hours for care. How would she avoid a similar or worse fate?

Had she gotten in way over her head? How in the world would she pull this off? And how could she be so sure that giving free medical care all day wouldn't attract even more customers who couldn't pay her?

She wrestled with thoughts of calling Jamar and enlisting his help, but he was already bogged down with his clients. Especially this one guy who seemed to call day and night. She'd never heard of someone so eager to get a divorce. However, she could never glean any information about the guy because Jamar would always leave the room when he called.

Maybe Jamar *could* help her out. She knew he was busy, but she also knew he had contacts. Maybe he knew someone who could make a nice, hefty donation. She quickly picked up the phone and dialed Jamar's office.

"J. Duplessis," Jamar answered.

"Hey, sweetie, you busy?"

"Unfortunately, I am, baby," he replied, apologies dripping from his voice. "I'm in with a client. Can I call you back in an hour?"

Alexis rolled her eyes in disappointment. She bet it was that client who was going through the divorce. "Okay, I'm sorry. You didn't have to answer, you know."

"I know, but if I didn't I wouldn't have been able to tell you I love you," he said.

She smiled. "You're so silly. Make sure you call me back because I need to ask you something."

"I'll call you back as soon as I can."

Alexis's mind was too wound up to wait that hour. She needed an answer, and she needed it now! She stuffed her feet deeper under the sofa cushions and folded her arms as she racked her mind for an option she hadn't yet explored. What about Brenda? She was a nurse. She was bound to have options. *No, I'd better save her for rounding up the volunteers I'm going to need*, Alexis thought. *She has enough on her plate getting ready for that move.*

"I've got it!" she said aloud, snapping her fingers.

Selling vendor space. People with medical books or dietary supplement businesses would love to get in on something like this. Then again, even if she sold ten tables, it wouldn't bring more than two thousand dollars. She'd still need help.

She thought back to Shalonda and how she'd urged her to call Reggie for help. She was determined to do this without him, but it looked as though she was going to need to pull in all the help she could. Maybe enlisting Reggie Morgan's help wasn't such a bad idea. Not only could he donate money or big door prizes, but just him and a few of his friends walking around signing autographs could attract thousands.

The more she thought about it, the more the excitement returned. But what had she done with his business card? She closed her eyes and thought back to the day he had shown up at her job last month. Which purse did she have? Had she thrown his card into her messenger bag? She didn't throw it away, did she?

She hopped off her bed and made a beeline for her closet. She pulled out her messenger bag and dumped the contents all over her bed, turning over every scrap of paper that even looked like a card. Nothing. She then grabbed her favorite designer purse, the black leather one with the giant gold lock. She toted that bag every weekend, so there was a chance that the card had been inadvertently passed into one of the pockets during one of her many purse changes. Unfortunately, except for finding a twenty she didn't know she had, dumping that purse out onto her bed yielded no positive results.

She stood in the middle of her room with arms folded, nervously tapping her foot. Her eyes landed on the camel-brown slacks she remembered wearing that day. Had she placed the card in her pocket? *Shit!* It wasn't there, either, she realized after feeling through her pockets.

She then snapped her fingers, remembering that she'd gone to the gym that day. She pulled her gym bag from behind her door and set it on the bed. She'd have to do some serious cleaning before she could lie in that bed again. But it was all worth it when she unzipped the bag and found the card sticking out from underneath her running shoes.

But now that she had the card in her hand, a wave of nerves attacked her. Didn't she curse this man out and call him everything but a child of God the last time they saw each other? And how many times before then had she seen him and turned the other way? Why in the world would he want to help her?

"I gotta play this right," Alexis told herself, holding the receiver with a death grip. "There's no way he can say no to this."

Before she could change her mind, she quickly dialed the number and paced the floor as she waited for him to answer.

"Boy, you crazy," Reggie said, holding his stomach in laughter.

He and Jamar had just finished their session and were laughing about Reggie's upcoming game against the Chicago Bears, the team that had kept the Saints out of the Super Bowl last year. If the Saints beat them this year, it would be poetic justice.

"I'm serious, though," Jamar said between chuckles. "If y'all don't win that game, I'ma have to wear a Bears jersey to work that Monday, and you know a brother got a image to protect. I'ma get my ass kicked tryna walk through this city!"

Reggie laughed even harder, picturing his street-wise lawyer running from his car into his office, trying to avoid a beatdown. It was almost worth it to lose just to see what would happen. A vibration in his pocket interrupted his thoughts. "Hold up a minute, man."

Reggie dug into his pocket and glanced at the number. It was nothing he recognized, but that wasn't unusual. He was used to getting calls from people he didn't know, many requesting public appearances or local product endorsements. He would just treat this one like the rest—politely direct whoever it was to his agent and move on. "Morgan."

"Reggie?"

Reggie snatched the phone from his ear and stared at it. The woman's voice sounded familiar, but he couldn't place it. Whoever it was, it had to be somebody he knew, because everyone in his circle either called him by his last name or just "Reg." "Yeah, this is Reg, who's this?"

"I'm sorry, did I catch you at a bad time? This is Alexis."

Reggie's eyes bugged. He glanced at Jamar, who waited patiently for him to finish his call. "Hold on. H-hey, J, I need to take this call. I'ma roll out."

"That's cool, champ," Jamar said, turning to his computer. "Handle your business. Just keep in mind what we talked about."

Reggie nodded. "Cool. I'll call you when I need you."

With that, he quickly made a beeline for the door. Once he was safely out of the office, he resumed his conversation. "Damn, I didn't think I would ever hear from you."

"Well, I ain't gonna lie. It took a lot for me to call."

"I understand," he replied, pressing the DOWN button for the elevator. "So, what's good?"

She paused before replying, "I just called to see how you were doing. Shalonda and Brenda told me I was too hard on you when you came to see me, so I figured I would call and make peace."

Reggie chuckled as he stepped into the elevator. He wondered whether he should call her back once he got off the elevator, but didn't want to risk her disappearing again. "Don't worry about it. I'm used to your mean ass. And if I lose you, it's because I'm in the elevator."

"Why does everybody think I'm so mean?" Alexis asked, a chuckle behind her words.

"Girl, I know we ain't seen each other in a while, but I'm sure you haven't changed *that* much."

Another pause. "You'd be surprised."

"I heard that," he said, stepping off the elevator. "I see you're still with me. I guess this phone is pretty good."

"I guess."

"So, you gonna let me try to take you to dinner again? This time, we might even be able to finish the meal and have a decent conversation."

"I think that can happen. Your wife won't mind? I'm not trying to have no drama."

"What did I tell you the last time you asked about my wife?"

"You said let you worry about that."

"All right, then. I got this."

"All right. Enough said on the subject."

"What time should I pick you up?" Reggie asked as he got into his car.

"You meant today?"

"No time like the present. It's been over ten years since we talked."

Pause again. "Is seven okay?"

Reggie looked at his watch. That gave him three hours to shit, shower, and shave after his team meeting. He was glad DeShawn was with his mother. That left one thing off his plate. "That'll work. Where are you living now?"

"Why don't I just meet you somewhere?"

"What? You don't want me at your house? I promise not to try to take advantage of you."

Alexis laughed. "It's not that. I'm still living at home. I just don't want my brother in my business."

"Your brother?"

"I'll explain later."

"That's cool. Why don't you meet me at Pampy's?"

"Sounds good. I'll see you there."

"Can't wait," Reggie replied.

He pulled out of the parking lot with a huge grin on his face. He'd finally come up with a plan to make his divorce go smoothly. He would spend Christmas with his son in a few days. And then, out of nowhere, Alexis had called him and waved the olive branch. It looked as though his day would turn out okay.

Well, the conversation didn't go as expected, but Alexis had to admit that it actually felt good to laugh and talk with Reggie. It brought her back to her college days when the two lovebirds could sit and talk about anything. Those were the Sexy Lexy days, the times when they both ruled the world. He was the campus football star, and she was every man's fantasy. Had they gotten past their issues, they could have been a serious power couple. They were the smart, beautiful people.

"Those were the days," Alexis said softly as she lay back on her bed. She hugged her pillow tightly, contemplating her next move. As much as she enjoyed talking to her former love, she needed to focus. Reggie was the past, and she needed to concentrate on her present and future. Her biggest priority right now was her health fair. She needed money. She needed incentives. She needed people. Reggie could be the answer to all three.

But how could she ask him for money right off the bat? They hadn't seen each other in years, and their last meeting ended in flames. Although they'd had a civil conversation, she didn't want him to think she was only using him for money.

But wasn't she?

*No,* she told herself. *This is strictly about business.* She would go to dinner, order some tilapia, then present her proposal. Once he saw how focused she was on this project there would be no way he would let his feelings get in the way. This wasn't about Alexis and Reggie; it was about the people in the city who needed their help.

Besides, it was more than obvious that Reggie was trying to play around on his wife, and she wasn't about to be an accessory to that. *Let me worry about my wife,* he'd told her. How many times had she heard that tired line? She wished she'd had a dollar for every married man who'd hit on her in her office. They acted as if they'd never seen an attractive female doctor before. Although she knew some of the male doctors went through the same thing—Tony used to brag about it— it didn't make it any better. She wanted her own man, not someone she'd have to sneak around with and see only once the sun went down.

Her thoughts nearly made her consider calling Reggie to cancel their dinner date. She would just call Jamar and take him out. Why not spend the evening with someone who truly loved and respected her? She would just ask Jamar to help her. He'd already offered his help when she first presented the idea to him a couple of weeks ago. She'd refused then because she thought she had it covered. She'd just have to tell him she was wrong.

Then again, could Jamar as a lawyer have the same type of pull that Reggie would have as a celebrity? Jamar might be able to give her some contacts with money, but who would want a lawyer's autograph? Most people still looked at athletes as heroes, while lawyers and police officers were seen as crooks. It wasn't right, but it was what she was dealing with. She'd just have to keep that dinner date and try her best to keep it professional.

Beyoncé's "Irreplaceable" rang from her cell phone. She turned and grabbed it from under her pillow. "Hey, baby."

"Hey, yourself," Jamar greeted.

"You finally finished with that client?" Alexis asked, scooting down on the bed so she could lie down. "I don't know why you have to work every Saturday, anyway."

"We don't all run our own business. Some of us have bosses."

"I work on weekends. Every first and third Saturday. The rest are mine."

Jamar laughed. "Like I said, some of us have bosses. So, what did you need earlier?"

"Your help."

"With what?"

Alexis took a deep breath. "Look, I know I said I wanted to do this health fair on my own, but this thing is costing way more than I thought it would."

Jamar laughed again. "I know you didn't think it would be free to put on something like this."

"No, Mr. Smart-ass," Alexis snapped, sucking her teeth. "I'm just saying I underestimated the cost. Now, are you going to make fun of me or are you going to help me?"

"Wow, I love the way you ask for favors," Jamar said dryly. "It really turns me on."

*Calm down, Alexis. Put the attitude in check.* She took a deep breath and softened her tone. "I'm sorry, but sometimes I think you don't take me seriously."

"Why would you think that?"

"I know you respect that I'm a doctor, but I don't always think you respect my feelings. It's like you always know better."

"Alexis, it's not like that. You know me. It's impossible for me to love someone I can't respect."

"Don't just tell me what you want me to hear, Jamar. Tell me the truth—do you really think I can pull this off?"

"Baby, you can do anything you want, and I mean that. You've already proven that."

Alexis smiled. Guilt could be a powerful tool, but she had to admit that it felt good to hear her ego being stroked. "Thanks, baby. I needed that."

"So what do you need me to do for you?"

Alexis bit her lip. "You have any friends looking for a tax break?"

"Let me see what I can do. In the meantime, why don't you come over tonight and spend some time with me?"

"I can't tonight," she said quickly. "I have to talk with another potential donor in a couple of hours."

"That shouldn't take all night," he pushed. "Just call me when you're done."

Alexis pursed her lips. She had no idea when she would be home. "I'll do that."

"Make sure you do," Jamar said before hanging up.

Alexis slammed the phone down on the bed and kicked her feet in frustration. Why did men have to make everything so difficult?

Reggie sat patiently at the bar, sipping on a Hennessy and Coke. The excitement that pounded in his chest surprised him. It made him feel like a teenager going on his first date. He had to remind himself that this wasn't a romantic date. It was just two old friends getting together over dinner. She had a boyfriend, and he was nowhere near the state of mind to deal with a new girlfriend.

He laughed to himself as he thought of the so-called advice Levi had given him after the team meeting.

"Man, you better knock the back out of that woman," he'd told him. "After what she put you through in college, and what Nikki is doing now, you deserve to get you some!"

Levi just didn't know who Reggie was dealing with. Alexis might have been fast in college, but from what he'd seen over the past few months, she'd definitely slowed down. And that mean streak was still there! Alexis was likely to knock his head into next week if he even looked as if he thought he was getting sexed that night!

He began looking around the small tastefully decorated restaurant in order to get his mind off Alexis. Pampy's Creole Kitchen was a welcome return to the reviving city last year. Their executive chef, Austin Leslie, died shortly after Katrina, and the city sent him off with its first jazz funeral procession, traditionally called a second-line, since before the storm. The restaurant opened later with a slightly different menu, but the thought of the restaurant's Creole-style soul food never failed to make Reggie's mouth water.

But it wasn't just the food that he loved. The restaurant's walls were adorned with pictures of the city he'd learned to call home. There were even photos of some of the post-Katrina cleanup in the restaurant's location, the Seventh Ward, and even in the Lower Ninth Ward, which was hit hardest in the storm.

It was Saturday night, date night, and Pampy's was packed. Every table was populated with couples or groups socializing over dinner before going out on the town. A few people approached Reggie for autographs, while others were bold enough to try to give him advice on how the Saints could win tomorrow's game against the Philadelphia Eagles.

"I'm tellin' you, man," one guy told him, Heineken

wafting from his breath, "all y'all need ta do is find that soft spot in the middle. Philly ain't got no defense."

Reggie laughed and leaned back to avoid the funk. "I hear you, man."

"Shiiiiit," the man went on. "Y'all take care of Philly tomorrow, and Chicago ain't gonna be no kinda problem. Y'all in this!"

Reggie smiled and gave him a soulful shake. This drunken man had more faith in the team than he did sometimes.

"Goddamn!" the man exclaimed, looking toward the door. "Now, that's a fuckin' woman."

Reggie looked in the direction where the man gawked and smiled even harder at the espresso-colored beauty standing at the door running her fingers through her long, wavy hair. Alexis was definitely a woman. And with those fitting jeans and that low-cut top she was wearing, every man and woman in the place knew it. The male tables had no shame in the way they stared, while the women glanced at her and sucked their teeth, a sure sign that Alexis was looking good. She slid off her leather coat, seemingly oblivious of the attention, which Reggie felt was a real point of growth. The old Alexis relished the attention she received from men and would look around to ensure that all eyes were on her. But this new Alexis only seemed to be looking for the person she needed to see—Reggie.

He stood up and waved at her until he got her attention. She waved back and made her way across the dining room.

The drunken fan was in awe. "That's you, man?"

Reggie chuckled, a bit embarrassed by the fan's outburst. "Naw, man, she's just an old friend."

"Well, if he don't want you," the man told Alexis as she reached the two men, "then you always got a friend in me."

He kissed her hand and went back to his table.

Alexis scrunched her eyebrows and looked at him in confusion. "What was that all about?"

"Just a man who seems to be a fan of us both," Reggie said, pulling out the neighboring bar stool for her. "I hope you don't mind, but we'll have to sit here until our table is ready. It shouldn't be much longer."

"That's okay," she replied, placing her jacket on the back of the stool. "I can see it's crowded."

After taking her seat and ordering a hurricane, she said, "Sorry it took me so long. I actually had to run into my office real quick."

Reggie asked the waitress to refresh his drink. "Everything okay?"

"Yeah, I just needed to grab some paperwork for a project I'm putting together."

"What kind of project?"

She shot him a winning Colgate smile. "I'm putting together a health fair at the convention center."

Reggie was visibly impressed. There was no way this could be the same Alexis he knew and loved. "Look at you! That's big."

She rolled her eyes in exhaustion. "Bigger than I thought. I started this wanting to help some of my patients, but the deeper I got into it, the more it required. I got a few organizations to help, and some of my friends who run their own private practices are going to participate, but I'm almost at the point where I'll be glad when this is over."

"Don't say that. Sometimes the fun is in the journey."

"That's true, but the rest is at the end."

They shared a laugh as the bartender set their drinks in front of them. A few minutes later, a young, petite waitress approached them and placed her hand on Reggie's shoulder. "Mr. Morgan? Your table is ready."

"Thanks," he replied. He looked at Alexis and lifted his hand toward the table. "After you."

"Thank you," she said with a smile. Once they were seated, she remarked, "You know your little waitress friend rolled her eyes at me when you turned your head. I think she wants you for herself."

Reggie laughed and waved off the comment. "I ain't nobody. Don't nobody want me."

"Whatever."

"Do I detect a little bit of jealousy?"

Alexis smirked. "Please. I don't have anything to be jealous of."

He shot her a flirtatious smile. "You don't love me no more?"

She nearly choked on her drink. "I don't think so."

"Not even a little bit?" he asked, holding his index finger and thumb close together.

"Uh-uh, so you better get your little friend's phone number."

Reggie leaned back, undaunted. "Still mean as hell."

"Just real."

"Okay, *real*, so tell me why you called me today. I gave you my number almost two months ago."

She took another sip from her drink, but before she could reply, the waitress came to take their orders. They each placed their orders; then Reggie quickly returned to the business at hand. "I ain't forgot. Answer the question."

"What question?" Alexis asked innocently, her index finger slowly tracing the rim of her glass.

"Oh, so now you have amnesia."

"What are you talking about?" she asked with a grimace.

Reggie could read the sarcasm all over her face, but it was nothing new for him. If he could handle Alexis when she was a twenty-year-old wild child, he surely could handle this more refined woman sitting in front of him now. The jitters he had felt when he walked into her office two months ago were a thing of the past. "All right, keep being difficult. I'll let you answer my question when you're good and ready."

Alexis smiled and took another sip from her drink. They then stared at each other, each practically daring the other to blink first. Most men would have found the entire ordeal a frustrating hot mess and would have ended the drama before it could get started. However, Reggie was never one to give up easily.

"This place is beautiful, isn't it?" Alexis asked, her eyes scanning the pictures scattered throughout the restaurant.

"Yeah, it is," Reggie replied. He still wished Alexis would stop playing with him, but he knew she would come around sooner or later. "This is one of my favorite spots, although I haven't been here in a while."

"Why is that?"

"Between football and other stuff, I just haven't had the time or energy to go out, so I must say that you are a welcome distraction."

She smiled. Reggie smiled back once he was sure her action was genuine.

"Glad I could help," she said.

"Me, too."

Their food arrived, and the table went silent as they each blessed their food and savored the first few bites.

"So, what's this other stuff you've been dealing with?" Alexis asked after a few long moments of silence.

Reggie laughed, knowing she couldn't hold back her curiosity for long. He had planned to tell her about his impending divorce tonight, but he wasn't sure how to bring it up without making it sound like an announcement. By planting a piece of ambiguous information, he was sure she would take the bait.

"Now, how are you gonna ask me some personal information, and you still haven't answered my question from earlier?"

Alexis smiled again and took a big bite from her fish. She took her time chewing. Once she finally swallowed, she replied, "You got me."

"You gotta give a little to get a little," he pointed out. "We go back too far for you not to know that."

She laughed. "Okay. I called you because I was curious. I couldn't understand why, after all this time, you had shown up in my office like that. I know we had seen each other a few times, but I also know you've been married for a good while."

"Is that the only reason?"

She smiled again. "Well, there is one more tiny reason."

"And what's that?"

She bit her lip. "Promise not to get mad?"

Reggie contorted his mouth and folded his arms.

"Okay, okay. I was kinda hoping that you would help me with my project."

Reggie's facial expression softened, but his arms remained folded. "Alexis, this isn't a business meeting for you, is it?"

"No, I promise it's not," she said quickly. "It took a lot for me to call you. Shalonda told me I should have called you weeks ago, but I refused. Then I thought about it and figured you might be able to help me, but I didn't want you thinking I was just coming to you for money. Then when I finally called you today, I had such a good time talking to you, that I really wanted to see you."

"And I guess that's where the curiosity comes in," he surmised.

She shook her head and took another bite from her fish. "I knew you wouldn't believe me."

"I'm just saying," Reggie said, "I get people every

day asking me to help them with something. I was just hoping tonight could be a night without all of that. You know, just two old friends having dinner."

"Isn't that what we're doing?"

"Yeah, but now that I think about it, you didn't waste any time bringing up that project when you first got here."

Alexis glared at him. "I know you're not calling me a liar."

"I didn't call you anything."

"Look, if you didn't want to know the truth, you shouldn't have asked. You don't have to help me with a damn thing. I'll do it on my own."

Reggie smirked at her and finished his drink in one gulp. He then signaled to the waitress to bring him another. Remembering he still had a game the next day, he shoveled some food into his mouth to counteract the alcohol. Tomorrow's game was too important, and he couldn't afford a replay of his pathetic performance against the Panthers. "Let's be real, Alexis. If you could do it yourself, you wouldn't have come to me. Now, let's enjoy our dinner and go back to having a pleasant conversation. I really don't feel like fighting tonight."

Alexis looked at him in confusion. On the inside, Reggie gloated, knowing he'd shut her down. Maybe life had given him a little bit of growth, too. But his small victory would have to be short-lived. He had to change the subject quickly or else Alexis would shut down tighter than a bank after six o'clock.

"Excuse me, Mr. Morgan."

Reggie and Alexis both looked up at the same time and found a woman dressed in a tight minidress and too much weave standing over them. Alexis made a face, but tried to hide it while Reggie sat up straight in his chair and cleared his throat. "Can I help you?"

The woman stole a quick look at Alexis and rolled

her eyes before replying, "My friends and me was just about to leave, but I was hoping you would sign this napkin for us."

Reggie looked again at Alexis, who had propped her chin on her hand and seemed to be enjoying how he would handle this situation. "Um, Miss—"

"Charlene."

"Charlene, I'm sorry, but I'm in the middle of dinner with a good friend of mine."

"I know, and I'm sorry, but I figured since she didn't look like your wife that it was nothing serious," the woman said, stealing another glance at Alexis.

"Uh," Alexis hiccupped.

Reggie's eyes grew as big as saucers, as he prayed to God that Alexis wouldn't go off. A quick flashback of him carrying her out of Tabu popped into his mind. He looked around the restaurant, hoping this woman hadn't caused a scene. Only the couple at the next table seemed to take an interest in the conversation. "Uh, um, Miss Charlene, I don't think who I'm having dinner with is any of your business. This lady is a good friend of mine, and I'm not gonna have you stand here disrespecting her like that."

"Uuum," Charlene said. "I guess she *is* a good friend. Y'all have a good night."

With that, she strutted toward the door where her two girlfriends awaited her. After a few words, they all left the restaurant in a huff.

"That bitch had her nerve," Alexis said.

"Don't worry, girl," said the lady at the next table. "It looks like he had your back. I wish a bitch would approach my man like that."

"You ain't gotta worry about all that," her date said. "That ain't even your business."

Reggie and Alexis laughed at the couple and returned to their meals.

"Thanks for handling your business," Alexis said once she recovered from her laughter. "I guess your wife has to put up with that all the time."

"More like I have to put up with that from her," Reggie corrected. He hadn't meant to spill the beans this way, but there was no time like the present.

"*Que paso?*"

"That girl has a fan club that can outdo mine anytime," he replied, shaking his head.

"You know, now that you mention it, I have seen her in a magazine before," Alexis said. "She's very pretty."

"And she knows it. Too well."

"Uh-oh. Sounds like trouble in paradise."

"Girl, you don't know the half of it."

"She cheating?"

"Every chance she gets. I'm actually in the process of divorcing her."

"Oh," Alexis said. "Sorry to hear that."

"It's all good."

"How do you know she's cheating?"

Reggie booted his mouth again at Alexis and commenced to telling her the whole story, including her Internet pictures, his impending retirement, and the athletes who made it no secret that they'd been with Nikki. He also divulged his fight for DeShawn and how he wondered if the custody battle was worth the child's well-being. He even wondered aloud if he even deserved to be loved, since he'd never been successful in that area.

"Wow," Alexis said. "You've been through a lot the past couple of years."

"You ain't bullshittin'."

"So I guess there's no chance that you two will work things out."

"Alexis, there's a better chance of Osama bin Laden flying here and having lunch with Mayor Nagin."

Alexis let out a loud laugh, then quickly tried to contain it when she saw some of the other patrons turn and look at her. Even the couple next to them thought she'd lost her mind. "Reggie, you are crazy."

"Just telling the truth."

"I hear you."

"So, tell me what's going on with Alexis," Reggie said, hoping she'd mention the status between her and Jamar. It was funny. He'd started off wanting nothing more than friendship from Alexis. But after talking and laughing with her, he realized how much he'd missed these times with her. Maybe it was vulnerability from his impending divorce, or maybe it was nostalgia, but something made him want to explore this woman further.

"Not much to say," she said, shrugging her shoulders. "You already know I'm still living at home while I get my practice off the ground. I did almost get married once, but that didn't work out too well."

"What happened?"

"We evacuated to Houston, which is where he's from. We were supposed to move back to New Orleans eventually, but he got a job there and refused to come back with me."

"So you left him."

"Yep, especially when he told me he didn't need me because I couldn't give him a baby."

"Damn," Reggie said, noticing her roll her eyes as if she hadn't meant to divulge that much information. "You can't have kids?"

Alexis shook her head slowly, seemingly struggling to hold back tears.

"He still didn't have to jump off like that," he said, hoping his words would soften the year-old blow.

"It's over now," she replied. "I'm over it. I'm even seeing someone new. He's a good guy."

*So it begins*, he thought. "Sounds like love is in the air."

She smiled weakly. "I don't know about that, but I enjoy being with him."

"That's good. Is he a doctor, too?"

"No, he's a lawyer."

"You two serious?"

"I don't know yet," Alexis said quickly.

Reggie already knew the answers to these questions, but he convinced himself that he needed to confirm them just in case he tried to pursue something with this woman. He hated to admit it, but the more he talked with Alexis, the more he knew he wanted more than just friendship with her. But how could he honestly pursue a relationship with a woman who was already in a relationship, while he himself was still trying to get out of his own? How would he be being fair to Alexis by making her sneak around with him while he finalized his divorce? And could he really convince her to leave Jamar for him? Even if he could, he knew there was no way in hell he could make her stand by while he worked through his issues. The way things looked, he would just have to settle for being the good buddy.

# Chapter 15

# This Christmas

"Merry Christmas!" Brenda sang into the phone.

"Merry Christmas, yourself, sister-cuz," Alexis replied. "How you doing?"

"Just fabulous," Brenda said, taking a sip from her hot chocolate. "My baby just bought me a new computer."

"Dude, you're getting a Dell?" Alexis exclaimed, mocking the boy on the popular computer commercial.

Brenda laughed. "Girl, this one is better than a Dell. This thing has every gadget you can think of. It even has a built-in webcam. My man hooked me up big time!"

"All right, now. Do your thang," Alexis congratulated. "So, what are you guys up to?"

Brenda cleared her throat, wondering if bringing up a certain name would dampen the mood. It had been a long time, but some wounds didn't heal over time. "Andrea and Christopher surprised us last night and spent the holiday with us."

"That's nice," Alexis replied absently. "How are they doing?"

"They're good. Little Latrise is getting so big, and Dee is still the principal at her school."

"Oh yeah? How old is she now? Should be about seven or eight now."

"She's eight, and she looks just like Andrea."

"That's nice. I'm glad they're happy," Alexis replied quietly. "But anyway, I was just calling to wish you a merry Christmas."

"I'm sorry. I'm just going on and on. How are you and Aunt Mary doing?"

"We're good. Mama cooked dinner last night, so we're about to tear into that. Roman brought his little girlfriend over, and Frank's brother is over here, so we have a full house."

"What about Jamar? Is he coming over this time?"

"Yeah, he'll be over here later."

Brenda scrunched her eyebrows in suspicion. "You don't sound happy about that."

"No, I am," Alexis said. "It's just that, that, I've been spending the last couple of days with Reggie and now I'm all confused."

"Hold up, back up. You've been spending time with who?"

"Reggie."

"When did this happen?"

"Well, Shalonda told me I should ask for his help with my health fair. I wasn't going to call him, but when I saw how much this thing was going to cost me, I figured I would call him," Alexis explained. "But we wound up having such a good time that we've been communicating ever since."

"So are you two together now?"

"No, we're just friends. But, Bren, it feels so good

to be with Reggie again. He still knows me so well, and I feel like I don't have to pretend with him."

"Did you feel like you had to pretend with Jamar?"

"Not really, but Jamar doesn't know everything about my past, so I'm careful what I bring up in front of him. But Reggie knows all about the abortion, and how things were in college. I've never been able to talk that freely with Jamar."

"Have you tried?"

"No," Alexis admitted.

"Then how do you know you can't talk to him?" Brenda asked. "From what you've told me, that man loves you. You're not being fair to him or yourself if you're not giving him a chance. You can't split your time between him and Reggie for too long."

"It's not like I'm trying to. Why do you think Jamar is coming over here, and not Reggie?"

"I don't know," Brenda replied with a shrug. "Isn't Reggie married?"

"He's getting a divorce."

"Girl, every man who's cheated on his wife claims he's getting a divorce. How is Reggie any different?"

"Because I know Reggie. Believe me, I thought the same thing about him, but I think I actually believe him."

"Well, let's just hope decent and honest Reggie hasn't changed over the years."

"Bren, whatcha doing, girl?" Andrea yelled up the steps. "We're about to play Taboo, and you know we can't let these men think they're gonna win."

"I'm coming!" Brenda yelled back. "Girl, lemme go and get back to our company, but this conversation isn't over. Just tell me one thing before I go, though."

"No, we haven't slept together, Brenda."

"Just checking, don't get all huffy," Brenda replied

with a laugh. "I'll call you tomorrow. Better yet, call me when you open my present."

"I'll do that," Alexis said. "Mama won't let us open presents until after dinner."

"Girl, I know Aunt Mary like a book. That's why I know you haven't seen the gift yet," Brenda said with a laugh.

Once she hung up with her cousin, Brenda trotted back downstairs to her company. Darnell was passing out drinks while Christopher and Andrea sat together on the sofa watching their daughter Latrise sing a song she'd learned in Sunday school. Once she finished, the adults gave her applause, as if they hadn't already heard the song six times before. The little girl took a bow, and then Elizabeth grabbed her hand and led her to her bedroom.

"Call us when it's time for cake!" Elizabeth called back before closing the door to her room.

The adults laughed.

"Girl, she is so grown," Andrea said with a smile.

"I know," Brenda agreed. "She's going to be a teen-ager before I know it."

Darnell grabbed his heart and shook his head. "Don't say stuff like that."

They laughed again, although Brenda knew they all harbored the same fears about their daughters.

"So, Chris, I never did ask you how my boy is doing," Darnell said as he set up the cards for Taboo.

"Man, you ain't gonna believe this," Christopher said with a laugh. He took his arm from around his wife to help make his point. "Your boy, Byron, is finally getting married."

"What?" Darnell asked in surprise. It had been about five years since they'd spoken, but the Byron he knew and was once thick as thieves with had sworn that he'd never get married because he loved the game too much. That Byron could be with three different women in the same week and walk away with no worries as he looked for the next victim. Byron respected marriage, but he knew there was no way he was ready to make that type of commitment, and didn't desire to any time soon. "When did this minor miracle occur?"

"He met this shorty named Rayna, and the sista didn't take no shit," Christopher explained. "She told him it was going to be her only, or else she was gone."

"Damn, and he went for that?" Darnell asked.

"Not at first, but when he saw that she was a good girl, he went ahead and gave her a chance," Andrea replied. "I told him he better not lose that girl. She could cook *and* go to church."

"That was certainly different from the women he used to date back in the day," Brenda commented. "I remember the oceanfront was his main place to pick up girls."

"Or the club," Andrea added.

"Or blacksingles dot com if he was really in a rut," Darnell said with a laugh. "Remember that one girl who claimed she looked like Tyra Banks and she showed up for their date looking more like Lloyd Banks?"

"Yeah, and she had the beard and everything!" Brenda added with a cackle. Everyone howled in laughter.

"Y'all gonna get off my brother," Christopher snapped.

"Oh, boy, lighten up," Andrea retorted, tapping him on his leg. "We all know your brother got around. Shoot, you did, too, back in college."

Christopher cleared his throat quickly. "That was then, this is now. Byron is happy now, so we should be happy for him."

"I know," Andrea said. "He came and talked with

me about her. He's really into her. He just had to be sure he wasn't making a mistake."

"You two sure have gotten close over the years," Christopher replied with a sniff.

Brenda caught her friend's eyes dart quickly before she said, "Byron needed a woman's opinion. Who else was he going to ask?"

"Yeah, all right," he replied, turning his attention back to Darnell. "So, you gonna come to the wedding? He's getting married in June."

"How long has he been seeing her?" Darnell asked, fully aware of the elephant standing in the room. Brenda had never hidden anything from him.

"About a year now," Christopher said. "The wedding's going to be in VA Beach."

"They ain't wastin' no time, are they?" Darnell said, squeezing his wife's hand.

"Shit, I said the same thing," Christopher replied.

"Well, when it's right, it's right," Brenda said. "And yes, we will definitely be at the wedding."

"Girl, you sure you're gonna have the time?" Andrea asked. "You're moving to New Orleans in a couple of months."

"Yeah, and you're still coming down to help me move, right?"

"Of course, girl," Andrea replied with a smile. "You know I got your back. And Chris is coming, too."

Christopher's head snapped at his wife at the sound of his name. "I am?"

"Now, you don't expect me to drive down here by myself and do all that packing without you, do you?"

"Doesn't the military move you for free?" Christopher asked Darnell.

"That's true," Darnell replied, "but look at it this way: if you come out, you'll be in town for Mardi Gras and we can score some tickets to the All Star Game. You know it's gonna be in New Orleans this year."

"That's true," Christopher said, rubbing his mustache. "In fact, I might be able to get us some free tickets through the newspaper."

"That's right, Mr. Big-Time Journalist," Darnell exclaimed. "I forgot about that."

"Lemme work on something and I'll let you know."

"Bribing my husband with sports," Andrea said. "Whoever said the way to a man's heart is through his stomach obviously didn't know Christopher Lee."

The group laughed again, making Brenda thankful that the topic of Andrea and Byron had been dropped. The kiss they shared thirteen years ago was a thing of the past, but Andrea had always felt guilty about it. It had come at a low point in Andrea's life. She'd just found out about Christopher's affair with Alexis, and she'd pushed everyone, including Brenda, out of her life. So when Byron, who was going through his own issues with his brother, came over one night to check on her, they both gave in to a moment of weakness. Nothing more than a kiss happened between them, but it was enough that the two of them could never look each other in the eye when Christopher was around. They each tried to pretend nothing had happened, but it just wasn't that simple. To this day, Christopher had never learned the truth, but he always suspected something wasn't right.

"Hey!" Darnell snapped. "There's absolutely nothing wrong with sports. It's a good, pure, and wholesome American way of life."

Brenda looked at her husband as if he'd lost his mind and smacked him on the back of his head. "Boy, shut the hell up!"

The group laughed again.

"Okay, we gonna play this game, or what?" Andrea asked, grabbing the cardholder.

"What makes you think y'all are going first?" Christopher asked, trying to take the cards away from his wife.

She snatched them out of his reach. "Ladies always go first."

Darnell laughed. "Man, let them go ahead. No matter who goes first, you know we're gonna win."

"True, true," he relented.

Brenda stood up quickly. "Before we get started, Dee, let's go in the kitchen and go over our strategy."

"What?" the men asked in shock.

"Aw, just chill," Andrea said. "We'll be right back. Don't get mad because we know how to make a plan."

"Let it go, bro," Christopher said, waving his hand at them. "Y'all just hurry up."

"Be right back," Brenda assured them.

The two women had barely reached the kitchen when Brenda grabbed Andrea's arm. "You are one slick woman."

"What are you talking about?" Andrea asked.

"All these years and Chris still hasn't figured out that you and Byron kissed."

"Shhh! And he won't find out. I didn't sleep with his brother; it was just one funky kiss that didn't mean anything."

"If it didn't mean anything, then why not tell him?"

"Because it didn't mean anything!" Andrea repeated. "Just leave it alone. Why are you so concerned about it?"

"Because you know Chris would go ballistic if he found out the wrong way. It would be better if it came from you."

"How is it going to come out the wrong way, Bren? The only people who know about it will never say anything, right?"

Brenda put her hands up and stepped back in

retaliation. "Okay, Andrea. You're right. It happened a long time ago. I just hope you're right."

"I am," Andrea reassured her. "We're going to be fine. Just relax."

"Daddy!" DeShawn exclaimed. "A Wii!"

Reggie laughed as he watched his little boy run around the room, holding the computer game over his head as if he'd won the lottery.

"Can we hook it up now?" he asked.

"Why don't we wait until we finish dinner?" Reggie suggested. "Then we'll see if your cousins want to play, too."

"Ooookay," the little boy whined.

They had planned on having a quiet Christmas at home, but Shirley Morgan, Reggie's mother, wouldn't hear of it. "I'll be damned if you and that boy sit in that big old house feeling sorry for yourselves," she'd told him. "Now as soon as you finish your game, y'all pack up and come spend Christmas with your family."

"Okay, but I'm staying in my own house," Reggie stated.

"The hell you will," Shirley retorted. "You ain't got decoration the first over there. That house is fine. You two can stay here in your old room. Shawn deserves to have a nice holiday."

Reggie knew his mother was right, but he really didn't feel like packing up and driving out to Atlanta. He didn't feel like answering any questions about why he was divorcing Nikki. And he damn sure didn't feel like being cooped up in a room when he had an empty four-bedroom house sitting across town.

Yet he had to admit that being around his family was a welcome distraction after their 38–23 loss to the Eagles. The team had played their hearts out, which made it even more of a disappointing loss. They still had hopes of making it to the play-offs if they beat Chicago next week, but with morale being as low as it was, it didn't seem likely.

Reggie needed to get his mind off football for a while, so the day after the game, he and DeShawn rode to the Louis Armstrong New Orleans International Airport and flew first class into Atlanta and his mother's home cooking.

As happy as he was about seeing his family again, he was a little disappointed that he wouldn't be able to see Alexis. After the game Sunday, he called her and asked her to meet him at the Aquarium of the Americas. He then called his babysitter, Necee, and asked her to watch DeShawn for a few hours.

They spent the rest of the afternoon strolling through the aquarium while catching up on each other's lives. Reggie had even come this close to telling her the truth about his relationship with Jamar, but every time he looked in his former girlfriend's eyes, he lost the nerve. He knew he had to say something, but when would be the right moment? Besides, he told himself, she made it clear that she cared about Jamar, so maybe there was no need to say anything.

A knock at the door shook Reggie from his thoughts. "Yeah!"

"Uncle Reggie!" yelled a teenager's voice. It was his older sister's son, Kevin. "Grandma Shirl said come down and eat."

"All right," he replied. "We'll be down in a minute."

"Okay, but hurry up. I'm hungry as hell."

"You'll be all right," Reggie snapped. "You probably had a plate already, anyway."

"That's not the point," Kevin said.

Once he was sure Kevin was gone, Reggie turned back to his son. "You ready to eat, big man?"

"Can we still hook up my Wii after dinner?"

"Promise."

"Then let's get some food!"


"Merry Christmas, baby," Jamar whispered into Alexis's ear as she took a seat on the floor in front of him. She almost sat between his legs, but once she saw the disapproving look radiating from Mary's face, she quickly scooted next to his left leg and leaned against the couch.

She looked up and smiled. "You've told me that five times since you got here."

"I know, but it hasn't gotten old yet," Jamar said.

"Dinner was on point, Mama," Roman exclaimed as he walked into the living room.

Tameka followed close behind him, rubbing her full stomach. "Yeah, Ms. Mary, I can't even think about eating another thing."

"Well, I'm certainly glad you enjoyed it," Mary said, leaning back in her favorite recliner.

"Can we open presents now?" Roman asked like an expectant five-year-old.

"Where's your daddy?"

"Out on the porch with Uncle Charles," Roman said.

"Tell him to come on in here so we can get this over with. I'm tired now," Mary ordered.

Just as Roman walked toward the door, Alexis heard her cell phone ringing from her bedroom. "That's my phone. I'll be right back."

She scampered to her room, then jumped on her bed, wondering who would be calling her cell on Christmas Day. Shalonda was with her family and would have called the house, and Jamar was with her, so it obviously couldn't be him. She hoped none of her patients had an emergency. However, once she saw the number, her big smile stretched across her face. "Hello?"

"Hey, you," Reggie greeted.

"Hey, yourself," she whispered. "Merry Christmas."

"Same to you," he replied. "You enjoying the holiday?"

"Yes, but I can't talk right now. Jamar is over here."

"Oh, okay, well, I won't keep you long," Reggie stammered. "I just didn't want the day to go by without wishing you a merry Christmas."

Alexis smiled again. "Thanks. How's your little boy doing?"

"Gettin' spoiled as hell," he replied with a laugh. "I have something for you when I get back. Can I see you tomorrow night?"

"Boy, you gonna cause my man to break up with me if I keep sneaking off from him like this," she remarked, glancing at the door to make sure no one had walked in on her.

"Please?" he begged. "I miss you."

This was one of those moments Alexis was thankful for her dark skin, because if she was lighter, her blush would have been obvious. "I'll try to work something out."

"You do that," Reggie said. "I'll let you go so you get back to your man."

"Um, okay, I'll, uh, see you tomorrow."

"Looking forward to it."

Alexis pressed the END button and stared into space. She thought back to Brenda's words. It had only been a few days, but the feelings she once held for Reggie were becoming real again. When she first began dating him years ago, she was very carefree about the relationship. But the relationship ended before she realized how much she really loved him. She wondered if she would have felt this giddy over his phone call back then.

."Alexis!"

The sound of her brother's voice nearly made her jump out of her skin. "I'm comin'!"

She walked back into the living room, where Frank, Mary, and Roman were already tearing open their gifts. "Y'all started without me?"

"Shit, girl, how long was we s'posed to wait?" Mary snapped. "You acted like you forgot about us."

"Sorry," Alexis said, taking a seat next to Jamar.

"Everything all right?" he asked, placing his arm around her shoulders.

She nodded nonchalantly and replied, "It's all good."

Roman ran up to her and gave her a long kiss on the cheek. "Thanks for the Jordans, sis!"

The sudden display of affection nearly knocked Alexis off the couch. She didn't know whether to hug him back or hold on for balance. "You're welcome, lil' bro."

"Girl, I'm so happy, I don't even care if you call me little, even though I'm still a grown man!" Roman remarked. He then pulled a smaller box from his baggy pocket and handed it to her. "Here's a little something for you for all you've done for me."

Alexis gave her brother a look of understanding as she took the perfectly wrapped box from him. She unwrapped the box and pulled out a gold bracelet. "Aw, Roman. This is beautiful."

"You deserve it, sis," he said, giving her another hug.

"Lord, is that our children?" Frank asked Mary.

"It sure looks like 'em, but I ain't too sure," she replied.

"It's us," Roman said. "We've just finally come to an understanding."

"I wonder how long this is gonna last," Mary said.

"Who's taking bets?" Frank asked. Everyone except Alexis and Roman raised their hands.

"Aw, that's messed up, y'all," Alexis said with a laugh.

She turned to Roman. "I guess we'll have to show 'em better than we can tell 'em."

Everyone laughed again. Jamar hugged her reassuringly. "I was just playing, sweetie. And your brother gave you a nice gift. It'll go good with what's in this box."

He handed her a small felt gift box that he'd retrieved from his jacket pocket. Alexis took the box from him carefully. "What is this?"

"Open it and see," Jamar told her.

Everyone held their breath as Alexis opened the box. She then let out a sigh of relief when she found a pair of solid gold hoop earrings.

Jamar laughed. "I know what you thought it was, but you're not ready for that yet."

"You ain't never lyin'," Roman remarked, placing his arm around Tameka.

"See?" Frank said when he saw Alexis's head snap toward Roman. "You startin' already. Get out of your sister's business."

Jamar laughed again. "Don't worry, it's coming one day, just not today. I just wanted to give her something to go with this."

With that, he pulled out a gold herringbone necklace and clasped it around his girlfriend's neck.

"You are just full of surprises," Alexis said with a smile. She hugged him tightly. "Thank you, sweetie."

Mary then picked up an envelope and handed it to her daughter. "This is from Brenda. She made me promise not to let you open it until today."

"So this is the mystery gift. She told me to call her when I opened it," Alexis said, opening the envelope. Inside it was a letter. She read it silently, but as she got to the end, tears streamed down her face. "That girl is too much!"

"What is it?" Jamar asked.

"Is she pregnant again?" Mary asked.

"Mama, you know good and well Brenda's not pregnant," Alexis said as she wiped her face with her fingers. "Something tells me you had everything to do with this."

"What are you talking about?" Mary asked, trying in vain to hide her smile.

"This letter says that Brenda is sorry she and Darnell couldn't afford to make a financial donation to my health fair, but she still wanted to help," Alexis explained. "So she made a few phone calls, and on the day of the fair, I'm going to have three hundred volunteers from Dillard, Tulane, Xavier, and UNO helping me out. On top of that, the volunteers from Dillard and Tulane are medical students!"

She fanned dry the new tears that streamed down her face. "How did she know I would need this kind of help, Mommy?"

"Let's just say more people than you think understand what you're going through," Mary said. "The day you told me about this idea you had, I called your cousin and asked her to make a few phone calls for you."

"Mama, I love you," Alexis exclaimed, rising from the sofa. She rushed over to her mother and hugged her tighter than she ever had. "Thank you."

"That's what mamas are for. Now go call your cousin."

# Chapter 16

# Tell Me
# Your Secret

"Hey, lady," Alexis greeted as she walked into her office.

"Hey, Alexis," Latonya said, looking up from the book she was reading.

"We missed you last night," Alexis said, picking up the appointment book. She flipped to December 26 and scanned her appointments for the day. Two in the morning and three in the afternoon. A fairly slow day, but it was to be expected on the day after Christmas.

"Don't worry, I betcha somebody's gonna walk in with a child with a stomachache from all that food yesterday," Latonya said. "And I went to my man's house yesterday, and you know my mama ain't missin' a chance to cook Christmas dinner."

"Yeah, that's true," Alexis said, closing the book.

She reached for her lab coat and slipped it on. "Who all came over?"

"Quisha and Auntie Mildred, Donna and them, and Victor and his wife."

"Oh yeah?" Alexis asked with a smile. "I ain't seen Victor since the Essence Fest in Houston. What that boy been up to?"

"Same old, same old," Latonya said. "Still hustlin', tryin' to get something for free."

They laughed together.

"Yeah, that's him," Alexis agreed.

"Dr. White! Thank God you're here!"

The commotion nearly made the cousins jump into combat position. Once their hearts returned to their chests, they found Tavarious Johnson and his mother standing in the doorway. Tavarious, who held a handkerchief over his mouth and nose, was in the middle of a bad coughing fit. His mother, tears streaming down her hardened face, held his hand tightly as she tried to console him. No one moved an inch.

"Dr. White, T is worse," Ms. Johnson explained, finally breaking the ice. She moved closer to Alexis and Latonya, gently pulling Tavarious by the hand.

Alexis, finally shaken from her stupor, walked quickly toward Tavarious to ask him what was wrong. However, she was greeted by large spots of blood once she moved the handkerchief from his face. "What happened?"

"He woke up like this," Ms. Johnson cried.

Instantly, Alexis wished she hadn't given Ms. Kay the day off. It was times like this when she needed her wisdom and calm spirit. Without her, Alexis could feel the panic rising inside her. She swallowed hard and turned to Latonya. "Take him into the examining room."

\* \* \*

Alexis was still shaking as she pulled into the Lakeside Shopping Center's parking lot. She'd managed to take care of her five scheduled patients, but her mind never left the scare that Tavarious had given her.

It turned out that he had developed hemoptysis, resulting from a serious bronchial infection. She wanted to choke his mother for remaining in that fucking trailer. How many ways did she have to tell her that trailer wasn't good for the boy's health? Even though the weather had gotten cold, the trailers still posed a threat because of the heating system. The heat would just intensify the formaldehyde in the cabinets and wood that surrounded them.

"This is why this city needs this health fair," Alexis said aloud. "I'm not about to have one of my patients die on me because his parents refuse to face the facts."

She thought back to her mother and how she struggled to rebuild Grandma Margaret's house. If she could just convince her to sell the house, maybe the Johnsons would purchase it and move out of the FEMA trailers for good. But could they even afford a major purchase like a house? Alexis knew her mother wasn't just going to give it away, and she wouldn't dare let her be taken advantage of.

But buying a house was currently a pipe dream. She needed to think of a way to get Tavarious the medical treatment he needed without it costing his mother an arm and a leg. And the health fair seemed to be her only option. It was the only way she could afford to give Tavarious the treatment he needed. And maybe the information distributed at the fair wouldn't fall on deaf ears. Just maybe if someone else told Ms. Johnson what she needed to hear, she might actually listen.

Alexis glanced at her watch, despite the thoughts that tormented her. As much as she cared about Tavarious, she couldn't wait to see Reggie. His smile would be just the distraction she needed from this day of madness.

She was still ten minutes early, but it was just enough time to stroll on her own time into the mall and maybe even buy a daiquiri. One thing she loved about New Orleans was the number of real daiquiri shops in the city. New Orleans was the only city she knew where she could pull into a drive-through to buy a 180-octane, and she didn't mean gas. This was the drink of the bravest of New Orleanians.

As she walked through the shopping center, Alexis wondered why Reggie would want to meet in such a crowded area. December 26 was known throughout the country as a premium shopping day, with consumers looking for after-Christmas deals. Then she figured that maybe he chose the area because it would be so crowded that there would be less of a chance of them being noticed. She had to admit that if one more person interrupted their conversation asking for an autograph, she was going to scream!

Just as she'd figured, Lakeside was packed. She could barely walk three feet without bumping shoulders with someone. It was amazing how people could be slaves to twenty-five percent off! But then, she knew she couldn't judge because the only reason she owned half the designer purses she did was that she had a friend at the navy base, where items were at least twenty percent cheaper than in the rest of the city. And if that same item was another forty to fifty percent off, she felt she'd be a fool to pass it up!

Besides the shoppers, there were a number of teenagers just hanging out. Many window-shopped, but a few sat on the benches in the center of the walkways and seemed to scope out the customers. Alexis tried not to feel uppity, but she couldn't help holding her favorite black designer purse just a little tighter.

Slowly, but surely, she made her way to the daiquiri shop, ordered her drink, and strolled over to the food court, where she was to meet Reggie. She checked her watch again. It was now a quarter after seven, which meant he was fifteen minutes late. Alexis looked around impatiently, hoping Reggie would walk up any minute to save her from this madness.

"Um, hello," greeted a young-looking man dressed in an oversized T-shirt and even bigger faded blue jeans. "You lookin' good this evenin'."

Alexis rolled her eyes up to where the man stood. His skin was just a touch darker than hers, but what threw her off was his sparkling gold grill and wild cornrows. She pictured herself walking down Canal Street with him and nearly laughed. "Uh, thanks."

"Why a pretty lady such as yourself sittin' here by your lonesome?" he asked, taking an uninvited seat across from her.

"Well, actually, I'm waiting for someone."

"Well, I can keep you company till your friend shows up."

Alexis smiled nervously as she looked behind him. Three similarly dressed men were standing a few feet away, seeming to enjoy the show. She wondered if her so-called company had made a bet with them that he would walk away with her "digits." *Sorry to disappoint you.*

"I think he'll be here pretty soon," she assured him. "He's just running a little late."

"Sounds like your friend is married," the man said. "You know you deserve better than that."

"I know, but I'm just gonna wait for him, okay?"

"Why? He got some kinda hold on you?"

Alexis had grown disgusted. Why couldn't some men take no for an answer? She tried being nice, but this idiot was too dense to receive the message. She looked at him and scrunched her eyebrows. "Why is it a woman can't say no and mean it? Maybe I'm just not fuckin' interested."

The man cocked his head back in shock. "I was just tryin' to make conversation with your seditty ass. You ain't gotta act all stank."

"Oh, so now I'm seditty?" Alexis asked, wondering if this guy even knew what seditty meant. "You need to walk on and find some chickenhead to bother."

"So what, you think you too good for me or something?"

"You know what? I am," Alexis snapped, hearing the group of men behind him cackle like a group of hens. She thought only women laughed that way. "Now you need to walk on and let me finish my drink in peace."

The man rose from the seat and glared at Alexis. "That's what's wrong with you bitches now. Y'all make a little money and fuckin' act like your shit don't stink."

"Who the fuck are you calling a bitch?" Alexis snapped, keeping her seat. She was pissed, but she was no fool. This man could probably wrap her up like a pretzel. "I think it's time for you to go."

The man moved closer to Alexis and put his finger in her face, but before he could utter the words formulating in his brain, a man's voice interrupted him.

"Hey, man, she ain't gonna be too many more bitches."

They both looked up to find Reggie standing behind Alexis. She took a sigh of relief, then took another sip from her drink. The man, on the other hand, wasn't impressed. "So what, you Captain Save-A-Ho, or somethin'?"

Alexis started to curse at the man again for speaking to her that way but Reggie placed his hand on her shoulder, subtly telling her to let him handle the situation.

"You ain't gotta worry about all that, man," he said,

keeping his composure. "All you gotta do is leave the lady alone."

"Come on, man," one of the man's friends said, pulling him away from the table. "It ain't even worth all that."

The man listened to his friend and silently backed away. Once he'd backed out of the food court, he turned and walked away, but not before calling out, "Stuck-up bitch!"

Alexis rolled her eyes in disgust as Reggie sat in the seat once occupied by the man with the wild cornrows.

"I just can't leave you anywhere, can I?" Reggie asked with a smile. "You all right?"

"Now, you know I can handle myself," Alexis replied, "but if you had been on time, that drama would never have happened."

"I'm sorry," Reggie said, placing his hands in the prayer position and fixing his face to look like an innocent schoolboy. "Do you forgive me?"

Alexis folded her arms and looked away. "Um-um."

"Aw, come on," Reggie pushed, still smiling. "I was late trying to make sure your Christmas present was right."

"You got it out of here?" Alexis asked in surprise.

"No, I got it while I was home, but I got the engraving done here. I'll bet you you'll like it."

"We'll see."

"Mean ass," Reggie said, sliding a black velvet box toward her.

"I ain't marrying your ass," Alexis snapped, grabbing the box before Reggie could take it back.

"Good, because I never asked you to. I have enough problems. Now open the damned box!"

"No, you didn't just curse at me," Alexis said as she opened the box. It wasn't a ring, but the diamond tennis bracelet shone just as brightly. She could do nothing but smile. "It's beautiful."

Reggie smiled boldly, seemingly proud of himself. "I told you you'd like it. Now read the inscription."

She pulled the bracelet out of the box. "How did you put an inscription on diamonds?"

"You didn't know? This is the new millennium. You can do anything these days."

She looked at him quizzically and turned the bracelet every which way, trying to find the message. "I don't see anything."

"You can't?" he asked. He pulled out a small magnifying glass. "Try it now."

Alexis took the glass and held it close to the bracelet. Instantly, the message "My true blue friend" appeared. Her smile spread almost as instantly. "Aww, this is sweet."

Reggie smiled back, then leaned toward her. "Let me help you put it on."

She admired the shiny stones that now surrounded her wrist. The last diamonds she owned had been attached to the engagement ring that Tony had given her. That one-carat treasure was spectacular, and it really hurt her heart to throw it smack in the middle of his forehead the day she left him. But sometimes that's the price you pay for a broken heart. One thing was for sure, though. No matter how mad she got at Reggie in the future, she was determined that this bracelet would stay bound to her wrist!

"I'm guessin' you really do like it since you haven't taken your eyes off it in the last few minutes," Reggie said, breaking her trance.

"I love it," Alexis said. "You give all your friends gifts like this?"

"Just the special ones."

She frowned slightly, a look that didn't go unnoticed.

"Look," Reggie said, "before you say anything, I know you have a man, and I'm not trying to get in the middle of that. Like I told you before, I want to be your friend. You're a special lady, Alexis, and you deserve the best. And if your man is giving you that, I'm happy for you."

She looked at him suspiciously. "You sure about that?"

"Have I ever lied to you before?" he asked, looking directly into her eyes.

She had to admit that he hadn't. In all the years that she'd known him, she'd never known him to play games with her. Back in the day, she had played more games than the New Orleans Hornets, but Reggie had always been straight with her. She could never figure out why, but she was glad he did. Not many women are blessed to find a man who only knows the truth.

She also had to admit that she was a bit disappointed that he was telling the truth. Although she had deep feelings for Jamar, to the point where she could fall in love with him, she knew a piece of her heart would always belong to Reggie.

She wondered, if Reggie had never come along, would she have completely fallen in love with Jamar? As much as they battled each other, Jamar had given her everything she'd ever asked for in a man. Not only was he generous with his wallet, but he was generous with his time. He told her things no one else knew. And he listened intently whenever she wanted to talk. On top of that, he tried his best to be patient with her as she sorted out her feelings for her failed engagement. She knew she gave him a hard time every chance she got, but she couldn't help it. As tough as she tried to be, she didn't want to be hurt again. Jamar knew and understood that, which actually drew her closer to him.

Then Reggie had to come along and turn all of that upside down. Before he walked into her office, she'd accepted the fact that he was the one who got away. She knew they would never get back together, and she was fine with that. But when he waltzed back into her life, she was no longer sure about anything. She actually even grew afraid to commit to Jamar, thinking Reggie might one day want to be more than friends. But then she wondered if memories could be better than reality. What if being with Reggie now was nothing like what it was when they were back in college? What if he'd turned into a slob? What if he was a control freak? What if the years and past hurts had turned him into a selfish bastard? What if he had a girlfriend in every town? What if there was some chickenhead waiting for the Saints to get to Chicago this weekend so he could break her off? What if? What if? What if?

"Earth to Alexis."

Alexis shook her head and smiled. She knew she was reading a lot into the situation. Maybe Reggie really did just want to be friends. She decided to just enjoy the moment and see what happened. Whatever the case, she'd stay prepared. She refused to let anyone but herself control this situation.

"Irreplaceable" sounded from her purse. She quickly slipped her hand into the purse and pulled her cell phone from the little pocket inside. That ring only meant one person. "Hey, Jamar."

"Hey," he greeted. "Whatcha up to?"

"Um," Alexis stammered, her eyes drilling holes into Reggie. He looked away, but didn't move from the table. She looked down and shifted in her seat. "I'm at Lakeside."

"You okay? You sound distracted."

"Yeah, I just had my hands full."

"Oh, okay, I'ma let you get back to your shopping. I was just calling to tell you to come by later."

"What time?"

"Just call me when you get back from the mall. I don't wanna rush you."

Alexis bit her lip and ran her hand through her hair. "I might be a while, but I'll call you when I get back."

"Do that," Jamar replied.

Alexis pushed END on her phone and stared at Reggie. "You got me lying to my man."

Reggie shrugged. "You didn't lie. You *are* at the mall. And you *will* be a while."

She smirked. "You play with words pretty well for a man who respects the truth."

He smiled. "You can't blame me for wanting to spend time with you."

He then scrunched his eyebrows and looked her in the eye. "You never told Jamar about me?"

Alexis shook her head. "I didn't see any reason to. You and I were together back in college, and we hadn't spoken since. He knew I was engaged to Tony, but I never brought up much more about my past. Plus, he loves the Saints, so I figured telling him you and I dated would just make him bring up a bunch of questions I didn't feel like answering."

Reggie nodded. "I can understand that."

"You ever tell Little Miss Nikki about me?"

"Actually, yes," Reggie replied. "Believe it or not, she was my first real girlfriend after you and I broke up."

Alexis cocked her head back in surprise. "You serious?"

"Yep. I mean, I did kick it with a few girls, but I always figured you and I would get back together."

"Then why didn't we?" Alexis couldn't help but ask.

Reggie shrugged again and shook his head. "I guess pride got in the way. I wanted you to sweat. I mean, you had hurt me bad, and I wanted you to feel what I felt."

She pursed her lips and glared at Reggie. "That's messed up."

"I know, but I was young then. I thought you were

going to beg me, but when you gave up, I figured I might as well move on, too."

Alexis sighed deeply. "I never gave up on wanting you back. I thought you had given up, and I wasn't about to make a fool of myself."

"Wow," Reggie said, tapping the table with his index finger. "Communication can be a motherfucker."

"I know that's right," Alexis agreed, her voice drifting off.

Suddenly Reggie slapped the table and stood up. "Well, that was the past, this is the present. Let's move on to bigger and better subjects."

Alexis blew out some air, thankful for the abrupt change in mood. "Good idea. Lemme tell you what happened at work."

# Chapter 17

# It's Getting Deeper

Jamar checked his watch for what seemed like the tenth time in the last thirty minutes. It was ten thirty-seven. Alexis should have called him at least two hours ago. There was no damned way she could still be at the mall!

This just wasn't like her. They'd had their share of problems, but she'd always been dependable. Even if she couldn't make it, she'd at least call.

But then again, she'd been acting different for the past few days. She seemed more distant than usual. Sometimes he would call, and his messages wouldn't be returned until the next day. And although he was happy to spend Christmas with her, he couldn't help but wonder about that phone call that had kept her away from the family for so long.

Thoughts of her seeing somebody else danced around his head, but he refused to succumb to them. He gave that woman everything she ever wanted and more. Women didn't cheat unless they were missing something, right? At least that was what he was always taught.

He thought about giving her another call, but decided against it. He didn't want to seem desperate. In fact, enough about thinking about her! She obviously wasn't thinking about him, or else she would be there with him.

"I don't know why I put up with her ass sometimes," he mumbled as he walked to the kitchen. He pulled out a Heineken and strolled back to the living room. After turning on the TV, he turned off the light and flopped on his sofa.

He wanted to go out, but it was the middle of the week. He really didn't feel like going to the casino, and the French Quarter was out. Real New Orleanians didn't hang out in the Quarter every day. In fact, most of them hated the area. The sights of drunk tourists, pissy bums, and overcrowded streets got old once he left high school. He felt he was better than that scene now, and only visited the Quarter when entertaining clients and visitors. He had become what many in New Orleans called *bourgie*, and he was proud to wear the badge.

It was this attitude that had attracted him to Alexis a year ago. He was a young, attractive, and successful attorney on the rise, and it only made sense that the woman on his arm be just as attractive and successful. So when he saw the beautiful dark-skinned, good-haired beauty drinking a white wine at the now-closed Jin Jean's Jazz Restaurant and Lounge, he knew he would need to do whatever he could to get her.

After countless phone calls and three bouquets of roses, she finally agreed to go out with him. However, no matter how much fun they had together, she always seemed to hold back. But Jamar hadn't become successful by being a quitter. He knew she had feelings for him, but she refused to show them. He also knew her hard heart had a lot to do with that clown she had left in Texas.

So instead of quitting, he chiseled bit by bit at her heart of stone. Soon, he sculpted a hole that showed a tenderness that only he could see. The hole had gotten bigger in the past month. They'd grown closer, and the passion had heated up. But it now seemed as though it was all coming to a screeching halt.

Why was she tripping all of a sudden? Didn't she know that despite all the women who threw themselves at him, he only wanted to be with her?

"This is some bullshit," Jamar said, before taking a long swig of his beer. "I oughta go find me a chicken-head tonight. Being a fuckin' good guy don't mean shit these days."

*Ding-dong.*

"The fuck?" Jamar said to himself. He checked his watch again. It was after eleven. "Who the hell is ringing my bell this time of night?"

*Ding-dong.*

He just knew it couldn't be Alexis. She'd had a key to his kingdom for the last three months. And no one else was allowed to visit without calling first.

He sat for a while longer, hoping the uninvited guest would go away. Instead, he heard the doorknob rattle, followed by the lock being popped. He froze, wishing he had his gun handy.

"Baby?"

"Alexis?" Jamar asked in surprise. Once she rounded the corner into the living room, his confused look turned into irritation. "What the hell you ringing the doorbell for? You almost got left out there."

"I'm sorry, but I couldn't find my keys in the dark,"

she explained. "Why didn't you turn the porch light on?"

"Ain't thought about it," he replied. He took another swig from his beer. "Probably the same reason you ain't called to tell me your ass was running late."

"Excuse me?" Alexis asked, cocking her head back in surprise. "I didn't think I was on a time limit."

"No, but courtesy goes a long motherfuckin' way."

Alexis put her purse and coat on the love seat. "You have about two seconds to stop cursing at me. Now, if you got something to say, just say it, but you won't disrespect me."

Jamar glared at Alexis until she took a seat on the sofa next to him. "You don't think it was disrespectful to just blow me off without calling?"

"I'm sorry," she relented. "I lost track of time. After I left the mall, I got some dinner, then hung out for a while."

"Who were you with?"

"Shalonda," Alexis snapped. "What's up with the twenty questions?"

"I just asked one," he retorted. "Let those defenses down."

Alexis sighed. "I'm sorry I was late, and I'm sorry I didn't call. I didn't think you'd mind what time I came over. Anyway, I'm here now."

"Yeah, you're here," he mumbled.

"You want me to leave?"

"If I wanted you to leave, you woulda been gone."

Alexis leaned over and kissed him. "And if I didn't wanna be here, I would never have come."

He leaned back and frowned. "Why did you come?"

"Because I wanted to see you. Why else would I be here?"

"Maybe you just wanted to keep your word. You

said you were coming, so you had to stick to that," he said, rising from the sofa.

Alexis shook her head and chuckled. "I don't believe this."

"Don't believe what?"

"As long as I've been with you, you would have the audacity to think I'm with you out of obligation," she replied, eying him as he leaned against the wall. "You of all people should know that I do what I want, I say what I mean, and I mean what I say."

Jamar matched her gaze and moved closer to her. "That's what I know. You always mean what you say. You're the realest woman I ever been with. That's why I don't get why you're trippin' all of a sudden."

"I'm not trippin'."

He leaned over the back of the sofa, close enough to see his girlfriend's chest move up and down with each breath. "I always knew you were a hard woman. Shit, that's what I love about you. But tell me—you love me back?"

Alexis grew silent and looked around nervously. "I love you."

Jamar's eyes remained hard. "No, baby. You said you mean what you say and you say what you mean, so tell me. Do you really love me?"

"I—I . . ."

He rose and walked away. "You ain't even gotta answer me. I already know the truth. Your ass wouldn't know love if it conked you in the damned head."

Alexis rose from the sofa and followed Jamar into his bedroom. "See, that's where you're wrong. I know love very well. And every time I've been in love, I've had my heart handed to me. You think I feel like going through that again?"

"That's the damned problem," Jamar snapped, walking into his bathroom. He closed the door, but kept talking. "You think everybody's the same. You think that just because you dealt with a few clowns back in the day, every man gotta be the same. You're so blind, you don't even know when you hit the fuckin' jackpot."

Alexis waited until she heard the toilet flush before she responded. Jamar washed his hands and retreated from the bathroom to find her sitting silently on his bed. "You don't know me as well as you think you do. And you don't know about every man I've ever been with. It's really not your business."

"I never asked you to tell me about the people you've been with," he snapped. "You must think I'm a fool if you think I believe the only man you loved was that nigga in Houston. I just know he's the only one you ever told me about. Maybe if you open up to me—"

He stopped in midsentence, his mouth agape. The words hung from his lips but refused to materialize. He had grown weary of having this conversation every month. He knew he was doing right by this woman, and if she couldn't see it, it was just too bad. Maybe she wasn't the woman he thought she was. For a moment, he considered ending this entire thing and putting her out. Yet the other part of him convinced him that he'd put too much work into this relationship to just end it like this.

"If I just open up to you what?" Alexis challenged. She stood over the bed, her hands defensively on her hips.

Jamar looked at her angrily, his chest heaving. As much as he wanted to put her out, he needed her to stay. As crazy as she made him, he loved her too much to let her go. How in the hell could one woman cause this much turmoil in his life?

"Whatcha got to say?" Alexis asked, still in her defensive stance.

Jamar softened his stance and turned his back to her. "Shut up, Alexis."

"Excuse me?"

"I said shut up," he snapped, facing her again.

"I know you didn't—"

Before she could finish, Jamar rushed her and kissed her as he never had before. Despite her feeble protests, he held her tightly, refusing to let her go. Once he felt her relax, he pushed her back onto the bed, crawled on top of her, and kissed her again. Electricity ran through him as he pulled off her clothes.

"You're *my* woman, Alexis," he told her, looking her in the eye. "Don't you forget that. You hear me?"

She nodded, draping her arms around his neck.

"I'm not playing, Alexis. Do you understand me?"

She nodded again, but he pushed harder. "Say you understand me."

"I do," she whispered.

"I'ma make sure you do," he said, moving down to her V section. He grabbed her thighs and held them atop his shoulders, entering her tongue-first. He didn't want to be rough with her, but he had to show her how serious he was about her. He could no longer play the cat and mouse game they'd been playing for the past year. He had neither the stomach nor the patience for it. Tonight would be the night that she would admit that she loved him, whether she liked it or not. He knew she loved him. He could feel it. There was no way she couldn't. He just needed for her to say it.

He continued to lick and suck, causing her to release moans that he had never heard from her before. Once he tasted her flow, he pulled back and released her right leg. After placing himself inside her, he put her leg back on his shoulder and quickly moved in and out, making her scream even louder.

"Why don't you understand how I feel about you, Alexis?" he asked breathlessly.

She refused to look him in the eye, so he continued

to torture her with pleasure. He'd never made love like this before. It felt as if every stroke moved him closer to saving his own life. He'd given it rough before, but with those women, it was just sex. This time, the roughness was mixed with passion. But what surprised him most was that Alexis responded. She refused to say anything, but he caught glimpses of her looking at him with a longing in her eyes. It was as if the sex made her go through an internal struggle. He hoped she would overcome it soon, though, because he wasn't sure how much longer he would last. In order to prolong things, he pulled out and began kissing and squeezing her all over.

"I know you love me," he said. "Just say it. You know I'm never gonna hurt you."

He again looked at her. He caught a glimpse of sadness in her eyes, but she quickly looked away.

"You want me to stop?" he asked.

She looked at him and shook her head, holding him tighter. What was she struggling with? he wondered. Finally, he stopped and rolled onto his back, pulling Alexis into his arms. She laid her head on his chest while pulling the covers over them.

"You okay?" he asked as he stared at the ceiling.

"Yes."

They lay quietly. Jamar wished he had turned out the light before they'd gotten started. It would just have to stay on for a while. There was no way he would ruin this moment by moving from his position.

He wondered if he should push forward and delve into their relationship some more. He knew Alexis thought he was pushy. It was true, but that was part of what made him successful. He knew what he wanted and wasn't afraid to go after it.

He'd heard what she said about being hurt every time she fell in love, but hadn't he proven to her that he wasn't the same as those others? Who had hurt her so badly, anyway?

"Do you want me, Alexis?" Jamar asked, stroking her upper arm softly. He felt her nod. "Then just let go, baby. I've done nothing but treat you like a queen for the last year."

He gently lifted her head so they faced each other. "Do I make you happy?"

She nodded again, a slight smile tugging at the corners of her mouth.

"Then marry me," he said. He didn't mean for the proposal to sound so much like an order, but he had to convince her that he meant what he said.

"You serious?" she asked quietly.

"I'm very serious," he replied, looking her in the eye. "We don't have to do it tomorrow, but I do want you to be my wife. I've known it since the first day we met."

"But why?"

"Because we're good together. We make each other happy. At least we do when we're not pissing each other off."

She managed to laugh a little. "I don't know, Jamar. It wasn't that long ago that I was engaged to Tony."

"Aww, there's the name again," he groaned. "Think about it. Have you heard from him since you moved back to New Orleans?"

"No," she admitted, looking down.

"Have you called him?"

"Hell, no."

"Then move on."

"I have moved on," she protested. "I don't want him back. I just don't think it's healthy to get married a year after I was engaged to someone else."

"First of all, it's been more than a year since you two broke up," Jamar pointed out. "Second of all, you never shoulda been thinking about marrying that guy in the first place. From what you told me, he was a fuckin' clown."

"So you think you're better for me?" Alexis challenged.

"I know I am. But like I said, we don't have to do this right now. You ain't even gotta answer me right now. Take a couple days to think about it. Let's get together New Year's Eve night. Is that enough time?"

Alexis smiled genuinely for the first time that night, then placed her head back on Jamar's chest. "I'll think about it."

"You do that," he replied.

He lay back on the bed with his free arm tucked behind his head. Alexis was really considering being his wife. He was so happy that he completely overlooked the fact that she still hadn't told him that she loved him.

# Chapter 18

# Not My Man

"Home, sweet home," Nikki said to herself.

She'd just stepped out of the Louis Armstrong New Orleans International Airport terminal. Her friend Shereese should have pulled up by now. She'd called Shereese on her cell phone as soon as her plane landed from Aruba to ensure that she was on the way. Her friend refused to pay money for parking, and was circling the airport until Nikki finished in the baggage claim.

She finally pulled up in front of Nikki, who sat impatiently on her large suitcase. She popped up as soon as she spotted her friend's silver Mercedes round the corner.

"'Bout time," Nikki snapped once she was seated in the passenger seat. "It's cold as hell out there."

"Sorry, girl," Shereese said. "Like three taxis were blocking the way, so I had to wait."

"Yeah," Nikki mumbled, staring out of the window. No matter how many cities and exotic islands she visited, nothing compared to New Orleans. Despite the trash that was still piled high in some areas, despite the houses that were yet to be rebuilt, despite the homeless bums whose tents lined the neutral ground under the overpasses, she would always love her city.

She had to admit, however, that she enjoyed her weeklong break from the cold. Aruba was beautiful. The white sand and crystal-clear water on the beaches looked just the way they did on the pictures. And the Spanish architecture nearly reminded her of her hometown in some places. But the most beautiful thing about it all was that she didn't have to pay for a thing.

*Hot Girl* magazine had called her for another photo shoot just a week before Christmas, and this time, they were paying big time. The shoot included an all-expenses-paid trip to Aruba, as well as a nice two hundred fifty dollars an hour just for looking good.

The icing on Nikki's cake came halfway through the week when she met an Italian businessman who happened to be vacationing in her hotel. She usually only did black men, but for this dark-haired sexy man, she had to make an exception. He wined her, dined her, and made the last few days of her vacation quite worth it. It almost made leaving DeShawn at home with Reggie for Christmas worth it.

"I guess you enjoyed your holiday, because you ain't said a word since you got in the car," Shereese commented as she pulled into Nikki's apartment complex. "Over there daydreaming and carrying on."

Nikki turned to her friend and smiled. "Girl, you wouldn't believe the time I had."

Once they parked in front of Nikki's apartment, they pulled her suitcases out of the car while Nikki filled Shereese in on all of the details.

"Girl, if you think only black men can throw down in bed, you better ask somebody!" Nikki exclaimed as she recounted her sex-capades with her Italian lover.

Shereese laughed. "I'll let you tell it. But leave it to you to go modeling on a beautiful island on Christmas and find you some booty in the process. You gonna keep in touch with him?"

"Girl, no," Nikki replied, waving off the thought. She poured two glasses of wine, then took a seat on the couch. "I got enough drama here. That was Aruba, and it's gonna stay in Aruba."

"That's good," Shereese said, sitting next to her. She took a sip from the wine her friend had offered her. "You don't want Reggie trying to find any dirt on you."

"He can try if he wants, but I'm not stupid," Nikki scoffed. "I might talk shit, but he can't prove none of it. He can try all he wants to try to take DeShawn and leave me without alimony, but I ain't the one. Acting like he can do so much better than me. Let his ass sit in that house by himself if he wants to, but I'ma live my life. He's just mad because I don't want his ass no more."

Shereese shook her head and set the wineglass on the lamp table. "Well, from what I hear, he might be trying to get over that."

Nikki eyed her friend suspiciously. "What are you talking about?"

"I heard he's been spending time with some girl."

Nikki cocked her head back in confusion. "What girl?"

"I don't know. I ain't never seen her before."

"And you didn't try to find out?"

"Shit, Nikki, that ain't my business!" Shereese snapped. "That's *your* husband. I don't see why you care, anyway."

Realizing she was showing more emotion than she

should have, Nikki leaned back and took a sip from her wine. Her friend was right—there really was no reason to care. In fact, she might be able to use this little piece of information to her advantage. "I don't care, Reesie. She probably ain't nobody to be worried about, anyway."

Shereese cut her eyes at her friend. "You sure about that?"

"I'm positive," Nikki boasted. "Reggie ain't slick enough to fool around. He knows if he's caught fuckin' around, I can get his ass for adultery. Why you think I'm smooth enough not to get caught?"

"I hope you're right, but I would still check it out if I were you."

"I already told you, Reesie. Ain't nothing to worry about. You just make sure he doesn't find out the real reason he got to spend Christmas with Shawn."

"I'm not trying to get caught up in y'all's drama. Like I said, that's *your* husband."

"Just as long as you know."

They sat silently for a few minutes, sipping their wine. The two women had been friends for the last two years. Shereese was also a native New Orleanian who had recently divorced her husband. She dated a number of athletes, which was how she and Nikki became friends. They each did their share of dirt, justifying their actions with the thoughts that their men were probably doing just as much dirt when they went out of town.

Nikki knew she hadn't handled everything the right way concerning Reggie, but if things kept working in her favor, she'd have her freedom and her son all to herself in a matter of months. She just had to keep being careful. It took a lot of threats to finally shut her boyfriends up. She knew they'd been making comments around Reggie, but he still had no solid proof that she'd been cheating. As far as he knew, those guys were just being assholes partaking in locker room shit talk.

"But how are you going to keep him from seeing the pictures once the magazine comes out?" Shereese asked all of a sudden.

"Those pictures won't be out until June for their swimsuit issue," Nikki explained. "Reggie never has to know when they were taken."

"Well, it looks like you have your shit together," Shereese said. "Just don't get caught up."

"Oh, you don't have to worry about that."


The thought of Reggie possibly seeing another woman still clung to Nikki's thoughts as she drove to his place to pick up DeShawn. She didn't know why it bothered her so much. She was sure she didn't even want Reggie anymore. As far as she was concerned, as long as he paid his child support and alimony, he could do whatever the hell he wanted.

Then again, she figured, his weak ass couldn't be seeing anybody. First of all, he was still in love with her. There was no way Reggie could have gotten over her that quickly. He'd been in love with her too long, and she knew for a fact that he was still in love with her when he called himself announcing their divorce.

She was sure that whoever this new woman was could only be no more than a friend. There was no other possible explanation. But she knew one thing—she would get to the bottom of this little mystery quick, fast, and in a hurry.

Her thoughts had consumed her so much that she hadn't realized she'd already pulled up in front of Reggie's house. Make that *her* house. She still wasn't through with that battle, but she would save that for another day.

She got out of her car and walked to the door with a purpose. She raised her hand to ring the doorbell, but stopped midmotion. *I don't think so,* she thought, digging out her keys. The lock popped loudly as if welcoming her back to her palace. She hadn't taken this liberty in months, but it sure felt good to not walk into her home feeling like an invited guest.

"Mommy!" DeShawn shouted as he ran from around the corner. He jumped into her arms and kissed her on the cheek. "When did you get back?"

Nikki hesitated for a moment, hoping her son hadn't blown her cover. She then remembered that she'd told both him and Reggie that she was going to her mother's house in Baton Rouge to clear her mind. "I got back today, man, and I came straight here to come get you."

"How's Grandma?" DeShawn asked.

"She's missin' you," she said. "We'll call her when we get back home."

"I knew it would only be a matter of time before you used that key."

Nikki looked up to find Reggie sitting in his favorite chair doing his favorite thing—drinking a beer. She sucked her teeth and rolled her eyes.

"Don't you have a game in a couple days?" she asked, still holding DeShawn in her arms. She put him down and waltzed into the living room, taking a seat on the sofa.

"Yep," he replied, not looking at her. "I leave tonight. I was just waitin' for you to get back."

"Well, I'm here."

"Now you can go."

Nikki drew her head back. This attitude coming from her estranged husband seemed new. They'd had arguments before, but his words never had the venom he seemed to be spewing tonight. She turned to DeShawn, who had followed her into the room, and suggested, "Hey, man, why don't you go play in your room for a while so me and your daddy can talk?"

"Okay, but tell me when you're ready. I gotta tell you about all my presents!"

"All right, baby," she called after him. Once he disappeared up the stairs, she turned back to her estranged husband and asked, "What's your problem?"

"Nothing, Nikki," he replied, finally looking at her. His eyes roamed her body before adding, "You have a good holiday?"

Nikki smiled. *I knew he wasn't over me.* "It was nice. Mama said hi."

Reggie held back a chuckle. "I didn't think she was still speaking to me."

"Oh, she doesn't like that we're breaking up, but you know she loves her Saints."

"Well, tell her I said hi right back," he replied, smiling a bit. "You look nice. You almost look darker."

"Shoot, I wish I could get some sun," Nikki said quickly, hoping her tan wouldn't get her busted. "I pretty much stayed in the house all week."

"I hear you."

"What did you do for your holiday?" she asked, grateful for the natural segue. Maybe she'd get to the bottom of this mystery woman sooner than she'd thought.

"Not much," he said, taking another sip from his beer. "Hung out with some friends, then we spent Christmas in Atlanta."

"Oh yeah? That's nice."

He nodded without saying a word.

Nikki wondered where to go next. She'd gotten out of him that he'd been with friends, but were they male or female? She didn't want to come out and ask.

That would make her sound jealous, or worse, that she was still interested. "You spent the whole week in Atlanta?"

"No, just the holiday. We were here the rest of the time."

Nikki looked around the living room. Very subtle changes had been made. Where she used to have plants surrounding them, Reggie had placed a few figurines and some of his trophies. Her bright floral colors had been replaced with earth-toned pillows and a throw rug. The place was nice, but had a more masculine feel to it. "I see you made some changes around the house."

Reggie looked around, as if noticing the changes for the first time. "Yeah, it was too girly in here."

Nikki laughed. "You didn't like my flowers?"

"They were all right," he replied with a laugh. "But I'm a man. Men don't live with a bunch of flowers and bright colors."

She laughed again. "Boy, you are too silly. But I gotta admit that the place looks really great. I like it."

"Thanks."

A few moments passed before Nikki noted, "You know, we haven't sat and talked like this in a long time."

"I know."

"Hopefully once all this is over, we can still be friends. At least for Shawn's sake."

"I don't have a problem with that. You always had been a cool person to talk to, even back in the day."

"Yeah," Nikki said absently. "I don't know how it got bad between us."

"Me, either."

"I'm sorry, Reggie. I didn't mean for things to go as far as they did. Whether you believe me or not, I still care about you. I always have."

Reggie looked at her through squinted eyes, seemingly shocked by her apology. "Did I just hear you apologize?"

She smiled. "I am capable of that, you know."

"I know you are, but I haven't heard those words come out of your mouth in a long time. You feeling okay?"

"I feel fine, Reggie," she said with a laugh. "Can't a woman have an emotional moment?"

"You're feeling emotional?" he asked, leaning closer to her.

"I guess going through this whole thing gave me some time to reflect," she said. "You know, put some priorities in order."

"What did you come up with?"

"That I miss you. I miss how things used to be with us."

"Is that right?" Reggie asked, leaning back into his chair.

"I know it's hard to believe, especially since we've been fighting for so long, but it's true," she pushed. She kicked off her high-heeled mules, hoping Reggie would get a look at her fresh pedicure before she tucked her feet underneath her bottom. She knew he always loved her toes. "Do you still love me?"

A look of shock again registered on Reggie's face. "Nikki, are you serious?"

"Very."

"Where is this coming from?"

"I just told you," Nikki pled. "You don't believe me?"

He rubbed his bald head, letting his hand linger at the crown. He scratched his bronze skin before replying, "It's been years since you showed me this kind of emotion. Now, out of nowhere, you ask me if I still love you. How am I supposed to take that?"

"Take it like I'm giving it to you. The new year is

coming, and I don't want to go into a new year with this same baggage. I'm not saying we have to get back together, but I just want to know if there's still something between us."

He sighed, never taking his eyes off Nikki. After a few moments, he said, "Yes, Nikki, I do still have feelings for you. You're the mother of my child, and you were there from the beginning. I'll never forget that."

Nikki smiled triumphantly, but the moment was short-lived when he added, "But no, Nikki, I can't say that I love you anymore. I've been hurt before, and I've been cheated on before, but what you did to me is something I can't forget or forgive."

"Damn, you really mean that, don't you?" Nikki asked dejectedly, rising from the sofa. This wasn't how this conversation was supposed to turn out.

"In all the years we've been together, have you ever known me to lie?"

He had a point. "Then tell me this. Are you saying all this because there's somebody else in your life?"

"You think another woman would be the only reason I would fall out of love with you? Nikki, get over yourself. You slept around on me for two years. I just got tired enough of it to finally do something about it. Another woman had nothing to do with that."

Nikki folded her arms defiantly and glared at him. "You never answered my question."

"No, Nikki, there is no other woman. I have a friend, but that's all she is. We're not sleeping together, nor are we planning on it. Are you satisfied now?"

"You're such a fuckin' liar," she grumbled, turning and walking to the steps. "DeShawn! Come tell your daddy bye."

"Just a minute!" DeShawn called out. "I gotta put my game away."

"Nikki, I don't have any reason to lie to you," Reggie pled, following her.

She turned and glared at him. "You mean to tell me you're hanging out with some bitch and you're not sleeping together?"

"Nikki, I am capable of having a mature relationship without sex."

As DeShawn bounded down the stairs, she moved closer to Reggie and snarled, "You just make sure it stays that way, because if I find out you laid so much as one lip on her, it's gonna be a long fuckin' day in court."

"Bye, Daddy," DeShawn said, taking his mother's hand. "I had fun. When can we do it again?"

"Real soon, lil' man," Reggie said quietly. "Come gimme a hug."

Nikki watched as the boy obliged his father. She hadn't meant for the conversation to become as heated as it did, but just knowing that some other woman even had a chance of being with Reggie made her incensed. She knew she didn't want Reggie, that point was clear. But it was also clear that she didn't want anyone else to have him, either.

She quietly picked up DeShawn's suitcase, which had been sitting near the steps since before she arrived. "You ready, man?"

"Okay, Mommy," DeShawn said, releasing his father and taking his mother's hand. "Bye, Daddy, I love you."

"I love you, too," Reggie said. "I'll see you when I get back from Chicago."

"Okay. Good luck!" DeShawn said as Nikki led him out of the house.

Good luck, she thought. That's exactly what he was going to need when she got through with him. Just let him slip up one time, and she would make sure she and DeShawn were financially set for the rest of their lives.

---

Reggie stared at the door, wondering what the hell had just happened. Did Nikki really just walk in and announce that she still loved him? Had she been smoking crack?

The ringing of his house phone interrupted his thoughts. He strolled over to the phone, still wondering what had gotten into his estranged wife. "Morgan."

"Mr. Morgan, is this a bad time?"

His voice quickly softened at the sound of his baby-sitter's voice. "Oh, I'm sorry, Necee. What's good? DeShawn isn't here. He just left with his mother."

"Oh, okay. But actually, uh, don't kill me for this, but my sister is going to be in Chicago for New Year's and she wanted to know if she might be able to get a ticket to come to the game."

"Who is your sister?"

"Well, she's really my dad's daughter. She's older than I am, which is why you never see her. Her name is Janice."

"So she ain't never met me but she wants me to hook her up?" Reggie asked, shaking his head. *She got her nerve,* he thought. If he had a dollar for every person trying to get something for nothing, they'd all be rich. Then again, what else was he going to do with the ticket?

"I know what you're saying, and I'm with you, but I promised her I would at least ask."

"It's all good. Is it just her?"

"I think she wants to bring one of her sorority sisters. Do you think you could swing two?"

"Uh! Necee, you killin' me! I don't even know this

woman, and now I gotta hook her girl up, too? You lucky I love you like my own sister."

Necee laughed nervously. "I'm sorry, Mr. Morgan."

"No need to apologize. Nikki and DeShawn aren't coming, so they can use my box seats. Tell 'em to go to Will Call."

"Thank you, Mr. Morgan! I'll make sure she thanks you personally!"

"She better," Reggie remarked before ending the call. He tossed the phone on the sofa and kicked the air. If another woman called him asking for something, somebody was getting choked out!

# Chapter 19

# Push Comes to Shove

"This can't be happening."

Nikki paced the floor of her Metairie apartment and repeated the line over and over to herself, but it didn't make the situation any less real. Reggie was really going through with this divorce.

At first, she was all for it. He was hell-bent on throwing away his career to be some has-been trying to be a regular guy, and she wasn't having it. She loved being an NFL wife. She loved the excitement. She loved being recognized. She even loved the way people fell all over themselves whenever they saw her license plate, NMORGAN.

Yeah, she cheated on him, but so what? Lots of women were doing it. And besides, if he had been giving her what she needed at home, she would never have sought it somewhere else. Reggie was okay, but he just didn't have that street mentality that she'd grown up on in the Lower Ninth Ward. Back in those days, if you didn't know how to defend yourself, you'd better not come to the Lower Nine. Some guys were scared out of their minds to visit her for fear of getting jacked on the way to her house.

Nikki smiled as she thought back on those days. Men always knew they had to come correct when trying to step to her, because they knew she took no mess. She was known to embarrass a man for not bringing his A-game.

Reggie could easily have become one of those victims, but she saw something different in him. At first it was just a potential paycheck, but as she got to know him, she could see that his gentle nature could be deceiving. He definitely had a little street in him, but that was just it: it was just *a little*. She knew he was running with two other girls when she met him, but it was obvious that he'd had his feelings hurt by some chickenhead girl. He'd even told her a little about the girl, but she barely listened. All she knew was that she would pick up where that idiot ex-girlfriend of his left off.

Her feelings for Reggie eventually grew into love. Reggie must have sensed it right away because almost immediately, he proposed. She happily accepted and went right to work planning the social event of the year. She wanted everyone to know that Reggie Morgan, New Orleans Saints Rookie of the Year, was off the market, and that the new Nicole Harrison Morgan now held the key to his heart.

Together, they made the power couple they each always wanted to be. He kicked ass on the field, and she made sure he received the endorsements. Everything was going perfectly.

But then he had to go and mess things up by talking that retirement mess. The selfish bastard never even considered how that decision would affect the both of them. Well, if he was going to throw his life away, she refused to go down with him. So instead of arguing with him, trying to convince him he'd made a mistake, she went out and found one or two guys who had not only the street cred she craved, but the potential she needed.

Then when he popped up with the divorce, she figured she'd go along with it just to teach him a lesson. The way she saw it, Reggie would appreciate just how good he had had it with her once she left. He'd realize that they might have had their problems, but they were still a hell of a team. Soon, he'd beg her to come back. She planned to let him sweat for a while, but eventually she'd come back and maybe even suggest an open marriage. Hell, all the celebrities were doing that these days, and their marriages seemed stronger than ever. Why couldn't it work for them?

But this new woman was messing up the plan. How was Reggie going to grow to miss Nikki if this chick hung around him all the time? There was no way in hell Nikki could get him to beg her to come back like this. And there was no way she would bring up an open marriage now. He would only think she was succumbing to *his* terms instead of the other way around.

"I gotta get to the bottom of this," Nikki said aloud. She walked to the telephone, which sat beneath the leaves of her flowing green fern, and dialed the numbers as if her life depended on it.

"Hey, Coop?" she said once the male voice answered. "Yeah, this is Nikki. I need you to do something for me. There's a few dollars in it if you come through."


"I really wish I could spend New Year's night with you," Alexis mused.

"Why can't you?" Reggie asked.

"Because," Alexis said, absently flipping through a

patient's chart. She had no idea whose it was, but she needed to do something to keep her hands busy. She'd been staring at her left ring finger all day, wondering what it would look like dressed in diamonds. She'd then look over at the diamond bracelet on her right wrist and wonder if she even needed to be considering marrying Jamar. "Jamar is taking me to a New Year's Eve party at the W Hotel."

"That sounds fun."

"Yeah, but I'll take a quiet night at home anytime. The city's getting crazy."

"Yeah, I was watching the news this morning and there were three murders overnight," Reggie agreed.

"That's what I'm saying. It's ridiculous out there."

"Well, why don't you just tell Jamar you'd rather stay home?"

"Because he already bought the tickets, and—"

"And you need to answer his proposal," Reggie finished.

"Yeah." Alexis drifted off, looking down in guilt. She hadn't meant to tell Reggie about Jamar's proposal, but when he'd called her last night and told her how his wife had snapped on him, she'd admitted that she'd also had drama with her significant other. Only difference was that while his ended in threats, hers ended in a proposal. It was funny how life worked. What other drama could surface as a result of their friendship?

"Well, you gotta do what's in your heart," Reggie said, interrupting her thoughts.

"Huh?" she asked. "Oh yeah, I know."

Reggie laughed. "Caught you in la-la land, huh?"

"Yeah, I guess you did," she replied, giggling. "I know I have to do what's right for me, but frankly, I don't know what that is right now. Jamar is a good guy, and I do have feelings for him, but I'm not sure if I'm in love with him enough to marry him."

"Then tell him no."

"It's not that simple, Reggie."

"Why isn't it?"

"Because it's just not!" Alexis protested. She took a deep breath and blew it out slowly, tapping her desk impatiently with her knuckles. "It's not that I don't want to be with Jamar. I do care about him. In the year we've been together, he's been very good to me. But I've been down this road before, and I'm not making the same mistake. When I get engaged this time, I need to make sure I go all the way. No conflicts, no doubts."

"I feel you, but it doesn't sound like you love him," Reggie challenged. "In that whole little speech, you never once said you loved him."

Alexis opened her mouth to protest, but a knock at the door interrupted her.

"Dr. White," Ms. Kay called through the door. "Your next appointment is here."

"I'll be right there," Alexis replied, grateful for the distraction. She sighed, turning back to her original conversation. "Look, I gotta go. We'll have to talk about this some other time. Good luck with your game tomorrow."

She hung up the phone, not bothering to give Reggie a chance to agree or disagree. Who was he to pop up after all these years and start trying to read her? She didn't need to defend her feelings. Just because his marriage was ending didn't mean she needed to be alone, too. This wasn't a conversation to be having with her ex-boyfriend, anyway. She needed her girls.

By eight o'clock that night, Alexis and Shalonda were sitting at a table at Sweet Lorraine's listening to live jazz. The music was lively, and the crowd was jumping, but the mood at the table was anything but jovial.

Each of the ladies sipped her drink as Shalonda listened attentively to Alexis's latest drama with the two men in her life.

"I told you before," Shalonda said with a smile, "it's fire to have two well-to-do, fine men after your time."

"Shut up, 'Londa!" Alexis snapped. "I don't have two men. Reggie and I are just friends. Jamar is the only man in my life."

"Girl, if you believed that, you wouldn't be thinking this hard about marrying Jamar," Shalonda said, dismissing her with a wave of the hand. "You know that man has loved you since the day you two started seeing each other."

"Yeah, but it's not just about him loving me," Alexis protested. "I need to love him, too, or else I wouldn't be doing him any favors."

"How do you know you don't?"

"How do *you* know I *do*?"

Shalonda booted her lips at her friend. "How long do you think we've known each other?"

"I know, forever."

"And in all those years, we've stayed thicker than a chocolate shake. I know when you're hiding stuff."

Alexis averted her eyes, knowing her best friend was right. Shalonda was the only person outside of Brenda and her mother who knew her that well. Reggie thought he did, but they hadn't been close in a long time. Things had changed. She wasn't the same girl she was back in college, even though she felt that way every time they were together.

"Okay, Shalonda," Alexis relented. "I do love him, but I'm just not sure if the feeling is strong enough to be his wife. I mean, what if I marry him and find out it's not all that?"

"I'm with you on that," Shalonda agreed. "But I do know Jamar is nothing like Tony."

"I know he's not."

"And he's nothing like Reggie, either."

Alexis glared at her friend. "Reggie has nothing to do with this. He's just a friend."

Shalonda looked at her sideways. "You telling me in these couple of weeks, you haven't thought about what might have been?"

Alexis smiled slightly. "A little. To tell the truth, hanging out with Reggie has brought up some feelings I thought had died a long time ago."

"Are those feelings enough not to marry Jamar?"

Alexis shrugged. "That's what I'm trying to sort out."

"In that case, you've just got to do what's in your heart."

Alexis shook her head and turned her attention to the band. If one more person fed her that tired line, she was going to scream. Why did everybody think the answer to life's problems was that easy? If she knew what was in her heart, didn't they think she'd have followed it a long time ago?

"I really love you. You should know. I wanna make sure I'm right, girl, before I let go."

The lead singer sang Frankie Beverly and Maze's classic "Before I Let Go" as if his woman were standing right before him. He dropped down to his knees and sang the next few lines as if his well-being depended on this woman believing that he truly loved her.

She thought back to Jamar as she watched the show. He'd never dropped to his knees, but he'd never been shy about letting her know how he felt about her. Could she really love him that way? What if her prophesy was correct and she fell out of love with him after they were married? Or worse, what if he changed his mind about her once he found out about her not being able to have children?

Then there was Reggie. How could two weeks mess

her mind up the way they had? Before Reggie came along, she was sure that she was ready for a real relationship with Jamar. They were only friends, and he was technically still married, but part of her was curious as to where their friendship would take them. She didn't want him to be the one who got away twice.

"You talk to your cousin Brenda about this?" Shalonda asked once the song ended.

"I haven't really had the time," Alexis replied, her eyes still on the band, who had set down their instruments for a break. "Besides Mama, you and Reggie are the only people I told, and I shouldn't have told his ass."

"Why did you?"

"He called me last night talking about how his wife asked if he still loved her, and snapped when he said he didn't."

"Whaaaaat?" Shalonda asked, intrigued. "What happened?"

"He didn't give me all the details, but apparently she went crazy when he said he didn't want her back," Alexis said. "I guess she's not the one to be turned down."

"Well, I've seen her on TV a couple times, and she doesn't look like the type of woman who gets turned down very often."

"When did you see her on TV?"

"A while back on WWL when they did a special on him."

"When was that?"

Shalonda burst out laughing. "Girl, you really need to get out of that office every once in a while."

"Girl, you know I don't watch much TV," Alexis replied with a laugh.

All of a sudden, Shalonda's eyes grew wide as she stared at her friend. "You two hit the sheets, didn't you?"

"What?" Alexis asked in shock. "Why would you say that?"

"Girl, you don't have to hide anything from me. I don't have a heaven or a hell to put you in, so you might as well tell the truth."

Alexis rolled her eyes. "No, Shalonda, we haven't slept together. We haven't even kissed."

Shalonda booted her mouth at Alexis. "Yeah, right."

"We haven't! Not that I haven't thought about it, but we just haven't. We've always met in public, so we haven't even had the opportunity."

"Oh, there's been opportunity," Shalonda said with a smirk. "You two just haven't taken it."

After a few minutes, she added, "Maybe you two are in love."

"What are you talking about?" Alexis asked, scrunching her eyebrows.

"You two spend two weeks together with no sex and he's already got your mind spun up," Shalonda surmised.

"Hmph," was all Alexis could manage to say. She refused to believe her friend might be right.

"You going to watch the game tomorrow?" Shalonda asked, tapping her foot while watching the crowd dance to "Cupid Shuffle."

"Of course! It's the last game of the season and I need my boys to get into the play-offs."

"Yeah, they've gotta win this one."

"They will, I have faith in him," Alexis assured her friend. "I mean *them.*"

# Chapter 20

# Decisions, Decisions

The weekend ended as quietly as a lamb. Neither Brenda nor Darnell dared to move from their just-right positions in their king-sized bed. If Brenda had snuggled any closer to her husband's muscular body, she would have been inside him. She knew they needed to get up for church, but she reasoned that since they were going to watchnight service tomorrow night, it was okay to sleep their Sunday away.

It was moments like these that Brenda relished. Neither one of them slept, but just lying there with their eyes closed brought a sense of solace. No TV played, no radio blasted. The only sound in the room was the tick-tock of their old-fashioned grandfather clock that sat in the living room near their bedroom. This was what made being married worth its weight, because only the truly blessed could experience the security of being wrapped in love.

Unfortunately, their solitude wouldn't last for long, as the phone's ring cut through their silence like a buzz saw.

"Tell Alexis or Andrea or whoever that is to call back later!" Darnell grumbled, refusing to move from his position. "Can't we have a break? It's Sunday morning!"

"How you know it's for me?" Brenda asked, also remaining in her position. "People call for you, too."

The phone rang two more times before Darnell forced his eyes open and grabbed the receiver. "You know, you are one hardheaded woman sometimes."

He begrudgingly placed the receiver to his ear and bellowed, "Yeah!" A few seconds later, he sucked his teeth and said, "Hold on, Alexis."

Brenda turned over and took the receiver, a bit embarrassed. She had really hoped the phone was for Darnell so she could prove him wrong for once. That man thought he knew everything!

"Hey, Lex, what's going on?"

"I'm sorry to wake y'all up, but I really need to talk to you."

"What's wrong?" Brenda asked, cutting her eyes at Darnell. He glared at her and mouthed the words *hurry up.*

"Girl, tomorrow night could make or break me, and I need you to be straight with me."

"Girl, what's wrong?"

"Jamar asked me to marry him a few days ago and I have to give him an answer tomorrow."

"Well, do you love him?"

"I think so. He's been so good to me, and when we're not fighting, we get along well."

"Sounds like a friend to me," Brenda said, lying back on her pillow.

"But I don't just see him as a friend," Alexis protested. "How did you know Darnell was the one?"

Brenda again cut her eyes at her husband, who'd risen from the bed and stormed into the bathroom. She loved so many things about him, but that attitude was definitely not one of them. "Well, besides the fact that my man is smart and fine and is sweet and understanding most of the time, I found myself being able to talk to him about anything. I started thinking about him throughout the day, and he respected me from day one to wait until I was ready to pursue something deeper with him. He understands me and balances me in a lot of ways. But most of all, I didn't feel like I had to work hard to get or keep his love, and that was a big one for me."

"I feel a lot of that with Jamar," Alexis admitted.

"Then what's the problem?"

"I can't get Reggie off my mind! Ever since we started hanging out, I've been fantasizing about what it would be like if we ever got back together."

"Are you willing to wait two years for you two to be together?"

"I thought separation periods were only a year?"

"Yeah, but after that, you have to go through the actual divorce," Brenda explained. "Reggie is a star athlete with a grip of money. You think his wife is going to just walk away without getting all she can out of him? And if you don't think he'll fight for his, then you're crazy."

"That's true," Alexis replied quietly.

"What's going on with you two, anyway?" Brenda asked. "I thought you were supposedly just friends?"

"We are, but I've been feeling so comfortable with him that I can't help but wonder what might happen between us."

"Hmph. Sounds like you just have a case of nostalgia. You have to do what's right for you, but if you're asking me what you should do, I say think with your head as well as your heart."

"That's what I'm trying to do," Alexis protested.

Brenda felt the bed sink behind her, followed by her husband's arm sliding around her waist. He kissed her gently behind her ear, cuing her to end this phone call quickly. Alexis was just going to have to solve her own problems this morning. "Hey, Lex, I gotta get off this phone. Just think about what I said. I'm not sleeping with either one of those guys, so I can't tell you who you should choose."

"Choose the one who doesn't mind being woke up by early morning phone calls!" Darnell shouted, pulling his wife closer.

"Boy, shut up!" Brenda snapped. "Alexis, lemme get off this phone before I hurt this man."

Alexis laughed. "Go ahead. Tell Darnell I'm sorry for disturbing y'all."

"Girl, don't worry about that. I'm just glad you're really thinking this thing out before you make any decisions."

"I am," Alexis assured her, "but I'm going to let you go so you can get back to your husband."

"Okay, sweetie, but one more thing. Remember to pray and ask God to help you to make the right decision."

"I will."

Brenda reached over her husband to hang up the phone, then stared at him in mock anger.

"What's wrong with you?" Darnell asked, matching her gaze.

"Why are you so mean?"

"How am I being mean?"

"That girl really needed someone to talk to. Do you know what it's like to be in love with two men?"

Darnell pretended to think for a moment. "No, I can't say that I do."

Brenda glared at him even harder. "You know what I mean."

"Yes, I do, but frankly, I don't think she's in love with either one of them."

"What makes you say that?"

"I love Alexis to death, but that girl has always had tunnel vision," Darnell explained, propping his head on his hand. "I do think she had feelings for that guy Tony, but since then, the only thing she's ever put any energy into is her career. You said yourself that she was always hard on Jamar, and Reggie just popped up out of nowhere. She ain't had time to fall in love with either of them."

"Unless she never fell out of love with Reggie," Brenda pointed out.

"In which case, there's no possible way she can love Jamar."

"You don't think she can love two people for two different reasons?"

"If we were talking about anybody but your cousin, I might say yes," Darnell replied. He lay back on his pillow and pulled Brenda on top of him. "But like you said, that's a decision she has to make for herself. In the meantime, you need to give me some lovin'."

Brenda let herself be pulled on top of her husband, but she used her arms as a barrier between them. "Don't think I'ma give you some just because you demanded it."

He sucked his teeth and looked at her as if she'd lost her mind. "All right, but by trying to deprive me, you're really depriving yourself. I can feel how much you want this."

Brenda thought for a minute, then realized that she'd gotten wet as soon as he pulled her on top of him. She both hated and loved the fact that her husband could still excite her after all these years. "Okay, but only because *I* want it."

Darnell laughed. "Whatever makes you happy."

But just as their lips touched, a young feminine voice called, "Mommy, can I have some breakfast?"

Brenda laughed, placing her head on Darnell's chest. "Give me a minute, baby."

She then rose from the bed and put on her robe. "I'll be right back."

She left the room to the sound of her husband kicking the bed and cursing the phone.

For New Orleans, the Saints and Bears was the most important game of the year. It would determine whether their struggling team would get into the play-offs. No one was sure what would happen, but everyone would be glued to their television sets to find out.

That is, everyone except Alexis. Still troubled by the choice she would have to make tomorrow, she couldn't bear to watch the game. It would only warp her thinking because she'd be too busy watching Reggie. She'd managed to avoid Reggie's calls, which had been a feat since he called her almost all the way up to game time. She wondered if he'd gotten any practice in at all.

Jamar, on the other hand, had been great. He'd stayed true to his word, not putting any extra pressure on her. Ever since he'd popped the big question, he avoided bringing it up in their subsequent conversations. He'd even purposely not called her the entire weekend, except once on Saturday to confirm their plans for New Year's Eve.

So instead of tainting her thoughts with either man, she went to the one place where she knew she could clear her mind. The lake.

The lakefront was pretty quiet because of the weather, but a few people braved the cold, anyway. She figured that not every New Orleanian was concerned with the Saints. Either that, or they were listening to the game on their car stereos.

She longed to take her usual spot on the steps, but the bitter cold refused to let her out of her car. Instead, she kept the engine running and turned on the heat. As she watched the waters, she noticed a couple of kids running in the grassy area near the shore. They wore long-sleeved sweaters, but neither had on coats.

"Where are their mama and daddy?" Alexis asked aloud. "They won't be satisfied until those children get pneumonia in the ass."

She chuckled a bit at the phrase her mother would use whenever she even looked as though she wasn't dressed for the cold. Although she knew it wasn't medically possible to get pneumonia in the ass, it was always fun to say. Plus, it helped make her point that one should dress sensibly in cold weather.

Her thoughts on sickness reminded her of her upcoming health fair. It was only two short months away, yet she hadn't given the project much thought since Christmas. It was always amazing to her how relationships could sometimes get in the way of what was important. Some girls had failed school because of their excitement over their new boyfriend. Others had given up on the career of their dreams in order to marry the man of their dreams. Alexis refused to let that happen. Once the holidays were over, she vowed to get back down to business, whether she decided to marry Jamar or not.

Jamar, Jamar. Why did that man love her so much? All she did was give him reason after reason to leave her, yet he still hung in there. He listened intently to her problems, remembered all of the important days in her life, showered her with affection, and wasn't afraid to tell her the truth. When had she returned those qualities? What had she done to deserve his love?

Maybe he enjoyed the challenge of trying to win her heart. But what would happen once she married him? The challenge would be over. Would he lose interest? Would she very quickly become just another pretty face?

One thing she could say about Reggie was that he never treated her as just another pretty face. Sometimes it seemed as if her looks didn't matter to him. Instead, he saw the beauty inside her. He made her feel like a queen, even when she didn't always carry herself that way.

But so did Jamar. He never once treated her like a trophy. He constantly told her how beautiful she was, but he also complimented her intellect and drive. He never played her cheap, nor did he take her for granted.

Yet she could say the same thing about Reggie. Back in college, he would tell her that she had so much to offer the world. That wasn't the catalyst for her pursuing her career, but she loved the fact that a man saw through her looks and tight clothes and saw that she would actually make something of herself.

But that was then. How much did Reggie actually know about her now? He knew who she was in college, but had he really taken the time to know who she was today? And in fairness, had she gotten to know Reggie the man, and not just Reggie the sought-after college student? Were they living in the present, or trying to recapture the past?

Realistically, they'd had two nice weeks together, but she and Jamar had clocked more than a year in their relationship. Jamar was there through it all. The long hours, the depression, and the celebrations. They had always been real with each other. Even when they fought, they never had to put up fronts.

But Jamar didn't know her past. He didn't know how wild she'd been in her younger days, although she was sure he could imagine. She never told him that she couldn't have children. Would he even want to marry her once he found out? Tony didn't. What made Jamar any different?

On the other hand, Reggie knew all about her past, and understood that she couldn't have children. She felt comfortable around him because she felt he truly knew her. Maybe it wouldn't take him long to get to know the woman she'd become.

Then again, if it were that easy, why not just bite the bullet and let Jamar in on her past? Maybe she didn't feel like she loved him fully because she never trusted him enough to let him in.

She continued going back and forth between Reggie and Jamar until her head ached. She wasn't sure if she was any closer to a decision, but it felt good to finally have some time to herself to truly think things through.

# Chapter 21

# Auld Lang Syne

"Hey, baby," Jamar greeted.

"Hey," Alexis mumbled. She sleepily lifted her head from her pillow and glanced at the clock. Why was Jamar calling her at eight in the morning? She wasn't supposed to see him for another twelve hours.

"I know it's early, but I'm going to be busy tying up some loose ends in the office today so I wanted to call you early," he explained, as if hearing her thoughts. "You going in today?"

"Uh-uh. Long night."

"Oh, you went out last night?"

"No, but I have a big decision to make today so I put a lot of thought into it," Alexis said, clearing her throat in a vain effort to sound less husky.

"Oh yeah," Jamar said quietly. "Well, I won't keep you long. I just wanted to let you know I'm gonna pick you up about seven thirty. We'll have dinner at the W before we go into the party."

"Sounds good, sweetie," she replied. "I'll be ready."

"I know you will. I'll see you tonight."

"Okay," she said. "And hey! Sorry about the game."

"Aww, did you see that shit?" Jamar exclaimed, lamenting the Saints' 33–25 loss to Chicago. "I just knew we would make a miracle happen. We just made too many mistakes."

Alexis smiled at the way Jamar kept saying "we" as if he were part of the team. "Don't worry. It's hard to repeat a season like the Saints had last year. But I bet you they won't repeat this season."

"I sure hope not. I am not looking forward to wearing this damned Chicago jersey into work today."

Alexis laughed. "You're wearing it now?"

"Hell, naw! I'm not putting this thing on until I'm safely inside!"

They laughed together.

"Well, baby, go ahead and get you some more sleep. I'll call you when I'm on the way over," Jamar said.

"Okay, have a good day today," Alexis replied.

Once she pushed END on her cell phone, she lay on her back, replaying the conversation in her head. The fact that Jamar had quickly changed the subject when she mentioned her decision hadn't gone unnoticed. She wondered if he'd changed his mind.

Her cell phone rang again before the thought could take root in her mind. Thinking it was Jamar again, she quickly hit SEND and said, "Hey."

"Hey, yourself."

Reggie.

"Hi, you already back from Chicago?" Alexis greeted, sitting up in bed. It was obvious that she wasn't going back to sleep. Why everyone chose to call this early in the morning was beyond her. But when she remembered she'd done the same thing to Brenda the day before, she couldn't get mad.

"No, I'm still here," Reggie replied. "We board in a half hour or so."

"Oh, okay."

"Can I see you today?"

"You know I'm going out with Jamar tonight," Alexis reminded him.

"I know, I thought we could do a late lunch. I promise not to keep you too long."

She bit her lip as she wondered what to do. "What time?"

"I'll be back in a couple hours. Let me get home and get some rest. Can we meet at two?"

"Where?"

"Look, I just really need to talk to you. I don't care where we go."

Alexis sighed, wondering why he had such an urgency in his voice. "Okay. Call me when you're ready. Just remember I have to get back home so I can get ready for tonight."

"I know you do."


The couple ended up at a local sandwich shop near the Seventh Ward. No tourists frequented this spot, so it was easy to sit and go relatively unnoticed. Since neither of them was very hungry, they decided to split a hot sausage sandwich.

To Alexis, Reggie seemed more uncomfortable than usual. He sat on the edge of his seat, rubbing his hands together. His eyes darted around the room, as if he were trying to avoid eye contact.

"You okay?" Alexis asked.

"Yeah, I'm good," he replied, taking a deep breath.

"Look, I need to say something to you before I lose the nerve."

Now it was Alexis's turn to look nervous. "What is it? Is everything okay?"

"Not really. I don't know any other way to say this, so I'm just gonna come out with it. I don't want you to marry Jamar."

Alexis scrunched her eyebrows in confusion. "Excuse me? Why not?"

"It's like this," he explained, taking her hand. "I never stopped loving you. I thought I had gotten over you, but spending the last couple of weeks with you brought out a lot of feelings I thought were gone."

Alexis blinked and turned away. This was not the conversation she needed to be having right now. This decision was hard enough without Reggie trying to add extra drama to it. "Are you sure about that?"

"I'm positive."

"Okay, because it's funny to me that you never bothered to say anything until the day I have to give Jamar my answer."

"I know, it's really fucked-up timing on my part, and I'm sorry. But I had to tell you. I don't know if it will make a difference or not, but I needed to be honest with you and myself and let you know how I feel. I know we're supposed to be friends, but I've noticed the way you look at me sometimes. I also noticed how you sometimes avoid talking about Jamar around me."

"You're right, Reggie," Alexis said angrily. "This *is* fucked up. You noticed all that but never bothered to say anything until now. You haven't changed one damned bit since college. You still think you hold all the cards and make all the decisions. Nobody else fits into your master plan unless you allow them to, right?"

Reggie's eyes grew wide as Alexis went on her tirade. "Alexis, where is all this coming from?"

"You know exactly where it's coming from," Alexis replied, struggling to fight back tears. Why did love have to be so complicated? Why did happily ever after have to lie at the end of the rockiest, curviest road imaginable? "Do you know how hard it was to see you with your wife, or even by yourself for that matter, all those years? I wished it could be me standing next to you. All those years. I wished like hell I could rewrite history and make that affair go away. I beat myself up for a long time after our breakup. Sometimes I still do. Now here you are, on New Year's Eve, the day I'm supposed to start my new beginning, telling me that the past was just a big misunderstanding."

"It was a misunderstanding, Alexis," Reggie pleaded. "We were both young then. We both made mistakes."

"Yeah, but you held me to such a high standard that my mistakes were unforgivable," Alexis surmised.

Reggie sighed deeply and looked away. "We don't have to go down that road. I've apologized to you about that. I'm just letting you know how I feel."

"What am I supposed to do with that, Reggie?" Alexis asked, holding her arms out to the side in resignation. "Do you want me to sneak around with you for the next year or so while you work out your divorce? Or maybe we can be out in the open and you can rub me in her face since she fucked around on you for so long!"

Reggie's eyes narrowed into slits. "You really didn't have to go there, Alexis. You can say some fucked-up shit sometimes, but you *really* didn't have to go there."

"Just saying what I feel," Alexis remarked, leaning back in her chair and folding her arms. Deep down, she felt bad about the remark, but it had to be said. What did Reggie expect her to do in this situation?

He knocked lightly on the table and pushed away his untouched sandwich. He then stood up and prepared to leave. "Look, Alexis, just like you said what you feel, I said what I felt. Do what you have to with the information. Just know that I know the whole you and I know what I can offer you. Jamar might be cool and all, but he will never know you like I do. Shit, what kind of name would Alexis Duplessis be, anyway? Sounds like a damned nursery rhyme."

His words struck her harder than a lightning bolt ever could. Had she just heard him right? "How do you now Jamar's last name?"

"Huh?" he asked. "You told me, didn't you?"

"Bullshit! I've never told you anything about him other than his name and him being a lawyer. Now, I ask you again, how *in the fuck* do you know his name?"

By this time, the few people in the restaurant had become captivated with the drama unfolding at their back table. Alexis wasn't sure how many of them recognized Reggie, but at this point, she didn't care. They needed to know that the man they revered was just as imperfect as the rest of the mere mortals in the world.

"I'm waiting on an answer," she pushed, rising from the table. She walked up to him and looked him right in the eye. "You gonna tell me the truth, or are you formulating your first-ever lie?"

"Damn," remarked a young guy sitting across the room. "She's pulling your punk card, man."

Reggie looked around the restaurant angrily, then grabbed Alexis's arm and pulled her out of the restaurant. He loosened his grip once they were outside and away from an audience. "Why do you always have to resort to getting loud when you don't get your way?"

She crossed her arms in defiance. "You gonna answer my question, or what?"

"Stay strong, bro," the young guy from inside said to Reggie as he walked out of the restaurant. He looked back again and smiled, then disappeared around the corner.

Reggie eyed him curiously, then shook his head and backed away. "I'll answer you, but not now. When you calm down, give me a call."

With that, he turned and walked away. *Bastard,* Alexis thought as she walked to her car. *No wonder he lost the game yesterday. All those secrets must have weighed him down.*

Reggie walked back into his house feeling dejected and drained. This was not how his day was supposed to turn out. He knew he'd jumped the gun by even telling Alexis how he felt. He was nowhere near a divorce, and Nikki had already flipped out when she found out that he and Alexis were friends.

But something good did come out of his day from hell. He'd learned that whatever he and Alexis had shared was definitely over. Maybe if he'd made his move sooner, things would have been different, but he'd played his hand too quickly, panicking when he'd heard about Jamar's proposal.

He wondered if he'd taken her back years ago, how different things would be. The more he thought about it, it was his own fault that he was in the situation he was in. He knew she truly regretted the affair she'd had in college, but his pride wouldn't let him take her back. Even his A Team wouldn't fill the void. But when he was drafted, he couldn't bear to begin his career without a woman on his side. It just didn't fit with the vision he had for himself. Yet, in his haste, he wound up marrying a woman who turned out to be ten times worse than the one he tried to avoid. It's funny how life works.

The vibration of his cell phone startled him, nearly making him jump out of his chair. He grabbed the phone and glanced at the incoming number. Nothing he recognized. He pressed TALK and barked, "Morgan!"

"I'm sorry, did I catch you at a bad time?" asked a female voice he didn't recognize.

He scrunched his eyebrows. "Who is this?"

"This is Janice. Necee's sister?"

"Who? Oh yeah, you got the tickets for the game yesterday."

"Yeah, and I never got a chance to thank you. I was hoping to see you after the game, but you were nowhere to be found."

"Yeah, I'm sorry about that. I had a lot of things on my mind."

"I understand. I was just wondering if I would ever be able to return the favor," Janice said.

Reggie again scrunched his eyebrows and stared at his cell phone. Could this day get any more crazy? Who the hell was this woman, anyway? Whoever she was, and whatever she was up to, he would make sure he nipped it in the bud before it even got started. "Look, um, Janice, I don't know if Necee told you, but I'm going through a divorce right now, and until that shit is resolved, I need to be careful who I'm hanging out with."

"Dag, I just wanted to buy you some coffee," Janice replied, sounding insulted.

"I'm sorry," Reggie said with an embarrassed laugh. "You wouldn't believe the amount of drama I've had today."

"I'm sorry to hear that. I'm not trying to add to that."

"No, it's not you," Reggie said with a sigh. He needed to do something to get out of this funk. Never before had he let other people's moods dictate his own. Maybe talking with someone who knew absolutely nothing about him outside of him being a football player just might be what he needed. "I'll tell you what—don't worry about returning the favor. Why don't you let me buy *you* a cup of coffee?"

"You sure?"

"Yep. That way you can thank me in person, and I can see who this mystery woman is who used up my box seats," Reggie said, a smile finally taking over his face. "And by the way, tell your sister don't be passin' out my number."

Alexis returned home just in time to see Frank and Mary dancing to Frankie Beverly and Maze's "Back in Stride Again." Immediately her anger with Reggie subsided as she laughed and leaned against the wall, watching her parents have fun together, barely noticing that Alexis had walked into the house.

Roman came out of his room and walked over to his stepsister. "They been like this for the last hour."

"What's up with them?"

"Mary finally got the insurance company to give her a decent payment," Roman explained. "On top of that, she talked to Louisiana Road Home and they said they're going to pay her enough to finish the house."

Alexis clapped her hands and joined in the dancing. "That *is* something to celebrate!"

Roman looked at his family as if they'd all lost their minds. "Y'all crazy. It's just a house."

"Hey, boy," Mary snapped, still stepping to the music. "That's the house I grew up in. It ain't just no house."

"Yeah, and I had memories in that house, too," Alexis added. "That's where we really had Saints parties. And every holiday was spent in that house."

"That's right," Mary agreed. "I tell you, when God blesses, he really blesses. All this in one day. Looks like next year is gonna be all right."

"I'm happy for you, Mommy," Alexis said, giving her mother a hug.

"All this celebratin' is fine, but we gotta get ready," Frank broke in. "Dinner is at eight-thirty."

Alexis looked at her watch. "Dag, Frank, it's just after four o'clock. You still have a couple hours."

"Girl, I live with two women and a boy who thinks he's God's gift to women," Frank said. "If y'all don't start gettin' ready now, we'll never get out of here in time."

Everyone laughed.

"Daddy, you know it don't take me but a minute," Roman said once the laughter subsided.

"Boy, please, you 'bout slower than these women."

"I'm gonna leave that alone," Mary interjected. "But Frankie is right. Let's go ahead and start gettin' dressed. We all goin' in separate directions, and I want us to pray together before we leave. God has been good to us and we need to thank him."

Roman and Alexis looked at Mary, wondering who had taken over her body. Mary was hardly the model Christian. Alexis guessed that her mother's recent good news made her start seeing things differently. In a way, it was kind of refreshing to see this rare side of Mary.

"I'll go ahead and get my shower first," Alexis said, breaking the silence. "Jamar's picking me up at seven thirty."

"That's nice," Mary said. "He's a nice boy."

"He is, isn't he?" Alexis agreed.

"Yeah, yeah, just don't be too long in the bathroom," Roman remarked. "I got next in the shower."

"We really have to get a house with more than one bathroom," Alexis said, shaking her head.

"Or you and Roman can move y'all grown asses out and me and my wife can have our bathroom to ourselves," Frank said.

"Woooooo," everyone said at the same time.

"Dag, Frank, you don't love me no more?" Alexis asked in mock hurt.

"I love you enough to tell you the truth, baby girl," he replied, giving her a kiss on the top of the head.

"Don't feel bad, Lex," Roman said. "He's been trying to kick me out since the beginning of college, but I ain't goin' nowhere!"

"Shit, that's what you think," Mary remarked, showing that her old side hadn't completely gone away.

"Roman, let's go get dressed before both of us get kicked out tonight," Alexis said with a laugh.

"I know, huh?" he agreed, walking to his room. "Whatever happened to the black family unit?"

The family laughed again as they went to their separate rooms to prepare for the upcoming new year. As planned, Alexis took her shower first, then searched her closet for the perfect dress for tonight. She still wasn't positive as to whether or not she would marry Jamar, but she did know she wanted to have a good time tonight. Jamar always knew how to spoil her, so she was excited to see what he had in store for tonight.

She picked out a champagne-colored, formfitting after-five gown that she'd bought months ago. The dress was on sale at Macy's and she couldn't bear to pass it up, even though she had no idea when she would wear it. Tonight seemed to be as good a night as any to wear it. Champagne always had a look of sophistication to it, which was exactly how Alexis wanted to portray herself. Whatever she told Jamar tonight, he would know the answer came from a woman of distinction.

As she sat in front of her mirror and applied her makeup, she thought back to Reggie's accidental admission. How could he possibly know Jamar's last name? Jamar was pretty well known in the city, but if Reggie knew him before, why hadn't he said anything? Why would he hide that from her, unless . . . Could it be possible that Reggie had been one of Jamar's clients? Maybe, but why wouldn't he just come out and say that? Why would she have cared that they had done business with each other in the past?

Or maybe they were still working together. Jamar never told her anything about his clients. He was always worried about violating attorney-client privilege. He figured if he didn't discuss them at all, he wouldn't wind up saying something he shouldn't. What if Reggie was that needy client who took up all of Jamar's time?

Alexis shook off the thought, thinking it would be too much of a coincidence. What were the chances of her boyfriend handling her ex-boyfriend's divorce? She laughed to herself. That would be some true Jerry Springer stuff right there. But then again, the way Reggie acted today, the possibility could be a reality. She would make sure she found out, though.

She looked at the clock. It was nearly six-thirty. Her dress, shoes, and stockings were already set out, and her makeup was flawless. She checked her hair, which she'd swept into a soft updo with tendrils framing her face. It was time to put the entire look together. Jamar wasn't going to know what to do with himself when he saw her.

"Alexis?" her mother called softly from outside her bedroom door.

"I'm here," she replied as she slipped on her dress. "Y'all ready to pray?"

Her bedroom door opened and Mary walked in, already dressed in a royal-blue pantsuit. "Not yet. I just wanted to talk to you for a minute."

Alexis turned from her mirror and faced her mother. "Okay. Is everything okay?"

"Oh yes, it's more than okay," Mary replied, smiling. "I just wanna make sure you're okay. You look beautiful."

"I'm good."

"No nerves?"

"Why would I be nervous?"

"I know I would be if I had to make a decision like you're about to make," Mary said, looking her daughter directly in the eyes.

Alexis cast her eyes downward, avoiding her mother's knowing stare. She'd told her mother about Jamar's proposal, but she never admitted to her how she'd been going back and forth in her mind as to what to tell him. She'd also never admitted to Mary her feelings for Reggie, although after today, she wasn't sure how she felt about him.

"Now, I never said much about you and Reggie seeing each other, because you told me you were friends," Mary said, taking a seat on the bed. "But I know how you felt about him back in school and how it affected you when you two broke up. Does this friendship have anything to do with why you're dragging your feet on Jamar's proposal?"

"A little," Alexis admitted, still looking down. Mary could always see right through her.

"Well, I'ma tell you like this: sometimes fear will make you run from something you need most. You planning on answering Jamar tonight?"

"Yes."

"Have you weighed all of your options? Are you absolutely sure about what you wanna do?"

"I think so. I was so sure about what I wanted to do, but Reggie called me this morning and asked if he could see me. Then when we saw each other, he told me he still loves me."

Mary's eyes widened in surprise. "What did you say?"

"I went off! He knew I've been going back and forth with this proposal for days, and he waited until today to tell me something like that. You know better than anybody that I don't like people trying to manipulate me."

"Nobody does," Mary said, shaking her head. "But just like it was hard for you to tell him how you felt, it was probably hard for him to tell you that. He's seen your temper before. Besides, he's probably panicking because he thinks you're going to choose Jamar."

"That's true," Alexis admitted. She finally looked up. "Mommy, who would you choose if you were me?"

"Girl, don't even put me in this," Mary said, chuckling a bit. "That's a decision for you to make, and I don't want to taint that by giving you my favorite. I told you before that Jamar is a nice boy. He's very respectful and he seems to love you very much. Reggie is also a nice boy, and I know you've loved him for a long time. I can see why this is hard for you. I'd be proud to call either one of them son-in-law."

Alexis smiled. "I do have good taste in men, don't I?"

"I don't know. You did choose Tony."

"Man, am I the only person who loved him?"

They laughed together; then Mary rose from the bed. "I know you'll make the right decision. Just make sure that you're ready to go all the way. Each time I was married, I knew it would be forever. If your daddy hadn't died, he would be sitting in here right next to me giving you all the support in the world. Make sure the one you pick has the capability to do that for his own daughter."

Alexis stared at her mother with wide eyes. Could she have forgotten?

Mary held up her hand. "Before you say anything, I didn't forget that you can't have kids, but miracles can happen. But even if it doesn't happen for you, I know you love children too much not to adopt one one day."

"I thought about it," Alexis said quietly. "I just don't know if the man I marry would be willing to do that."

"Well, if he's willing to accept you, I'm sure he would be willing to give you the child you want," Mary assured her. "We can't change the past, but it doesn't stop you from doing something about the future. Now, let's go pray so we can get out of here."

The two women hugged each other, then joined the rest of the family in the living room.

"It's about time," Roman snapped, looking at his watch. "My girl's gonna be here in a few."

"Boy, shut up," Alexis retorted. "You know that girl ain't goin' nowhere without you."

"True, but I can't keep my public waiting for too long."

Frank and Mary groaned.

"How in the hell did you raise such a vain boy?" Mary asked Frank.

"The same way you raised Ms. Black America over there," he replied.

"Wait, how did I get in this?" Alexis asked, covering her chest in defense.

"Girl, you always in it," Roman replied.

Mary cleared her throat. "Okay, that's enough. Now let's join hands so we can pray and get out of here."

Everyone did as they were told, but just as they bowed their heads, there was a knock at the door.

"See?" Roman said in disgust. "All that chatterin' and now my girl is here."

"How you know it's not for me?" Alexis asked.

"Well, somebody open that damned door so we can get this over with!" Mary snapped.

Roman broke from the circle and looked through the peephole. "Hey, Alexis, it's Perry Mason."

"Shut up, boy," she snapped as the family laughed. "Open the door for him."

"Hey, everyone, happy new year," Jamar greeted once Roman let him in. His eyes sparkled when they landed on Alexis. "You're beautiful."

Alexis smiled and blushed. All her life, she'd been called pretty, fine, sexy, and cute, but nothing made her feel as special as the word *beautiful*. Anybody could say *sexy*, but only a man who truly appreciated a woman said *beautiful*.

"You're just in time to join us for prayer," Mary

interjected, breaking the couple's trance. "Join the circle."

Jamar did as he was told, but never took his eyes off Alexis. Finally, he bowed his head after taking Roman's and Frank's hands.

"Okay, Frankie, do your thing," Mary said.

"Dear Lord, Heavenly Father," Frank began, "we come to you with humble hearts thanking you for allowing us to see a new year. We thank you for blessing us over and over again, even though we don't always deserve it. You've been good to us, and for this we give you the praise and the glory. Now, tonight, as we go our separate ways, we pray for your angels of protection. Keep us safe, and help us to remember to put you first in all we do. All of this we ask in Your name. Amen."

"Amen!" everyone repeated. They then hugged each other.

Alexis took Jamar's hand and led him to the door. "Okay, we're going to hit the road. Y'all have fun tonight and we'll see each other in the morning. Love y'all!"

"Bye, love you, too," the family replied.

"That was nice," Jamar said once they were outside. "I thought I was going to miss out on prayer. My family does that every year at midnight."

"That's nice," Alexis said as the chauffeur opened the door to their white stretch limousine for them. "This is our first year. Mama's happy because the insurance finally paid for my grandmother's house."

"That's good!" Jamar said once they were settled. He leaned toward the driver and told him, "Take us for a ride around the city, then end up at the W."

He then turned back to Alexis and shook his head slowly. "You really look beautiful tonight. I mean, that dress, your hair, your nails, you're breathtaking. And on top of that, you're smart, successful, and you pray— you're the total package."

Alexis smiled. "Well, I don't pray as much as I should."

"Not many people do, but you're willing to do it."

"So, what do you have planned for tonight?" Alexis asked.

"I just want tonight to be about us," he said, rubbing his fingers across her cheek. "And I know you're supposed to give me an answer tonight."

"Yeah, I know—"

"But save it. No marriage talk tonight. Let's have fun like we used to do. We can discuss the engagement later. Is that a deal?"

Alexis studied him, wondering where he was coming from. This wasn't the same pushy Jamar whom she was used to. She liked this guy. "That's a deal."

"We're going into a new year, so we're going to do things differently this time," he assured her.

"I'd like that," she replied, moving closer to Jamar. He sure looked good in that black-and-gray-striped Sean John suit. She laid her head on his shoulder, relishing how strong his arm felt. If this was a beginning, the rest of the story would work out just fine.

# Chapter 22

# New Year,
New Problems

"I got his ass," Nikki mumbled as she clicked through the photos her friend had e-mailed her. Reggie just didn't know who he was dealing with. While he was having his lovers' tryst two days ago, Nikki's friend Coop sat at a nearby table taking in every word. He'd even pulled out his cell phone and taken a few quick shots while the scene unfolded.

She smiled as she printed the pictures on her photo printer. That little fight in the sandwich shop had given her all the ammo she needed. She was going to stop this divorce and get rid of that Alexis bitch all in one fell swoop. All she needed to do now was figure out who Jamar was.

She gently rubbed her long fingernails back and forth across her brow. Why did those two names sound familiar? She thought and thought until finally it hit her. Jamar was the first name of Reggie's lawyer. Could Reggie really be trying to sleep with his lawyer's girl-friend? *Nah*, Nikki thought. *Even* he's *not that desperate.*

Now, who was this Alexis chick? Nikki knew the name sounded familiar, although she didn't know anyone with such a name. It just seemed she'd heard it before. She stared at the pictures, but was unable to place the face. Finally, she dug her cell phone out of her purse and dialed.

"Hey, Coop," she said once he picked up. "This is Nikki."

"What's up, Miss Lady?"

"Tell me again what happened at the sandwich shop," she ordered.

"I told you already, Nik," he said. "Reg kept goin' on and on about how he still loved ole girl, but she went off on him, talkin' about why did he wait so long to tell her? She asked him if he expected her to wait until his di-vorce was final."

"Like that shit's gonna happen," Nikki mumbled.

"I know, right? As fine as old girl was, she could have a new man by tomorrow. Apparently she does because they kept talkin' about that dude Jamar."

"Did they say anything else about him?"

"Reggie said his last name," he said. "Du-something." Nikki scrunched her eyebrows. "Duplessis?"

Coop laughed. "Yeah, that's it. You know him?"

"That's Reggie's fuckin' lawyer! That motherfucker."

"Whoa. That's deep."

"You damned right that's deep," Nikki said. "Lemme call you back."

Nikki was so mad and excited that she couldn't sit down. She began pacing the floor, trying to think how best she could use this information. She could tell her lawyer, but that wouldn't stop the divorce. She could confront Reggie, but all it would result in was another fight and the divorce would still happen.

Finally, it hit her. She wasn't exactly sure how to pull it off, but she knew it had to be done. She smiled and rushed to her room to get dressed.

"Katina, can you pull the Morgan and Jackson files?" Jamar requested. "I need to go over some things before their appointments this afternoon."

Katina turned to the file cabinet behind her desk and pulled out the two folders. She handed them to Jamar with an overanxious smile. "Here they are. You need anything else?"

"No, I'm good," he replied, matching her smile. "You can go back to playing computer solitaire now."

"That's cold, Mr. Duplessis," she said with a laugh. For your information, I was looking up articles that may relate to some of the cases you're working on."

"Oh yeah? You come up with anything good yet?"

"Just this one article about a guy who won custody of his three kids."

"Sounds interesting. E-mail that over to me."

"It's as good as done," Katina said, another smile plastered across her face.

"Thanks," he said, turning and walking back into his office. "Dr. White is coming over later this afternoon. Let me know when she gets here, even if I'm with a client."

The smile immediately left her face. "Yes, sir."

He smirked a bit as he closed the door to his office. He'd always known Katina had a little bit of a crush on him, but she also knew his heart belonged to Alexis. But truth be told, even if Alexis weren't in the picture, he would never date one of his employees. That was almost as bad as shitting where he slept.

He checked his e-mail, and, sure enough, the article Katina found sat at the top of his e-mail. He clicked on it and began reading. If this guy could win custody, surely Reggie could.

The phone rang after a few minutes. He looked down and recognized the number as Katina's. "What's up, Katina?"

"Um, Mr. Duplessis, there's a lady here to see you."

He checked his watch. "Dr. White's here already?"

"No, she said her name is Nicole Morgan."

"Nicole Morgan?" Jamar repeated with confusion. *Wasn't that Reggie's wife?* "Send her in."

The door to his office opened, and in walked a tall, mocha-colored beauty with an air of confidence that almost made her seem regal. Her entire outfit dripped with a designer touch, from her shoulder-baring sweater to her white furry boots. She stood above him as if awaiting an invitation to have a seat.

"May I help you, Mrs. Morgan?" Jamar asked cautiously.

"More like I can help you," she replied, setting down her designer purse, which matched her all the way down to the fur. She pointed to the plush chair that sat in front of Jamar's desk. "Mind if I have a seat?"

"Be my guest, but know that it's not a good idea that you be talking to me without your lawyer."

"Oh, I'm not here in a legal capacity," she said, crossing her legs. "Yet."

"Excuse me?"

"I'm here to let you know a couple things."

"Like what?"

"Like the fact that my husband isn't being totally honest with you and you might want to drop this case before this thing blows up in your face."

"Mrs. Morgan, what are you talking about?" Jamar asked, leaning back in his chair and folding his arms.

He'd heard this woman could be the devil incarnate, but he was never prepared for this. Yet, as appalled as he was with her nerve, he was also a bit intrigued. "You should know that your husband will be here shortly and I really don't need no drama up in my office."

"You ain't gotta worry about that from me, but you need to watch my husband," Nikki said, leaning forward. "He's playing dirty, and I don't think you wanna be involved in that."

"I'm a big boy," he replied, shrugging his shoulders.

"Big enough to handle Reggie's case while he tries to steal the woman you love?"

The look of professionalism quickly turned into one of worry, but he wiped it away before it had time to set in. He couldn't let Nikki know that she was getting to him, but what was she talking about? What did Alexis have to do with this? She didn't even know any of his clients. "Mrs. Morgan, I don't think my personal life has anything to do with this, and it's really not your business."

"On the contrary, Mr. Duplessis, it has everything to do with this, and yes, it is very much my business."

He leaned forward and placed his elbows on his desk. "Okay, Mrs. Morgan. Break this thing down for me."

She smiled and leaned closer to Jamar. "My husband, the great Reggie Morgan, has been running around with your girlfriend Alexis. I don't know for how long, but they have definitely been together."

"How do you know Alexis?" Jamar asked, the worried look making a return appearance. This time he couldn't hide it.

"I don't, but it seems that we have something big in common. So like I said, you might want to drop this case. I'd hate for something like this to hit the news. You seem to be pretty big in this town."

"That's kind of a wild story, and no offense, Mrs.

Morgan, but I've heard about some of your schemes," he said.

Anger seethed from Nikki's eyes, but she maintained her composure. "Oh, you don't have to believe me, but you gotta believe your eyes."

With that, she reached into her furry purse and pulled out a small envelope. She handed it to Jamar. "Take a look."

He cautiously took the envelope and opened it. His heart jumped when he saw the photos of his woman and his client together. They weren't the best quality, but there was no mistaking who was in the pictures. One of them even looked as though the two of them were kissing.

This couldn't be happening. How did Reggie even know Alexis? And of all the people in this city, how could those two find each other? All of a sudden, his mind took him back to the men's room at Sweet Lorraine's.

*"I saw you were with somebody."*

*"Yeah, that's my girl. She's fine, huh?"*

*"Yeah, I gotta give you that. She in law, too?"*

*"Naw, man, she's a doctor."*

*"Impressive. Go do your thing."*

How long had that motherfucker known Alexis? Reggie really had his nerve trying to pick his brain about his woman. He'd probably been scheming on her long before then.

That certainly explained Alexis's behavior lately. The walls she constantly built. All the unreturned phone calls. The increased late dates. Her dragging her feet on marrying him. She just didn't want to mess up the two worlds she was obviously living in.

"You still with me, Mr. Duplessis?" Nikki asked.

"You gotta get outta here," Jamar said.

"I'll bet you believe me now," she gloated.

"Tell me something," he said, fanning the pictures

across his desk. "You could easily have gone to your own lawyer with this and probably could have helped win your case. Why the hell did you come to me? You wanted to rub this shit in my face?"

She sat back in her chair and placed her hands in her lap. "I told you. I want you to drop this case. I don't want this divorce, and I know you don't want to be embarrassed by this. I figured we could work together. And if Reggie gets his ass kicked over this, then so be it. I'll be there to patch him up."

"So you want me to be your teammate, huh?"

"We could work well together," she suggested. "You think?"

Jamar made a sound that sounded like a cross between a cough and a laugh. "You a trip."

"No, I'm actually more of a vacation," Nikki said, standing up. "I don't need an answer now, although I'm sure your mind is already made up. Think about it and give me a call. I'm sure you know how to reach me."

Before he could reply, she grabbed her purse and left the office. Once the office was quiet, Jamar leaned back in his chair and replayed the conversation in his mind. What Nikki was asking wasn't that simple. He prided himself on being able to separate his personal feelings from his profession. He'd defended some of the biggest assholes in the city, but never a man who was sleeping with his woman! How could he get past this?

He reached over to his phone and dialed Katina. Once she answered, he asked, "What time is my next appointment supposed to be here?"

"About four-thirty."

"Can you call him and try to reschedule for first thing in the morning? I need to take care of something."

"Will do. You want me to reschedule Mr. Morgan, too?"

He looked at his watch. "No, he should be here pretty soon. Have him come in as soon as he gets here."

"Speak of the devil, he just got off the elevator," Katina said.

He hadn't been prepared to confront Reggie this soon, but there was no time like the present. "Tell him to come on in."

He quickly scooped up the photos on his desk and dropped them into his drawer. He then took a quick swig from the water bottle sitting on his desk.

"Hey, what's up, J?" Reggie greeted once he was seated, ironically in the same chair Nikki had just left.

"What's up?" Jamar asked. "You see any familiar faces on the way up here?"

"No, why, did I miss something?"

Jamar shook his head and took another sip from his water. "Never mind."

Reggie looked at him curiously. "You all right? You don't seem like yourself."

Jamar pursed his lips, holding back the cursing he was ready to mount on his client. "Still trying to recover from New Year's Eve."

"You had a good night, huh?"

"Excellent. My girl and I went to the W, rode around the city, and then she made me breakfast in bed the next morning."

Normally, Jamar wouldn't have divulged this much of his personal life to a client, but he needed to show Reggie that he had no chance of stealing Alexis away. He'd put in way too much work in this relationship in order for it to end over some bullshit. He would just have to deal with Alexis later.

"How was your holiday?" Jamar asked.

"It was straight," Reggie said with a stretch. "I just went to the club with my boy Levi; then I slept in yesterday."

"Yeah, I guess it's been a long week for you."

"You just don't know."

*I'll bet I do,* Jamar thought. Suddenly the thought of Reggie sitting in front of him as if nothing had ever happened pissed him off. He and Reggie weren't friends; they were attorney and client. But that didn't give Reggie the right to sneak behind his back like this. How could he even look Jamar in the eye knowing what he was doing?

"Let's cut the bullshit, Reg," Jamar said, moving from behind his desk. He stopped right in front of Reggie and leaned on the edge of his desk.

"What's up?" Reggie replied, looking nervous.

"How do you know Alexis?"

"I figured she was gonna talk to you sooner or later," Reggie said, shaking his head.

"She did."

"She didn't tell you how we know each other?"

"Nope," Jamar replied. He really wasn't sure where Reggie was going, but he decided to be as elusive with his answers as possible in hopes of getting the truth.

"I dated Alexis back in college."

"You knew that when you approached me that day in Sweet Lorraine's, didn't you?"

Reggie leaned forward and rested his elbows on his knees. "I knew who she was, but I hadn't talked to her."

"So what's going on with you two now?"

"Nothing. We're just friends."

"That's not what you want, is it?"

"Honestly? No. I'm sorry, Jamar, I know you're my lawyer, and she's been your girl for a while, but I still have feelings for her."

"Well, you know we can't do anything about that, right?"

"She accept your proposal yet?"

"Awww," Jamar said with a smile. He folded his arms. "You just know all the business, don't you?"

"I know enough. I also know that those times when she was late seeing you was because she was with me, so I'm not so sure she's ready to marry you."

Jamar glared at him and returned to his chair behind his desk. "I'm not going to get into some kind of pissing contest with you. The fact is not only are you messing around when I clearly told you not to because it would fuck up your case, but you purposely chose my girl. And I don't play that shit."

"So what? You gonna quit my case? Because Alexis is my friend, and I don't plan on leaving her alone unless she wants me to."

*Rrrrring!*

"Yes, Katina?" Jamar answered, never taking his eyes off Reggie.

"Dr. White is here."

"Awww, she's early," Jamar said with a smile. "Tell her to come on in."

"But don't you still have a client?"

"That's all right. Tell her to come join the party."

No sooner had Jamar hung up the phone than Alexis came storming into the office. "Reggie, what the fuck are you doing here?"

"So you two do know each other," Jamar said, swiveling back and forth in his chair.

Alexis looked at him apologetically. "Jamar, I'm sorry about this. Is Reggie one of your clients?"

"He sure is. Didn't he bother to tell you that?"

"She didn't know we knew each other until a couple days ago," Reggie explained.

"But you knew," Alexis said, her head snapping toward Reggie. "How are you gonna try to play me like this? It's a good thing Katina told me you were in here, or else I would have left here letting you play me some more."

"She tell you who else came by?" Jamar asked, almost

enjoying the drama unfolding before him. As long as it was contained in his office and no one was shouting, he had no problem with it. Although he would have to talk to Katina later for getting into his business.

"Who?" Alexis asked.

"*Mrs.* Morgan."

"What did she want?" Reggie asked, his eyes as wide as the Grand Canyon.

"Let's just say she knows what you're doing," Jamar said.

"What are you doing, Reggie?" Alexis asked, her arms folded.

"I'm not doing anything," Reggie said, his arms stretched out in surrender.

"That's not the way you tried to make it sound a little while ago," Jamar said.

"Excuse me?" Alexis said. "Jamar, Reggie and I are just friends. He's never even touched me in that way."

Reggie pursed his lips and shook his head.

"Okay, I believe you, but why didn't you bother to tell me about him?" he asked. "You didn't even tell me you two dated back in college."

"I didn't think it was important to tell you about a boyfriend I had thirteen years ago," Alexis explained. "Who did *you* date thirteen years ago?"

"Okay, I'll give you that," he replied. "But that still doesn't explain why you never said anything about you two being friends."

Alexis contorted her face in frustration. "I didn't even know you two knew each other!"

"Which comes back to you," Jamar said, turning his head toward Reggie. "You knew Alexis and I were together. Hell, you even saw us together. Why didn't you say anything?"

"Because you're my lawyer," Reggie said.

"Correction. I *was* your lawyer," he retorted. "Now I think it's time for you to bounce on up out of here."

"That's messed up, Jamar," Reggie said. "All this over a misunderstanding."

Jamar replied by swiveling his chair so his back faced Reggie. "Step, bro."

Reggie silently left the office, leaving Alexis and Jamar in an uncomfortable silence.

"He the reason why you didn't want to accept my proposal?" Jamar asked once they were alone. His back remained turned toward Alexis.

"Partly, but not all the way."

"You still wanna be with him?"

"No, not anymore. But I do want us to be friends."

"You trust him?"

"I trust him to respect me."

"You think he respected you when he did what he did?" Jamar asked, finally turning to face his girlfriend. He found her sitting in the chair that Reggie had vacated. "He tried to make it seem like there was more between you than just friendship."

"That's all it was. I've never even been to his house," Alexis assured him. "And I don't know when he saw us together, but we've only been hanging out for a couple weeks. I called him before Christmas to ask for help with my project."

"You asked for my help, too."

"I asked for a lot of people's help. I can't do this by myself."

Jamar eyed her suspiciously. "Why did you come here?"

"I needed to tell you something."

"About him?"

"No, about me."

Jamar stood up from his desk and escorted Alexis over to the love seat that sat on the other side of his office. He rarely sat there. It was usually reserved for days when he had a group of people visit. He prided himself on always making his clients feel comfortable, and having enough seating was a large part of that. Once they were seated, he asked, "What is it?"

"I don't think this is the right time," she said. "I really wasn't ready for all that drama just now."

"I've been dealing with it all afternoon," he replied. "Whatever you have to tell me, I can handle it."

She looked around the neatly decorated office, seemingly struggling with whatever it was she needed to say. Finally she looked at him, tears threatening the corners of her eyes. "Do you want kids one day?"

"Of course I do."

She cast her eyes downward. "I won't be able to give them to you."

"What do you mean?"

Slowly and quietly, she recounted the story of the affair that led to her abortion that went terribly wrong. She also told him how Tony had thrown it into her face that she couldn't have kids, which was why she left him. She added that she loved children, and longed to have some of her own, but it could never happen. This was why she became a pediatrician in the first place. If she couldn't have children, she wanted to make sure other kids could grow to be strong and healthy. "Does all that make you change your mind about wanting to marry me?"

Jamar remained quiet for a moment, taking it all in. Her admission explained a lot. The walls. Her fear of falling in love. He loved this woman, but could he really go the rest of his life without having a child of his own?

"You know, I always wanted a son I could call my junior," he said. When he saw the tears fall, he quickly took her hand and continued. "But if I didn't leave you when you kept pushing me away, and I didn't leave you when I found out about you and Reggie, what makes you think I'm gonna leave you over this?"

"I'm too much drama for you," Alexis cried. "It's just one thing after another with me. I'm not good for you."

"On the contrary, you're very good for me," Jamar corrected. "You're my balance. You keep me grounded. And I keep you grounded. You need a man like me in your life."

Alexis smiled in spite of yourself. "How so?"

"Because I'm the only one not afraid to stand up to you," he replied, matching her smile. He then grew serious. "But I need to know. Are you sure you're completely over Reggie? I don't want you thinking down the line that you'd made a mistake."

Alexis shifted in her seat until she faced her boyfriend squarely. "I did a lot of soul searching over the last week. I had always thought of Reggie as the one who got away because it was my fault that we broke up. Back in college, he loved me just as much as you do now. Probably even more because he loved me despite my reputation. Hanging out with him the last couple of weeks brought a lot of that back, and made me think we had another chance."

Jamar groaned as he listened to her tell her story. This was not what he wanted to hear, but he struggled to not pass judgment until she finished.

"Then I thought about you and how you were always here for me," Alexis continued. "I thought about how you remember everything I've ever told you. You remember all the important times in my life. You buy me flowers for no reason. You pamper me with massages. And you don't expect anything but love in return. That's what a relationship should be based on. I realized that I'm not the same person I was back in college. Reggie is a great guy, and one day he'll find a woman who will give him the love he deserves, but this isn't the time for us. With Reggie, it's all about the memories. You can't build a future on that. With you, I see the present as well as the future."

Jamar looked Alexis up and down, wondering whether he should believe her. His eyes landed on the diamond bracelet that encircled her wrist. "Did he give you that?"

She nodded.

"That doesn't look like a friendship gift."

"I don't know what he was thinking when he gave it to me, but I promise you we're just friends. I know I should have been straight about our friendship, but you know how I am sometimes."

"I hear you talkin'," Jamar said, still cautious, "but I'm in this for keeps. Are you really ready for this?"

"Jamar, I love you, and I am very ready for this," Alexis said with a smile.

"You know that's the first time you've told me that?"

She nodded. "I just wanted to be sure I did before I said it. I don't take that word lightly."

"Neither do I," he said, squeezing her hand. "You sure you mean it?"

"Very sure."

Jamar stood up and pulled Alexis into a tight hug. "You don't know how long I've been waiting to hear that from you. I love you so much."

"You have the ring with you?" Alexis asked.

"I carry it in my briefcase all the time," he replied, releasing her from the hug. "I wanted to be ready in case you ever surprised me. You know, kinda like what you did today."

Alexis giggled as Jamar scrambled to his desk and rifled through his briefcase. He returned to her and immediately prepared to drop to one knee, but Alexis stopped him.

"What's wrong?" he asked.

"Are you sure my being friends with Reggie won't be a problem for you?"

Jamar shook his head. "I'm not going to lie and say I'm happy about it. If I had it my way, that nigga wouldn't come ten feet near you. But I trust you. As long as you stay straight with me, I don't have a problem."

"Are you going to continue representing him?"

"I don't know about that. It could be a conflict of interest for me."

Alexis nodded and looked away. "I understand."

"But I'll tell you what I'll do," Jamar said. "I'll refer him to my boy Henry. He's just as good as I am. I promise he'll take care of him. I don't like what he did, but that's no cause for him to lose his son. But after that, don't expect me to be invitin' that nigga over for barbecues and shit."

Alexis nodded again. "Okay."

"Now can I finish what I started, please?"

"Oh, sorry," Alexis said quickly. She straightened her body and stuck out her left hand. "I'm ready now."

Jamar laughed. "You are one spoiled-ass woman. I don't know what I'ma do with you."

"Love me forever."

"You've got that right," Jamar said, dropping onto his right knee. He took the ring out of the box and slid it onto Alexis's anxious finger. "Will you marry me, Dr. White?"

"I'd be proud to."


Alexis felt one hundred pounds lighter as she left Jamar's office. Her new year began with a myriad of emotions, but in the end, she knew she'd made the right decision. She just couldn't picture herself throwing away a year of unconditional love for a couple of weeks of nostalgia. And once she'd finally admitted to herself and to

Jamar that she loved him, there was no doubt in her mind about marrying him. It was as if her words had sent positive vibrations throughout the universe.

But before she could totally move on, she knew there was something else she needed to do. She called Latonya and canceled all of her appointments, then drove to the lake, where she knew she'd have the peace she needed.

The January wind blew bitterly through her hair, but she didn't care. She pulled a blanket from her car and walked to the steps leading to the water. After moving a few steps down, she took a seat and dialed Reggie's number, hoping against hope that he'd answer the phone. Three rings later, her prayers were answered.

"Hey," she said quietly. "You mad at me?"

"Nope," he replied. "You did what you had to do. And if that meant throwing me under the bus, then so be it."

"Come on, Reggie, I didn't throw you under the bus. I'm sorry about how things went down today, but how was I supposed to react when I found my ex-boyfriend in my present boyfriend's office just talking it up?"

"So is he your fiancé now?"

"Wow," she remarked, staring into the distance at a passing boat. "You're just jumping right to the chase, aren't you?"

"Alexis, I wasted too much time in the past, and it cost me big. Maybe if I hadn't, you'd be married to me today."

"You think so?"

"I know so. But I came to grips a while ago that it just wasn't meant for you and me to get back together. I realized that in the sandwich shop."

"I think I realized it then, too. You ever think that sometimes memories are better than the present?"

"In this case, yes. We just finally began talking to

each other at a time when we were both going through some major changes in our lives."

"Yeah, me struggling to fall in love, and you falling out of love," Alexis said with a laugh. "Maybe it was meant for us to come together at a time like this. If it weren't for you, I'm not sure I would ever have faced my feelings for Jamar."

"Yeah, and if it weren't for you, I woulda choked the shit outta Nikki a long time ago," Reggie replied, laughing. "You helped me keep my sanity."

Alexis laughed with him. "I'm glad we became friends again. Are you still my friend?"

"Alexis, I'll always be your friend. Anytime you need somebody to talk to, I'm here for you. That's if your fiancé doesn't lock you down."

"That was a real smooth way of asking, Reg."

Reggie laughed again. "Well, you never answered my direct question, so I figured I'd try a different angle."

"Very funny," she replied, smiling. "And yes, I accepted his proposal."

"Are you sure that's what you want?"

"I'm positive."

"And you're happy?"

"Yes."

"Then I'm happy for you."

"Are you sure?"

"Yes, Alexis. Like I said, I came to grips with our friendship already. All I want is for you to be happy."

"What are you going to do?" she asked curiously. As happy as she was about her engagement, she still couldn't bear to see a good guy like Reggie by himself. He deserved to be happy with a woman whom he could trust.

"Well, believe it or not, the day you went off on me in the sandwich shop, a young lady called me. I had hooked her up with some tickets to the Chicago game, and she wanted to thank me."

"Oh yeah?" she said dryly. "I'll bet she did want to thank you."

Reggie laughed. "Believe it or not, not every woman wants to sleep with me. We just went out for coffee and wound up having a really good conversation."

"That's nice. You going to see her again?"

"Shit, after the day I had, I might take her out tonight."

"What about Nikki? Isn't she going to trip when she finds out a different woman is in the picture?"

"Oh, believe me," Reggie replied, a smile apparent in his voice. "I have that situation well under control. Jamar might not be speaking to me anymore, but he gave me a fire plan that is going very smoothly."

"That's good," she said. "You should know he's referring your case to another lawyer in his firm. He said he's just as good."

"I understand," he said. "Don't worry about me. This is a new year and a new day. Reggie Morgan is gonna be all right."

"You will," Alexis said. "We both will."

# Epilogue

The health fair was more successful than anything Alexis had imagined. The event attracted thousands from all over the city and as far as Baton Rouge, the state's capital. Doctors from Touro and its affiliated medical centers converged on the Morial Convention Center, treating ailments from the common cold to hypertension.

Alexis stood back and just watched, unable to put into words what she felt. Her cousin Brenda, who'd just moved to New Orleans the week prior, led the volunteer staff, ensuring that they carried out their duties with competency and professionalism. Latonya busily registered patrons at the door, while Ms. Kay gave out lollipops and balloons to the kids who were brave enough to endure their vaccinations.

"Dr. White."

Alexis turned to find Paulette Johnson, Tavarious

Johnson's mother, standing before her. She looked nice in her money-green velour jumpsuit. "Hello, Ms. Johnson. Are you enjoying the fair?"

"It's really nice," she replied. "I just wanted to come over and thank you for everything. You've been very good to Tavarious over the years."

"I have to," Alexis said with a smile. "He's my little buddy."

"He's over there standing in line to get the rest of those shots I couldn't afford to get him," Paulette said. "This fair has been a blessing. I brought my whole family over here. My aunt just found out she has high cholesterol. I done tole her 'bout all that fried food. I guess now she'll believe me."

The two women shared a laugh.

"Well, that's what this fair is for," Alexis said. "How's the house coming?"

Paulette sighed. "It ain't. The house is too far gone to repair. I'ma have to start from the very beginning."

"I'm sorry to hear that," the doctor replied. "Can you excuse me for a minute? I have to take care of something."

"Okay, I'll be here for a while."

"Good. Don't disappear on me."

Alexis walked over to her fiancé, who was huddled in the corner making phone calls. "Don't you ever stop working?"

"I told you everybody doesn't have it like you," Jamar replied with a smile. "Clients have needs that I have to address."

She laughed. "If you say so."

"It looks like you got a good turnout," Jamar said, looking at the crowd that seemed to continually grow.

"I know, I still can't believe it," she replied. She caught the eye of Reggie, who was busily signing autographs with his friend Levi and some of the other players from the New Orleans Saints. "I'm glad Reggie decided to come out and support."

"Well, from what I hear, things have been going his way," Jamar said. "Once his mandatory separation is up in a few months, the divorce proceedings should go pretty smoothly."

"Well, hopefully he'll get his son," Alexis said. "Nikki has some shit about her."

Jamar looked around cautiously. "Believe me, he'll get his son. Her little trip to Aruba sealed the deal on that."

"What trip to Aruba?"

"The one she took when she left DeShawn with Reggie on Christmas."

Alexis gasped. "How do you know about that?"

"Let's just say that she had more than just modeling pictures taken of her during that trip," Jamar whispered. "Reggie needed proof that she was cheating, and he got it. My boy Antonio helped him out."

"But—"

"Enough about him," Jamar replied, cutting her off by placing his hand over her mouth. "When you wanna let me make you an honest woman?"

"Hmm," Alexis thought. "How about Sweet September?"

"Sounds like a plan. Just give me the date, and I'll be there."

She smiled and hugged him. "I love you."

"I never get tired of hearing you say that."

"Well, you're gonna love what else I'm about to say."

"What's that?"

"Watch," she said, turning toward the stage. She climbed the steps and walked straight to the microphone. "May I have your attention please?"

The crowd settled down, and everyone turned toward the young female doctor standing on the stage.

"My name is Dr. Alexis White, and I own a private

practice with Touro Medical Center. I first want to thank all of you for coming out today. Health care is not always the most affordable thing for many people, so when we medical professionals can come together and take away some of the pressure, we find it a real blessing."

The crowd applauded, while a few whistled.

"I'd like to take this time to bless someone else. This person has grown very close to me over the years. I've treated him some for a variety of things, and I've taken pride in watching him grow. Can Paulette and Tavarious Johnson please come to the stage?"

"Awwww," purred a few people as the audience applauded again. Once the mother and son made it to the stage, Alexis hugged them both, eliciting even more applause.

"As you might imagine, putting together something like this takes a lot of money," Alexis said. "We solicited support from a lot of different people, including Touro Medical Center."

More audience applause.

"Blake, Cheney, Duplessis, and Associates."

Jamar waved as the audience clapped.

"The New Orleans Saints organization."

Reggie, Levi, and the other players waved while their fans cheered.

"And countless other sponsors. Together, those organizations donated so much money that we were able to purchase a house from my mother, Mrs. Mary Joseph. Anyone who lost their home to Hurricane Katrina knows the value of calling a house a home. And a trailer is not a good substitute. I would like to present that house to Paulette and Tavarious. May this house become your new home."

Paulette's eyes grew wide, and the tears flowed as she grabbed Alexis into a tight bear hug. Tavarious also joined in by gripping Alexis's leg.

"Thank you!" Paulette cried as the audience cheered. "How can I repay you for this?"

"Just keep taking good care of my little buddy," Alexis whispered in her ear.

"You two deserve this."

She handed the keys to Paulette, then walked them off the stage. Soon the tears began threatening her own eyes as she rushed through the crowd to the safety of Jamar's arms.

"That was a wonderful thing you just did," he told her. "I'm proud of you."

"Yeah," Alexis cried. "Maybe I'm not so mean after all."